D1549793

Fear for Miss Betony

DOROTHY BOWERS

 Moonstone Press

This edition published in 2019 by Moonstone Press
www.moonstonepress.co.uk

Originally published in 1941 by Hodder & Stoughton

ISBN 978-1-899000-09-8
eISBN 978-1-899000-18-0

A CIP catalogue record for this book is available from the British Library

Text designed and typeset by Tetragon, London
Cover illustration by Jason Anscomb
Printed and bound by in Great Britain by TJ International, Padstow, Cornwall

Contents

Introduction

Fear for Miss Betony, originally published by Houghton & Stoddard in 1941, was Dorothy Bowers' fourth novel, and widely considered her masterpiece. The *Times Literary Supplement* declared: "*Fear for Miss Betony* is the best detective story of the year so far. The crime is cleverly committed and cleverly detected but that is not all. Besides providing all that is usually asked of this kind of fiction, the author makes her characters as interesting for their own sake as novelists untrammelled by the shackles of mystery would. The house, part school, part nursing home, where the fear lurks, is haunted by ghosts who are sound psychologically. Every page bears witness to a brain of uncommon powers." Edgar-winning critic James Sandoe included the book in his *Readers' Guide to Crime* (1944), a list of the best books in the genre.

The story begins with retired governess Emma Betony, aged sixty-one, reluctantly seeking refuge in a home for "Decayed Gentlewomen", where she receives a surprise offer from an old pupil, Grace Aram. Grace is now headmistress of an evacuated girls' school housed in an old nursing home. Although most of the elderly patients were removed, she suspects there has been a murder attempt against one of the remaining residents. Grace persuades Miss Betony to accept a part-time teaching position as cover for a nebulous investigation into the unexplainable events at the school, where everyone is affected by a pervasive sense of fear. Bowers' detective Chief Inspector Pardoe makes an appearance in the final chapters, but most of the detective work and the unravelling of a dazzling—and dangerous—plot is carried out by Miss Betony, who is a great deal tougher and more intelligent than her enemies had hoped.

Bowers was an advocate of the "fair play" school of detective novels, and displayed great ingenuity in piecing together the necessary elements of a baffling mystery—with clues freely shared with the reader. Bowers' skill in obscuring her characters' motives allows her to hide the identity of the murderer until exactly the right moment. Her perceptive descriptions of characters and situations are a cut above those of her peers; this is particularly true of *Fear for Miss Betony*, with the intuitive and likeable Miss Betony and the abrasive, defensive Grace Aram.

Dorothy Violet Bowers was born in Leominster on 11 June 1902, the daughter of a confectioner. In 1903, the family moved to Monmouth, where Albert Edwards Bowers ran his own bakery until he retired in 1936. Educated at the Monmouth High School for Girls, Bowers received a scholarship to Oxford and, displaying the dogged tenacity evident throughout her short life, sat the Latin entrance exam three times before she was finally accepted. Though women had only recently been able to take degrees at Oxford, Bowers' sister Evelyn joined her there, which suggests a family focus on education. In 1926, Bowers graduated from the Society of Oxford Home-Students (now St Anne's College) with a third-class honours degree in Modern History, and spent the next few years pursuing a career as a history teacher. Subsequent letters to her college principal documented her worries about family finances ("my father... our university careers have been a heavy expense to him") and her desire to break away from Monmouth ("I have a dread of finding work in a small pleasant county-town such as this. The temptation to crystallize would be too great"). Temporary jobs teaching history and English did not inspire her and she turned to writing; letters to friends documented the "slow, uphill" battle to get published. During this time, she supplemented her income by compiling crossword puzzles for *John O'London's Weekly* under the pseudonym "Daedalus". Bowers published four Inspector Pardoe novels in rapid succession: *Postscript to Poison*

(1938), *Shadows Before* (1939), *A Deed Without a Name* (1940) and *Fear for Miss Betony* (1941). The outbreak of war brought Bowers to London, where she worked in the European News Service of the BBC. Her final book, *The Bells at Old Bailey*, was published in 1947, with Pardoe replaced by another Scotland Yard detective, Raikes. Never of robust health, Bowers contracted tuberculosis during this period and eventually succumbed to the disease on 29 August 1948. She died knowing that she had been inducted into the prestigious Detection Club, the only writer selected for membership in 1948. Moonstone Press is delighted to reissue the novels of Dorothy Bowers for a new generation to enjoy.

With love to
M.E.G.
who, knowing their faults,
still likes my stories

Chapter I

THE LIKES OF US

At the age of sixty-one Emma Betony in a kindly light looked ten years younger. She was tall, and still slim, with a figure the Edwardians, among whom she must be counted, called willowy. It was a good simile, because from the waist up there was always that faint inclination that suggested being driven in an open landau and acknowledging an acquaintance across the road. Only in the absence of the landau it somehow had a deprecatory air. Indeed, everything about Miss Betony, the tired soft skin of the permanently pink-veined cheeks, the mild blue eyes, the timorous smile bestowed too frequently perhaps, proclaimed a gentility so inoffensive as to be uninteresting; for to seem innocuous in old age is to invite disregard.

This afternoon, on coming out of the Toplady Homes after her weekly visit to Miss White, she took the path across the quadrangle instead of returning by the archway into Plane Street and, fumbling a moment at the iron gate (locked at 8 in winter, 10 in summer), let herself into the recreation ground in front. On its fringe were seats placed comfortably at haphazard, here and there screened by accommodating shrubs. She sat down on one of them, her hands trembling.

Her own sensitivity to attack from such a quarter shook her now as badly as Mildred White's remark had done five minutes ago. Was she really so touchy that the absurdity and—yes, the senility of it failed to strike her? No, she wasn't. That at least was something to be thankful for. Blind resentment only implied in herself the existence of those very traits she condemned in Milly.

"You mustn't be disappointed if they consider your case unfavourably, Emma. The Homes were intended for gentlewomen, you know, and your dear father *was* in trade, after all."

Acidity might have sharpened the words to a point of individual malice that would have made them at once easier to accept and to forget. There could hardly be a communicant at St. Philip's unaware of the blow Miss White had sustained when the vicar gave into Emma Betony's charge the decoration of the great south window at Harvest Thanksgiving. True, it was nearly a year ago now; but an affront of that nature was not so lightly passed over. There had been, however, no touch of rancour in the reminder that Toplady (George Henry Bumperdown, 1818–79, when the distinction was acutely recognized) had indubitably separated the sheep from the goats in his design for eight almshouses in the borough of Churchway. On the contrary, it had struck a note whose sheer impersonality had shaken Emma Betony with much the same result as one got from agitating a tranquil glass paperweight so as to produce a miniature blizzard. While the storm was still raging she had glimpsed the pitfall into which her feet had narrowly escaped slipping.

For the net spread out for her took in more than the discreet boundary of the Toplady Homes. It embraced, as she saw now, all Churchway, and beyond Churchway a world of thought and living she need not make her own unless she would. If the committee which sat to consider her application looked upon her as a fitting neighbour for Miss White and the other six occupants with their professional and nonoccupational backgrounds, she would then be at liberty to take her place where Betony's greengrocery would be at once forgiven and unforgotten. So, she would dedicate herself to the service of their loyalties.

But these were the people who frightened her, so little were they moved by personal issues, so profoundly by those affecting their class. It was perhaps rather sweeping to describe them as being emotional only in the sociological sense, but that did more or less illustrate their desiccated quality. It took red blood, after all, to hate another woman for being prettier than yourself, but a much more anaemic fluid to feel the odium of rubbing shoulders with one whose entry and exit at her own home had been a shop door flanked by peanuts, potatoes and beetroot. Gentlewomen? Of course. But Mildred had omitted the qualifying term in the endowment. There they were known as "decayed." The hint of corruption conveyed in this charming ambiguity suggested an imaginative power of which Mr. Toplady himself must be held guiltless.

Emma smiled as she poked gently with her umbrella at the moist path. When in anger concentrate thought and vision on something wholly detached from yourself. She had taught it her pupils over a long range of years and had found that, unlike the majority of precepts, it worked well in practice. Now, as she watched the thin spirals of vapour the afternoon sun was drawing from the gravel the importance of Mildred White and her kind seemed of equal evanescence. They belonged to the most vulnerable order on earth, the little people with small incomes, smaller brains, and smallest talents, who led the circumscribed lives that made them the Aunt Sallies for every Smart Aleck. Castigating them was an old and not very laudable practice. It went on, mainly, she thought, because of their surprising continuity. As a class these pious spinsters and unadventurous widows and widowers and little professional folk who had no big names with which to disarm criticism were uncommonly good at survival. The herd instinct again, she supposed.

Well, I won't subscribe to it, Emma thought, flushing a little at such mental resolve. I won't, even if I have got the forty pounds a year which makes me acceptable to Toplady. (If it were thirty-nine, now, it wouldn't have been any use applying for the vacancy at all. Think of that.) But I've got too my independence, which is another way of saying myself. It may have to go, but not among the Topladies.

Father struggled hard to give me a good education—he was never properly alive to the inferiority of women—and it *was* a good one in the days when I had it. I've knocked about a bit, and seen and heard and known a few things that would make poor Milly goggle, though I am silly and antiquated now, and credulous in some ways still. But the one side of me, the one that got the edges knocked off, will always pop in to the rescue of the other. It always has and it always will. Because in the end I don't accept other people's shibboleths. My own may be even stupider, but they are my own. And one of them is that people can't finally be docketed and pigeonholed according to what their fathers sold or didn't sell. You can do it for a time, but ultimately it doesn't work. There's only goodness and wickedness—and it's no good sorting those too precisely, because they get mixed in the *most* confusing way however careful you are. So I won't have a Toplady. And *that* means asking for parish relief. Dear me, I shan't like it very much... But the parish won't either.

With which consolatory afterthought Miss Betony rose and went home to Mrs. Flagg's boarding establishment in Museum Road.

She had lived there four years, in the tall, self-effacing house in a back street where the pavements marched sheer with the front doors and coffee-coloured net screened from the infrequent passerby the occupations of the ground floors. Her sojourn there had been marked by a significant ascent. Beginning at the first floor with windows commanding the complacent features of the Toplady Museum over the way, she had moved eighteen months later to a small but pleasanter room up the next flight, whence she looked down on five strips of walled garden, a budgerigar house, and the backs of homes that early each week flaunted their laundry like festive bunting.

Climbing had indeed its compensations, for the next move which nine months ago had brought her to the attic floor, with two buckets of sand in grim attendance at the top of uncarpeted stairs and the homely world of Monday washing and apple trees and cage birds dropping away beneath her, had given her too what none of the other boarders shared, a view of sky and distant hills, and bright gleams of the river slipping smoothly away to the sea that lay somewhere behind them. Sometimes she fancied she could taste its breath on her lips. It was a salutary reminder that life had not been spent wholly in Churchway.

It was nearly teatime when she got in. The hall was dim and a little odorous still. Noon, with its attendant aroma, lingered overlong at Mrs. Flagg's. Emma glanced left at the table where the afternoon post might be found. There was nothing there, but as she went by to the stairs a door on the right opened and Mrs. Flagg, in a whispering brown dress, came out of her private sitting room. In the quick gush of light from her own window her rigid black hair looked more than ever like a wig. It seemed to Emma for one flickering second that she had moved towards the hall table. The next she was coming up to her with something in her hand.

"Your letters, Miss Betony." Her teeth were ingratiating. "That silly girl leaves the front door open so long every time she answers it, I took the post in for safety. The wind's up, don't you think? But of course we're near the time of the equinoxial gales, aren't we? I always say nobody would ever think this quiet street could be so boisterous till you see the mat lifting and hear things flopping about on the floor."

"Thank you." Miss Betony took the letters. "There isn't any wind today."

Mrs. Flagg opened her mouth with the gasp of a fish jerked to land, then, seeing only Miss Betony's ascending back, turned about smartly and went into the dining room where Winny was setting out tea. There were moments now and again when her fourth floor's conspicuous lack of guile made her grow red about the ears. It was all very well to remind yourself that some folk were born naturals anyway: the fact remained, it was often easier to meet, if not dispose of, the double-edged individual who indulged in a little subtlety at one's expense. Like that sarky Mr. Coburn on the second floor who pretended he'd always thought before becoming a p.g. there the Flagg "pension" was an annexe to the Toplady Collection on the other side of the road.

Emma's habit of not examining her post until reaching her room had become a sort of rule. On the top landing where a sword of the sun pierced the skylight the house was soundless and far more intimate. She took a key from her handbag and, unlocking the door, passed into her room through a delicate curtain of dust motes that gilded the threshold.

There were three letters. The first was addressed in a beautiful, pointed, characterless legal hand with which she was not familiar. She opened it neatly in deference to its outside. The same urbane script informed her, on a single sheet of notepaper stamped with a Holborn address, that at a meeting of the governors of the Toplady Endowed Homes for Decayed Gentlewomen she had been appointed to fill the vacancy occurring at No. 3 of the said Homes as from the first of the month following receipt of notice of admission to the said Homes, etc.

Miss Betony, her cheeks a little pinker, sighed, and laying the letter down flat on her dressing table, looked for a minute or two with a fascinated gaze at its burden of phraseology. Then she picked up the next missive. This would be either a newspaper or a small magazine about six inches wide, folded twice in a transparent wrapper. Two short pieces of soiled string loosely embraced the package, and as Emma slipped them off and inserted a thumb beneath the wrapping she flushed scarlet. For the second time in two months she had had through the post a copy of *Wings of Friendship*.

It seemed that this eight-leaved journal, appearing monthly in typescript and borrowing its title from a Dick Swiveller misquotation, circulated among members of the Pact-and-Picture Club, to whom it advertised itself as "a beautiful medium for enduring friendship and conjugal bliss, highly confidential, references rigorously examined, correspondence arranged, introductions effected, sympathetic partnerships set on the road to happiness. Sent to you in a sealed envelope (*but it isn't*). Stamp only: Secretary, Edenhaven, Parade, Whimby-on-Sea."

But Miss Betony had never sent a stamp, nor a reference, nor any request to become a Pact-and-Picture-ite. She had never been to Whimby-on-Sea. But years ago, in the last war, when emotions ran high and loneliness and doubt and feelings of insecurity could be appeased in all kinds of strange ways, when she had been thirty-six and pretty enough not to hesitate about sending a photograph to someone she had not seen, there had been a club—well, a matrimonial bureau really—and a secretary, and a man…

It was all so long ago. Shame and disappointment and disgust had built their cage, imprisoning it too closely for any but a Freudian escape. But there was none to know her dreams. And the puzzle remained, who was it who troubled to prod that old ghost, and why?

She looked more attentively at the wrapper. Yes, the Churchway postmark again; and again the scribbled address, badly written but with no effort at disguise. She did not recognize the hand. Who was there in Churchway who knew? Milly White? Mrs. Flagg? Old Miss Chancey, Milly's bosom friend and next-door Toplady? What, even then, was the motive?

Nothing more particular than vague spite suggested itself. That the paper was posted in Churchway was the disquieting factor. It must mean that somebody she knew, however slightly, met and perhaps talked with, had knowledge of an indiscretion of twenty-five years ago, and was stabbing back with it in this oddly purposeless and repetitive fashion.

A month had elapsed between the arrivals of the papers. All at once she ran through the leaves quickly in search of something. Here it was, a blue-pencilled cross scored thickly against a notice on the last page. "*Lonely bachelor, age 49, good health, comfortable income, seeks friendship of unattached lady with view to matrimony. Write, photograph if possible, Box 12B, 'Wings of Friendship,' Edenhaven, Parade, Whimby-on-Sea.*" Last month too her attention had been directed to a similar appeal. In that case the heart-free gentleman had been forty-five. She noticed that advertisements on the same page outlined in every case the qualifications of older swains. This time, as last, her unknown correspondent had selected for Miss Betony the youngest suitor.

Emma's face burned and her lips were a little unsteady. She covered the Holborn letter with friendship's wings and sat down weakly in the noisy basket chair, uncertain whether to laugh or cry. They had in turn offered her Home and Husband. And she would have neither. What next?

The third letter was still in her hand. She looked down at it, at first absently because mental vision was misted with other things; then the familiar writing brought her back to earth. Chagrin melted to anticipatory pleasure. She smiled. She had no need of opening this to identify the writer. It was from Grace Aram.

Chapter II

UNATTACHED LADIES

Though Miss Betony had been governess to successive generations of children for the best part of thirty-five years, there was not one of her pupils with whom she had since kept up a correspondence, except Grace Aram.

The reasons for this were inherent in her own character. In the first place, she had no sentimental feelings about children, whose obscure cruelties had never ceased to make her wince. Privately, she thought them odious, and wondered increasingly why the thought should have to be private. Why was it taboo to confess antipathy to the human young? The lip service universally paid to love of them was, she felt, defensible only on the grounds that we had got to make the best of a bad bargain. Children were the guardians of man's perpetuity. They were man's perpetuity. Cherishing them was simply a measure of self-preservation, part of the general struggle for survival. And since the task of caring for an object is made easier by first loving and idealizing it, the expediency was adopted. It was a colossal game of let's pretend. Man himself had conspired to disguise as adorable and adored the most disagreeable phase of his existence; because, poor fellow, it was a necessary phase. Like smothering a pill with jam. The jam made swallowing pleasanter, but the pill was there just the same.

It's such humbug, Miss Betony told herself, that you can hardly find anybody now to question its insincerities. We've got to like what we do if we're going to make a success of it, and that's all there is to it. And I suppose we've got to make a success of perpetuating the human race—though with the Heinkels chugging over my skylight one can't help doubting the worth of all the wear and tear that goes to it. Well, turning on the tap of affection for other people's children just isn't a gift of mine. I can't gush over them. I don't even like them.

So it was easy to understand why there had been no *Schwärmerei*, to evoke a passionate flow of letters. Or was it? Children confess to unpredictable attractions and, like cats, will sometimes orient towards those who dislike them. But Miss Betony's aversion was so meekly sustained as to parade for the most part a gentle indifference—discouraging soil for the growth of a "pash" in its initial stages. There had been no letters, then—except to Grace, whom Miss Betony had known as an adolescent rather than a child.

She had been the oldest of all Emma's pupils, sixteen when they met, eighteen on parting; a queer, gawky, discontented orphan with Burne-Jones features painfully disfigured by acne. After unpromising conflict with a number of boarding schools she had come to live in a huge house in Baden Square, the town residence of old Mrs. Martyr, who was mother-in-law to Lord Abel and some sort of relative to Grace. The girl herself was vague about the precise connection; indeed, the cousinship involved was removed so many times that when all the removals had been got out of the way the guiding string to the maze was lost with them. Nobody could say exactly how Grace fitted in, but there she was with old Mrs. Martyr for guardian and only servants besides in the house.

As a duenna Mrs. Martyr was both severe and neglectful. Insisting as she did on the isolation of the young, she was little concerned with it sartorially. Grace seemed to be in a state of constant mourning for somebody or other, and slouched through the house, where even noon was twilit, in dowdy black frocks that barely touched her knees and avoided her wrists altogether. Mrs. Martyr liked entertaining, but excluded her ward from the entertainment, a doubtful loss to the girl, perhaps, since the guests even when younger were unmistakably her guardian's contemporaries.

From time to time there were other incursions. The Martyr grandchildren, Abels and Martyrs alike, would break out spasmodically all over the house like measles, agitating the propriety of the old rooms and leaving in their wake the foam of ill-temper. On these occasions Emma noticed how much more irritable and difficult Grace was. Apparently unprovoked, she nevertheless threw her weight about in all sorts of odd ways, with the same heavy hand as the Abels used in throwing their abundant pocket money. Grace had little money, how little Emma was never quite sure. But there were times when she brusquely approached her governess for a loan and got instead a hasty gift, because Emma had an old-fashioned prejudice against lending. A generation ago an inferiority complex was not the glib password it has since become. Miss Betony put it all down to growing pains, a repressive guardian, and not enough sunshine in Baden Square, a combination of afflictions which in practice amounted to the same thing.

A sense of unity, at first reluctant, developed between governess and pupil. Grace was old for her age, Emma in some ways over-young. The score of years between them seemed of small account beside the loneliness each knew but did not admit. Trifling confidences were exchanged, then larger; Emma regaled her charge with anecdotes of past experiences abroad, vivid little sketches of the vanished world of Germany, Russia, the Balkans in the first years of the century—pouring out tea for the Kaiser's sister-in-law, buttoning the boots of a little archduchess in St. Petersburg, waking to the whispering tremor of an earthquake shock one summer morning in Sofia. Grace liked her stories coloured with snobbery. This made Emma uncomfortable until she remembered the girl was a poor relation with still poorer prospects; and then Grace herself cleared the atmosphere in a frank outburst that Emma never forgot.

"You'll think I'm a pretty low tuft-hunter, always wanting to hear about lords and ladies and the potty little tin rulers of your Ruritanias. Because I like hearing about them doesn't mean I like them. I don't. I hate them. Yes, I *do*, Bet—you can call it sour grapes if you like, I don't care! They've left me skulking on the edge of blue blood, sniffing it like the fee-fo-fum creature and not much liking what I can smell. And I can only hit back with vulgar curiosity, poking my nose into their shady pasts—or letting you poke it for me. But you're very tiresome, you won't tell me the really debasing bits."

"Indeed, I won't!" Miss Betony cried, adding with lamentable lack of truth, "I don't know any."

She dutifully tried then, as on like occasions, to demonstrate with Shakespeare's help the insignificance of that tide of pomp beating on the high shores of the world, but neither bard nor governess carried much conviction in face of the Hon. Monty Abel's tuck allowance and Grace Aram's darned combinations. And it was all apt to end with the same digression.

"Well," Grace would say with her bitter smile, "the magic circle's closed anyway—and I'm outside it. Tell me about Mary Shagreen."

And off they would go again. But this time the tale bore no aristocratic halo; or, at best, a borrowed one. For Mary Shagreen, who was half-sister to Emma Betony's mother, had been common clay. She was a dancer who, from the age of fifteen, had danced a way through the hearts and purses and capitals of three continents, tripping in and out of wedlock with a charm so sprightly that its unrepentant pace had been forgiven her. The tales about her told by Emma, who had seen her only twice, had an air of unquestionable veracity, together with a fine disregard for chronological sequence. More often than not they lacked beginning and end. Like thistledown they skimmed the hemispheres, jumped the calendar, hopped indecorously from pole to pole—or very nearly. But they dazzled; and such inconsequence was half their charm.

To Grace Aram they were meat and drink. Here was an enchanting creature, unprivileged and penniless like you and me, and not so wonderfully pretty either, who with nimble feet and a stout heart had burst the bleak barriers of caste and looked at the magic circle from the inside.

"She was happy, wasn't she, Bet?"

"I—don't know, dear. One hopes so. Her life was such a whirl, though."

"But she was once Duchess of Chazzo-Pitti—and after only a week in Milan!"

"Yes. And the Countess of Wyvoe afterwards—or was it before? But—"

"And that wasn't all. Tell me again about the last husband."

"I don't *know* that he was the last," Emma would say, frowning, but she told it all the same—the story of Jeremiah P. Hale of Michigan, who had wooed Mary Shagreen in the guise of a poor man and had then to lay at her feet, which had first lured him to such trickery, more than ever the Lord of Burleigh dreamed of possessing.

"I expect she knew all the time, don't you?"

"Oh *no*." Emma was shocked at the implied duplicity. But looking into the uncomfortably mournful eyes and seeing the full, smiling lips, she had thought, Am I an incurable romantic?

"My—my aunt isn't that kind of woman," she had said hotly, for she loved Mary Shagreen because she was the unacknowledged symbol of what she would have liked to be herself. "Full of faults, I know, and not doing the right things according to standards we must respect, but never proud, never cruel, never avaricious—and not too anxious about tomorrow. She was too gay for that—and I don't mean only frivolous, for there's a spring of gaiety in her that is the treasure of the humble."

"Oh, I know she must be a darling!" Grace cried hastily, afraid lest a hint too much criticism should dry up at the source the Shagreen saga. "But I mean, her other husbands were all rich, and butterflies like that always know where the money is."

"You think too much of money," Miss Betony had reproved her.

"It's all I can do about it—think," said Grace, and there they left it.

Sometimes Emma was visited with doubt of the propriety of such tales for the diversion of a seventeen-year-old. But they went on, chiefly because the dazzling aura of Mary Shagreen succeeded, as nothing else ever could succeed, in shedding light through that sombre house where morning and afternoon and at schoolroom tea they two were left undisturbed. She it was who, invisible, unmet, sealed the friendship between them and so started their correspondence.

Emma had not been the first to write. She left Mrs. Martyr's service shortly before the 1918 armistice, when she had been with them two years. It was not until the spring of 1920 that a letter with a Swiss stamp, addressed and readdressed, had reached her. Grace was at a finishing school in Lausanne and, her entry there having been put off too long by the postwar tidying up of the Continent, was once again finding herself odd man out as she had been in Baden Square, all the other pupils being younger than she. Would Bet write and cheer her up as she had cheered her in London all those centuries ago? Her guardian's letters were only to instruct or reprove, and the miserable brevities she paid twopence-half-penny a time for were like military dispatches. Nobody else wrote at all. With the Abel and Martyr kids it was out of sight, out of mind; and, really, she'd never been much in their sight.

No, she hadn't, Emma agreed. Poor child, she seemed doomed to have maturity postponed, first by an unimaginative old woman who had paid her dues not to love but to the call of a remote blood tie, and then by the war. She ought to be married, or using her brain and detachment in an occupation she could make properly her own. Instead, she had to kick her heels in a fashionably jejune setting she did not fit and had anyway outgrown. Of course I'll write to her, Emma decided. She was touched by a fidelity she had not expected. It was even a little flattering to have proof of the impression she had made on at least one pupil.

There had been, not unnaturally, gaps in the correspondence. Sometimes for almost as long as a year Emma could not have said where Grace was or what she was doing. But that she had neither forgotten nor grown tired of writing to her was made plain by the fact that it was always she who picked up the thread again, without apology or a too conscientious labouring of past silences. The queer absence of attachment to place or people that had characterized her from the first marked her progress still through the giddy twenties and disillusioned thirties of the century. She bobbed up unhappily in all sorts of places, took on secretarial work, advertising, posts as nurse-companion, companion-chauffeuse, chauffeuse-gardener, gardener-kennelmaid, and was admittedly a square peg in all of them. Mrs. Martyr died and left her some old and, according to Grace, spurious jewellery; that was all.

Then she got a succession of teaching posts in schools, confessing to Emma that she had become the perfect marm, which Emma found incredible. Imperfection, indeed, was suggested in 1934 when she abruptly scuttled her job in a training college halfway through term. Thereafter she turned up in control of an establishment of her own, a private boarding school in the Epping district, formally christened Makeways (no saints for me, Grace had declared), where individuality, her own particular fetish, might be had, it seemed, for an enormous fee.

Letters were desultory then. Grace was so busy steering her girls clear of the regimentation she had loathed and feared as a child herself that Emma and her affairs had been once more relegated to the background. War had seemed to seal the cleavage as final; but, as before, the lapse was merely temporary.

Only two months ago—yes, it had been July—an affectionate, hasty letter had reached Emma from Dorset. Grace had evacuated her school, or what was left of it, to the country after the fall of France. She wrote to ask Bet to join her and take a post at Makeways. The staff, going to swell the Land Army or the A.T.S., or one or another of the services, was dwindling; there was nobody she'd so much care to have by her side as Bet.

But Miss Betony had had other views. For one thing, a Toplady Home was in the picture by then, when penury on one's doorstep and a temporary amnesia regarding the way Betony had earned a living had made the prospect by no means unattractive. For another, it was with a reluctance that acted like a cold douche that she entertained the idea of teaching again after a blessed liberation from the chains five years ago. The truce had made her more than ever unequal to the conflict. She would no longer be able to dissemble her antagonisms; she had been off her guard too long. It was better not to court failure and humiliation. Besides, it was more than twenty-two years since she and Grace had met. Separation was now so habitual as to have become an accepted condition it would be unlucky to disturb. Might it not be tempting providence to meet in the flesh? (I'm an old woman, and Grace—bless me, yes—Grace must be forty if she's a day!) It wouldn't do.

So she had written, declining the offer and explaining about the almshouses. Almost by return a letter came, begging her to reconsider her decision and pouring ridicule upon the idea of Bet settling down to lavender-and-lace inactivity. Little she knows about it, thought Emma ruefully. It stiffened her resolve. She did not answer the letter.

But things wore a different complexion on the day Grace wrote for the third time. Independence must be surrendered in one direction or another; it was pleasanter far to think of its partial renunciation at Makeways than either an appeal to the parish or the body-and-soul business it would mean among the Topladies.

Besides, it was little less than a miracle that this should have fallen into one hand on the day the other had thrown aside the offer of a home. To reject it might surely be tempting providence to more dangerous purpose?

She read the letter again.

MAKEWAYS SCHOOL,

MARTINMAS, BUGLE, DORSET,

September 11, 1940.

MY DEAR BET—When I last heard, you were consigning yourself to senility and looking out for an almshouse in the autumn. But I think you said it wasn't even vacant yet, and you didn't suppose you'd settle in till October. That gives me hope I'm still in time to stop you throwing yourself away in this old-maidish fashion. It makes me angry to see women of your years (you *must* remember the changed values regarding age. What was old to our mothers is nowadays young, or comparatively so) resigning themselves to such footling ways of getting through what they like, actually *like*, to suppose is the closing stage of life. An almshouse for you is unthinkable. Now, do please look at this thing sensibly and stop short of the plunge. Remember all the riches of the past, the whole background to your life we used to get a kick out of when I was a kid in Baden Square. You simply can't put it all aside to take on half a dozen old women and a doddering padre whose visits will be the only high spots of existence.

I want you to come here, and while you are here take one or two of the senior girls in French and German. Not a class, as I believe I first mentioned. My Mam'selle is still with me, but she can't or won't undertake German, and conversationally anyway is too impatient. Your salary would be a resident one of eighty pounds a year.

But I told you all this before when you turned it down so quickly. That impulsive refusal hurt. I'd counted too long on your readiness to help. And it's more than teaching help I need. I've run my head into something very queer. I've a habit of doing so. But this beats all. It may take a worse turn suddenly, at any moment. I can't be more explicit in writing. I dare not give details when the whole thing is so formless and frightening. See how frank I am with you. This cannot be any inducement to you to throw in your lot with mine. But, oh, Bet, you were a tower of strength in the dark London days in the last war, and what I need above all else is a friend standing by.—With love,

Grace

It was the abrupt ending which really decided Emma. As a girl Grace had never known how to solicit help appealingly. Only the mute understanding which had grown up between them was responsible for Miss Betony's proffering it at the right times. Those closing sentences carried more than a hint of desperation. It was plain that Grace had broken off because she could not trust herself a line further.

Emma's quixotic heart swelled with the pangs of self-reproach. She did not know how she could have refused Grace two months ago; worse, how she could have ignored her second letter with its note of urgency now readily understood. Well, her mind was made up the more firmly, that was all. There would be no turning back this time.

At tea Mrs. Flagg observed how pinkly resolute her fourth floor looked.

"Good news, Miss Betony?" Her glance was arch.

Miss Betony looked her inquiry.

Mrs. Flagg flushed. How dull-witted the woman was.

"I mean, have you heard yet whether we are to lose you to our good friends in the playground?"

This circumspect allusion contrived to give the homes a local habitation without a name. Miss Betony had a sudden giddy vision of herself poking about in the sandpit, or, thin legs flying beneath fluttering skirts, hurtling through the air on a swing. It was not improbable that Mr. Coburn too glimpsed some such picture, for his sardonic glance trembled to a wink as he caught her eye.

"Oh, yes," said Miss Betony. "I've heard from the Toplady Homes. A vacancy has been offered to me."

"Well, isn't that *nice*!" Mrs. Flagg was shrill. "How soon must you go?"

"I'm not going."

The silence was weighty.

"But—I thought they had—you said—"

"Yes, they have. I did. But I'm not going."

"But, *why*—Miss Betony?"

Emma laughed. She surprised her own ears with the firmness and sincerity of her mirth.

"I really think it's because my father was a greengrocer," she said pleasantly.

Little Miss Stobart from the Public Library put down her cup with the tea untasted. The gulp she had foreseen would have been by way of anticlimax. The Baptist minister's widow, Mrs. Roe, chopped at a harmless-looking morsel of madeira cake with a vigour that made the table ring. She blushed furiously, but nobody took any notice. Mr. Coburn stared at Miss Betony with the widest stretch he had ever permitted his indolent lids; then he burst out laughing.

Tea broke up in some disorder. Mrs. Flagg was a rich purple. The sooner that Betony woman was out of the house the better. Never before had she knowingly harboured a mental case under her roof, and she wasn't going on doing so now either. The Homes could think themselves lucky they weren't going to get her. They might be odd fish there, but they weren't *that* kind; Miss Chancey's father, anyway, had twice been Mayor of Churchway. She waited until Emma had gone out of the room, then, mentally mouthing the syllables to ensure refined utterance, bent a dark look on Mr. Coburn.

"*What* vul-garity. One can well believe her father was a green-grocer—as I know he was," she added hastily.

"One can indeed," said Mr. Coburn gravely.

"It just shows what she is."

"It does. Takes time to show us all up."

Mrs. Flagg eyed his retreating back doubtfully. You never knew where you were. Then she decided that for once Mr. Coburn was taking the sensible view.

Chapter III

INTERVAL FOR TEA

There was nobody on the platform, nobody in the station approach. Grace had promised to meet her with the car, and Emma found her absence disconcerting out of all proportion to its importance. The bewildering sense of not knowing what she ought to do next annoyed her too; one who in her time had grappled with the vagaries of continental train service ought not to be put out because she was momentarily stranded in an English country town. For all she knew the house might be just round the corner. But no—for then why the car?

When she returned to the platform the train she had just left was steaming out.

"Martinmas?" The freckled porter rubbed his cheek. "The house, you say? I haven't been here long, ma'am." He hailed an older man.

"You'll be meaning the nursing 'ome, miss?" this individual said civilly, with an unerring eye for a spinster.

"No," said Emma firmly, not stopping to think. "It's a girls' school I'm looking for, Makeways School, kept by Miss Aram."

"Same thing," was the surprising answer. "That's to say, this school you're wanting 'as took over the 'ouse." He broke off and, slapping his leg, ejaculated with some violence, "*Blimey*—of all the rud— bad luck!"

Apparent commiseration with Miss Aram on a poor bargain was explained at once. Martinmas House was five miles further on, approached from Underbarrow Halt at which Miss Betony's train would stop in ten minutes' time. By leaving the platform to look for her friend outside she had let slip the chance of going on straight to her destination.

"And the next train for the halt?"

"In pre-cisely an hour an' twenty minutes. But there's always a taxi to be 'ad, miss, if you're in a 'urry."

Emma, totting up fast, shook her head. The acquisition of a job was too new yet to have undermined the thrift of years. Consulting her watch she found it was already teatime. She was both hungry and inquisitive. The afternoon was drenched in that kind of sunny somnolence that invites lingering; and beyond the limits of the deserted platform was a strange, unvisited town.

Her luggage bestowed, she walked out into the sunshine. Climbing the short ascent of the station approach between the marigolds and laurels and drooping heads of leopard's-bane filmy with dust, she had the odd feeling that the world was asleep. Not dead, as the solitude and silence might suggest, but persuaded to slumber, thought Emma, with memories of innumerable small charges' bedtime, by the liberal dispensations of the Dustman. There's more than enough for our eyes, she caught herself whispering as the stuff eddied round her shoes like flour. But the thought was discouraging on the threshold of her mission to rescue Grace from whatever Dark Tower she fancied she was coming to, and she put it from her resolutely. This was the more easily done because the turn in the road brought other images to mind. At the end of a row of cottages where no life moved, a large and odorous brewery marked the corner. Rounding it Emma understood at once how Bugle had got its name.

For a distance of a quarter of a mile the hot, white road in front of her climbed clean as a whistle, bordered by placid green verges and a pleasing medley of houses, well-spaced and mainly eighteenth century. At the top of the hill it flowed out gently left and right at oblique angles, the summit crowned on the far side by a curving line of houses and shops that bulged a little towards the visitor entering the town. It was for all the world like a hunting horn lifted to the lips. But this afternoon its notes were not sounded.

At the top of the road, before crossing the bell of the bugle, Emma stopped to take breath. Here the houses gave place to shops which still kept in their upper storeys a residential character. In the mirror in a hairdresser's window she caught sight of her moist face and, with a sudden uprush of relief at the miles which lay between them, remembered Milly's disgust for perspiration. It was so vulgar. A cup of tea seemed the only answer.

From where she was standing no fewer than five establishments might be seen offering her this incomparable beverage. Bent on reaching the top she had already passed others by, and wondered if the managements of the rather fearful array confronting her had weighed the psychological factor in their choice of a site.

She rejected at once the "Bugle Teahouse"; its brassy invitation in letters a foot high and the nasal blares already proceeding from its open door suggested the kind of fatigue to which she had never been able to succumb gracefully. Hattie's Hearth conjured up a vision of condescending maidens in linen smocks who made one feel that to ask for a pot of tea and bread and butter was simply not done after all; Ye Nookye Neste displayed some dead wasps rather prominently in the window, while the door of Cluck's Café stuck so hard that there was nothing for it but to try The Teashop, whose arrogantly simple, if confusing, announcement compelled attention. Besides, it lay furthest to the right, sufficiently round the corner of the bulge to command what looked like a whole tangle of little alleys running into the town proper, while the left-hand road quietly put commercialism behind it and made leisured tree-lined way to meadows and river. In the short time at her disposal Emma judged a window of The Teashop, if she could secure one, likely to provide the most diversion.

In that respect, at least, she was lucky. The ground floor was given over to a rather tasteless display of confectionery and handi-craft; it was not easy to say where the one began and the other ended. But when she had obeyed the direction of a tipsy sign up some atrociously dark stairs with deep, irregular treads, she found herself in a small, low-ceilinged room, newly washed in lime-green, with a sloping oak floor and plenty of window space. A man and a woman sat speechlessly consuming buttered scones in a corner of it, and, spying an arch at the other end, she explored further and came into a second room, still smaller than the first, its backcloth an immense hearth flanked by a gleaming copper warming pan, with five tables disposed in the foreground and a little worm-eaten door on a latch leading to the cloakroom. There was nobody here and, sighing contentedly, she sat down at a crumb-littered table that gave an excellent view of the street below.

Emma looked out to where the bugle's bell and tube met in a jumbled sweep of Elizabethan and medieval building. The streets that threaded it like veins were mere passages squeezed out of their proper course by the jealous encroachment of the houses. At night they must be a mazy knot in the darkness; now they were picked out by the brilliant sunlight while her own side of the street lay in shadow. Above the disorderly pitch of roofs, where century toppled across century and a whole age lay open to the eye, a church spire with a gilded weathercock rose aloofly, warmly grey as the sky itself. Pigeons strutted the roof gutters or preened themselves in the road below; then, wheeling abruptly, skimmed the steeple for a minute or two before settling down to a repeat performance. The glint of their snowy breasts delighted Emma.

She must not forget what she had come for. An unpolished brass monstrosity on the table leered up at her and, shaken, emitted a hollow, unpromising note. To her surprise, however, she had not to wait longer than five minutes before there appeared an underblown damsel in shapeless linen with a cultivated absence of manner, who confirmed all her worst fears entertained for Hattie's rival hearthstone six doors away. She stared frigidly out of window while Emma made her frugal request, then, sluggish and insolent of carriage, made off without a word to see if anything could be done about it. By the time she's my age, Emma reflected, she'll be the perfect Toplady—if only The Teashop is comfortably dead and buried by then.

Drinking her tea, she became absorbed in the view from the window. There were plenty of people about for that hour of the day, hurrying to and fro with the curiously purposeful and, it should be confessed, entomological air which human beings on their lawful occasions display to a detached observer. They suggested a large population for a small town until she remembered that a proportion must be due to evacuation from the cities. Some, no doubt, like the party of girl cyclists over there with painfully scarlet legs in shorts, were belated holidaymakers defying the war.

Her attention was drawn to a middle-aged woman who emerged hurriedly from the alley opposite the restaurant. Though she was flashily dressed, it was not her clothes which made her conspicuous. She was ducking her head first one way and then the other with the distracted air of one who does not know which direction she ought to take. Finally, muttering excitedly, she stopped at the curb with every sign of plunging across the road any minute. Emma guessed at the muttering, because the strong light showed the rapid movement of her lips; and excitement was patent in the uncontrolled wagging of the head, the lack of self-consciousness, the restless feet and twitching fingers. Emma, who had seen epilepsy in her time, wondered if it was the prelude to a fit.

All at once the woman dived back so precipitately that she landed square against a passerby, who lifted his hat nervously and went on at a quickened pace. In the shelter of the alley corner she started plucking at her gloves, tearing at the fingers with a frightened petulance not lost on a spectator even as distant as Emma was. The gloves off, she held up first one hand, then the other, splaying them horribly, and with head tilted back studied with fearful deliberation whatever it was she could see there.

Why, it's like the sleepwalking scene in *Macbeth*, Emma thought, only there's more mopping and mowing to it.

A sound behind her, so light it might have been only an intake of breath, made her turn sharply. At the next table, on a line with her own, a girl was standing, straining tiptoe to absorb the last detail of the view from the window. She ignored Emma; her prominent eyes, focused on the alley mouth, looked above and beyond her. Somebody else, Emma told herself, who can't help staring at the poor thing, though her observation doesn't seem quite so idle as mine. I wonder if she knows her. I didn't hear her come in.

Girl, after all, was not precisely the term for her. She was clearly older than the slim, small stature suggested. Her plain grey suit and scrap of unadorned hat were extremely smart, but the makeup showed such extravagant neglect of detail as to defeat its own purpose. It gave revolting prominence to small, rabbity, unpleasant lips that normally would have been bloodless, while bleaching still more unwholesomely the pallid skin. With its long nose and pouchy cheeks hugged too closely by crescents of hair of a negative shade of brown, the face looked sharp-set without being thin. And that sort of pudgy beakiness is just the kind of combination one doesn't know what to do with, thought Emma tolerantly. But she mustn't gape at her like this. She turned back to the window.

The woman whose odd behaviour had enlivened the last few minutes had disappeared. There was nothing peculiar about that. She had to go sometime, one supposed. What was funny was that the girl keeping watch still stared with furious concentration at the now deserted pavement. Indeed, to get a more comfortable view of it she left the table and came up behind Emma's chair, so close as to stub her toe on its leg, and there stood without apology, her knees brushing the low sill. Emma, who had been sitting a little sideways, found that by turning her eyes to the corners she could glimpse, without moving, the hands gripping the top of the bag she had rested on the windowseat. They were plump and disagreeable, with nails carefully trimmed into talons and polished a brilliant scarlet. Now and again they explored the surface of the leather with little scratching noises.

Emma poured herself another cup of tea and sipped it slowly. Not for the world would she get up and go and leave this chit with her mystery unravelled. Of course she couldn't miss her connection, but there was more than half an hour yet to run before the train left and, going downhill, she need give herself a bare ten minutes to reach the station. Surely something would have happened by then.

It was happening now. An atmospheric change had taken place which she could not have defined. Though the girl at her back had not moved, Emma was sensible of a certain satisfaction in her neighbourhood. And then she saw that it coincided with the appearance at the entry opposite of a woman who had just come down it and who, like her predecessor, stood a moment on the pavement with an air of disquiet. Unlike her, however, she laid no pantomimic emphasis on her indecision. She was thin and elderly and dressed in black. Distance did nothing to mitigate the hopelessness of her bearing.

What's the matter with people this afternoon, Emma asked herself; or, at any rate, with those who leave that dark lane? She began to find odious its few innocuous yards visible from "The Teashop." The woman had turned right and was following the wide curve of the bell into the broad street that led townwards. The handkerchief she took from her bag gleamed for a moment white against the black breast of her coat; then she lifted it to her eyes. The bag on the windowseat was pushed aside while the hands that had held it pressed, palms down, on the sill. Emma, reckless of appearances, turned her head boldly and looked at the girl beside her. She was bending forward so close to the glass that her breath misted it. The stooping pose added an indescribably sly touch to the intensity with which her gaze followed the woman in black till she was out of sight. When she was gone she drew back, swung on her heel and, clutching her bag, made noisy exit through the outer room.

Emma too left in something of a hurry. She had a mind to see more of this business, if more there was. But when she had stumbled down the ill-lit stairs and delivered her bill to an arty-crafty lady afflicted with the same dumbness as her sister above, there was nothing outside to remind her of the incident.

The hot streets were still and quiet. The tea-hour hush had properly settled on the town. But in the undulatory contour of the roads where they rose to the summit of the hill and spread out from it again, there was a hint of something feline and, in the peculiarly velvet-shod feline sense, something minatory too. How fanciful I'm getting, Emma thought, ashamed, for Churchway had discouraged fancy and she was only a few hours away from it—how fanciful, to see anything predatory in the sunny silence of a little Dorset town.

Nevertheless, she was reassured by the back of a policeman waiting to direct traffic at the more rural end of the bell where little was likely to appear. It was always difficult to imagine anything unpleasant going on under an English police constable's eye. The superiority of prevention to cure shone in his very aura, and Emma, who knew better in her heart, was still able to convince herself that the most sinful intent would harmlessly burn itself out at sight of that dark-blue figure.

"The little turning by the hairdresser's, ma'am? We call it the Lanthorn. And it must've needed one in the old days—and would now if only we could show a light." He swept a solemn glance round for vehicles in need of guidance. "Shops? Well, I wouldn't call it a business centre down there—not in a manner of speaking, that is, though business there is, and plenty of it. Why, that part of Bugle's just a warren of little 'ouses—the *old* part, you understand—and the Lanthorn's but one of the runs into it. Not but what you don't have to go far that way before you come up against the police station and lockup."

He gave a rumbling chuckle, abruptly cut off in face of an on-coming bicycle whose rider, unaware that it had been kept in hand for the past quarter of an hour, seemed overwhelmed by the wealth of official gesticulation. Emma, neatly dodging the indecisive swing of the front wheel, made her way to the train which would soon be due now.

A warren of little houses with a business of their own divorced from the business of counter and till? The alley itself one of many such runs, breaking away from the placidity Bugle presented to the tourist of an hour or two, dropping crookedly into the bowels of the real town. The bowels of the town—how gross Mildred would think it—the bowels of the earth, from which at intervals strange unhappy Proserpines emerged, to blink, bewildered, in the unaccustomed day. Or so it seemed to Emma, stimulated by travel and warmth and the bizarre experience at the teashop to flights of imagination she would be the first to deprecate in tomorrow morning's rational light.

On the last stage of her journey she thought no more about it. As the train chugged through stubble-fields, honey-clear in the burning afternoon, past distant horizons humped with the barrows of the more distant dead, only her eyes reflected the shining peace outside. Her mind was busy with a swarm of doubts. Like gnats they rose about her, and like gnats refused to be beaten down.

Was she really doing the right thing by responding so uncondi-tionally to Grace's appeal? The right thing by Grace? For was she these days equal to grappling with someone else's problems when the handling of her own had been so conspicuously unsuccessful? If material advancement were the measure of ability she had no tes-timonial to offer. Was it fair to Grace to let her cherish the illusion that she was still the more or less efficient counsellor and friend of the Baden Square days? Times change, she reminded herself, and with them people; in particular, people change relatively. It was so often a case of the man and the hour. Useful people might become comparatively useless, and *vice versa*; not because their characters had lost or gained intrinsically, but because the circumstances which had once given their potentialities full play had themselves changed. A tower of strength to a lonely child twenty-five years ago—and an honest searching of her heart could not discover that she had ever merited so resounding a title—might well prove a broken reed to a woman of the world today. Emma's scrupulous conscience began to be weighted with the guilt of sailing under false colours.

She was the only passenger to alight at the halt from which steps led down to a road between hedges smothered in the curling silver smoke of old man's beard. She looked round for a waiting car, but there was none; her suitcase and trunk, which would have to be fetched, were temporarily stowed away in a hut at the end of the wooden platform. The "couple uv minutes'" walk to Martinmas covered a good half-mile delving deep into the countryside. Between the halt—clearly erected for the benefit of the nursing home—and the house itself, no human dwelling appeared. Once, passing the gate of a rough pasture, she caught a glimpse through the gap of a distant farmstead and a square-towered church; for the rest, she walked in hot silence enlivened only by a cloud of midges shimmering in the evening light.

The house was suddenly revealed where you expected no house to be. Under oak and hazel and crabapple, rooted in the high banks and clinging together overhead, the road was all at once a tunnel, with here on the right two short brick piers sinking like gravestones into the herbage round them, and a pair of iron gates pushed wide open. At the back stood the low-fronted brick house with lawns in front that seemed a sudden flash of light in the prevailing gloom, because they were bare to sky and sunshine and free of the trees that clustered at the bottom, leaning on one another like timorous watchers up and down that empty road.

Emma turned in at the drive without hesitation. There was no board up to indicate that Makeways had taken up its abode at Martinmas, but considering that the outlook was a branchy lane leading to a farmhouse or two, advertisement of a private boarding school must have been foredoomed optimism.

A car at the bottom of the drive was pointing at the gates. Emma could see a liveried chauffeur sitting at his wheel with impassive features and closed eyes. A step or two further, the front door under the porch was standing open. There was a flash of white from a starched cap as somebody passed across the hall. A strapped suitcase stood on the step. A boy in buttons came out and, picking it up, went down to the waiting car. He was followed almost immediately by a tall girl dressed for travelling, who left the house with an angry step. In spite of the absence of conventional uniform, Emma instinctively gave her sixth-form status. Her face was inflamed with crying that no last-minute attention had been able to disguise. For an instant their looks crossed. The dark, swollen eyes were full of penetration. To Emma that air of furious defiance was not unfamiliar, and, recognizing an outraged sense of justice, the most shattering emotion the young are ever called upon to experience, she wondered what was wrong.

Chapter IV

PREPARE FOR POISON

T here it was again, a snuffling sort of noise not far away, breaking as one listened to a whimper that rose in turn to wailing, inarticulate speech. It stopped short as before, however, and Emma decided for the second time that it was none of her business. Quite likely one of the children was larking in dormitory hours. Only it hadn't sounded like a child; and, oddly enough, nothing about it was quite so unpleasant as the chilly silence which closed down upon the cry.

She went on arranging her belongings, her manner *distrait* because her mind was on other things. It had been a funny arrival. Grace's welcome, it was true, had lacked nothing of the warmth her letter had suggested, but after a hug which Emma felt was more like the clutch of a drowning man, and a muttered apology for the failure to meet her, she had disappeared on some urgent errand which had claimed her, except momentarily, the rest of the evening.

They had taken Emma to the room allotted her on the east side of the house. It looked comfortable enough with a wood fire flaking slowly on the hearth and marigolds in a blue bowl. They had sent to the station for her luggage. But there was the same air of abstraction about the maids who unpacked for her; and when dinner was sent up with the message that Miss Aram would join her later, it was less, Emma felt, as a concession to her own weariness after a tedious journey than because an upset had occurred today which absorbed the attention of the household to the exclusion of all else. It was that which had given to her arrival the false air of being unexpected.

It was past nine o'clock now. The square of light and warmth the room had become since the curtains were drawn was only a more marked reminder of the strangeness of the house outside its door. It was a little unsettling to realize that she had still to learn the geography of passages and rooms beyond this one, and that it would be no easy matter to find her way back alone to the front hall.

When tired, Emma thought, the imagination works overtime. These are foolish speculations. But I really am getting sleepy, so I hope Grace won't be long.

She moved a photograph of her mother and father from an obviously unsuitable place, and put the cracked and slightly spotty one of Aunt Shagreen in a less conspicuous one. The lustre mugs from Guingamp, showing one *La Vieille Fontaine*, the other the church of *Notre Dame de Bon Secours*, would look better spaced at each end of the mantelpiece than on that little bureau that rocked at a touch. And Lottchen's watercolours—gracious, it was 1903 the child had given them to her, so the backs said—it would be wiser perhaps to hang them tomorrow in daylight.

The thought made her conscious of the brilliant room. Two or three years with Mrs. Flagg had taught her to dispense with such indulgence. Force of habit prompted economy still; she turned on the reading lamp on the little table between bed and fireplace, switching off the main light. Immediately the small proportions of the room melted to mysterious perspective. Things she had not noticed sprang into the foreground, others sank into a well of indefinite shadow that blurred the outline of furniture and walls. The fire, quenched before, took on a flickering life.

Emma picked up her writing case to put it in a drawer of the bureau when both copies of *Wings of Friendship* fell out on the carpet. She stooped hastily. They were hardly the literature one cared to display in public, or to introduce to a school. But a curiosity she half hoped might never be appeased had prompted her not to destroy them. The suitcase was the place; she could lock that. She pushed it back under the bed, and rose sharply to her feet at a sound behind her.

She could see nothing, yet she had been sure—Was there a change in the room, something as imperceptible yet definite as a current of air in a stale atmosphere? Over there the lamp only emphasized the gloom it did not dispel. Her eyes were not what they were; for a moment she even forgot where the door was. She peered more closely. There—

The door was ajar. Though the short passage outside was unlit, there could be no mistake. The sound she had heard must have been the click of the latch as it slipped. That was all. Yet—

It was opening as she moved to shut it. A figure stood on the threshold. It was small and thin, clothed in a light garment disclosed in front by the darker folds of what might have been dressing gown or coat. It was murmuring softly from invisible lips in a voice which now and again sank to a whisper. At the motionless pose Emma's heart gave a sudden lurch. She was ashamed of it instantly, for ghosts might be numbered among her mild repudiations. But for a second she had thought that a wanderer from another world kept the entrance to her room.

"Is there anything I can do?" she asked, advancing quickly, and saw before her a little old woman with a yellow shawl round her head and slight, clawlike hands that groped at her breast and fumbled round chin and lips.

"I forget—oh, I forget," the apparition whispered, falling back a pace or two. She turned and, leaving the door open, made off down the passage on light, unsteady feet, spreading out a hand either side as she went to balance herself, now touching the wall, now recoiling, and all the time talking fast and breathlessly.

Emma stopped at the door. She had no possible excuse for pursuit. But curiosity, after a minute, was too strong for reluctance. She walked to the mouth of the narrow passage. Lights burned dimly in the main corridor which crossed it at right angles; from end to end it stretched empty and noiseless, with something of the aseptic air of a hospital. No door stood open; only from behind a closed one came the faint plash of water from a trickling tap. Emma could have believed that she had dreamed her visitor.

She returned to her room. The moment she was shut inside, the slobbering whine she had heard twice before broke out again. A gust of wind caught up the note and carried it away outside. But not before it had seemed so close at hand she could have sworn she had just closed the door in the face of the whimperer.

Somebody was there at any rate. Quick footsteps warned her before the knock. Grace Aram slipped into the room, staring back into the corridor in a way which made Emma uncomfortable until she took the knob from her cold hand and fastened the door.

"Who is it?" She spoke tremblingly.

"Where?" Grace asked below her breath, but with an intensity that made Emma feel she had wanted to shout it.

"The—the person who cries. Not all the time. She's been doing it at intervals since supper. It's not—pleasant. It doesn't sound like the usual giving way to grief or pain. It makes me think—"

"You're dreaming it? I know," Grace said harshly. She plucked Emma's sleeve and pulled her out of the shadows to the hearth, where the lamp burned and the silver ash of the fire lifted and throbbed in the chimney draught. She seated herself in a low chair on rockers, a little in front of the bedside table, and motioned Emma to the armchair opposite. "It's the echoes in this beastly house—"

"Oh, *no*—"

"I don't *mean* that!" Grace cried, control snapping. "Of course somebody is making these noises, but if it weren't for the booming passages and so many empty rooms—" She broke off to lean forward and toss a fresh piece of wood on the fire. The violence with which she flung it sent a quick smother of sparky ash into the fender and a brilliant spout up the chimney. "Oh, why did I have to take over a nursing home of all places on earth—"

She stopped again to listen. There was no sound but the flurried whisper of the flames and now and again a creak from the rocking chair.

"But why does that matter?" Emma asked gently. "It's only a house, after all. You didn't take over the patients."

Grace stared at her. "That's exactly what I did do. Surely I told you? They didn't all go."

She spoke with the patient air reserved for children. She thought how old Emma looked. She could not take her eyes off her. She felt shaken, not by compassion but because imagination had received a shock. Of course, everybody got older—she had herself, she supposed—and looked it, but visual memory, no matter how studiously disciplined, had not prepared her for this faded and conciliatory creature. In spite of the vague sweetness she could still recall across the bridge of twenty-two years, she remembered too an assurance, a hint of implacability even, in the handling of Mrs. Martyr which had won for her governess an admiration she rarely bestowed. Or was it simply that her own sullen defencelessness of those days had seen strength and resolution where was actually none?

"You didn't tell me," Emma said, her tone apologetic as if for an omission of her own. "I thought, when you took over and moved in, the house was—well, vacated by the former tenants."

How Grace had aged. I've missed, Emma thought with sudden poignancy, the years when she must have been beautiful. She had never, of course, had the immature charm which gives promise even to gaucherie, but a quality of latent strength none had been able to deny her. Memory endowed her with the darkly angelic force of the Pre-Raphaelites. It was a shock, then, to meet this ravaged-looking woman, nearer fifty than forty, one would have said, whose manner was a mixture of fatigue and arrogance, and to whom the years had brought self-assurance without poise. It was the old aggressiveness Emma remembered too well, that comes from being continually on the defensive. But there the likeness of the old to the new Grace ended; for this one eyed her like a stranger, while preoccupied, it seemed, with an indefinable fear she was quite unable to dismiss. Well, it would perhaps be brought out into the open in good time. Wasn't that what she had come for? Meanwhile, here at last was Grace confronting her like the bewildering echo of a past one had never properly related to the present.

Lamplight was giving the bony structure of her face and unrelieved black frock the light and shade quality of an etching. Jets of flame from the crumbling wood were reflected for an instant in her restless eyes which sought the shadows and the door and the empty space behind Emma's chair while she talked.

"I took Martinmas off the hands of two doctors, both women. They'd been partners in this nursing home, and charged unheard-of fees for coddling the rich who wanted to be coddled. They got the kind of patient—they aimed at getting her—whose only real complaint is one she never admits. They must have done pretty well out of it for years, so well, in fact, that prosperity went to the head of the weaker partner. I don't know the details—nothing, that is, beyond what Dr. Wick, who carried through the negotiations, told me and what somehow gets round among people who know or think they know—but it appears she took to drink and messed up her cases. The senior partner, I mean, whom I didn't meet. And as soon as that happened there was a noticeable falling-off in the number of patients."

"Naturally," Emma murmured. "Only, if they really had nothing wrong with them—well, there wasn't much she could seriously bungle, was there?"

"Oh, wasn't there?" Grace drummed impatient fingers on the chair arm. "There was even more. Wealthy hypochondriacs are insensitive to everything but their own importance to their doctor.

I've done my share of unprofessional nursing, and I know. It's expedient to handle them with all the delicacy you'd bring to a major operation. And Dr. Fairman didn't. Pretence was gradually stripped off. She let them see, with less and less compunction, what humbugs they were and how very secondary as far as she was concerned to the consolations of the bottle. So they went—in various stages of huff. And Dr. Wick was left to hold the baby—that is, until I stepped in and relieved her of it."

Emma frowned. "And when you took over, there were patients in the house?"

"Still are." She bent towards her, wringing one hand slowly in the other till the knuckles shone white. "Bet, I'm worried. I'm sick with worry. No, *don't*—don't say a word. Let me tell you first. There are two of them here. They wouldn't leave when the home was given up. They were as stubbornly determined to stay as the rest had been to go. In fact, for several months before I came along Dr. Wick had had only these two on her hands and at least twice in that period had seen prospective tenants turn down the house because of the conditions on which it was to be let."

"So I should think," Emma said, struck with the absurdity of the situation. "But why didn't you too? Couldn't you have insisted—?"

"I couldn't," Grace said frankly. "Bet, you don't understand. The school's not what it was. Maybe I should have moved from Epping sooner. Even in the weeks of the phoney war there were people who thought the west healthier than London, and who acted upon it. Besides that, a wave of regimentation is sweeping the world—standardized schooling, like everything else out of a tin, is cheaper, easier, and certainly safer than my sort of venture. In the educational sense, as well as every other, individual effort is going to be swamped. Yes, I know it's the old bee still buzzing in the old bonnet—but there's no getting away from facts. And the fact is, my numbers are down and my pocket pretty light—and I dare not sneeze at the twelve guineas a week Miss Thurloe pays for her fancies. Humiliating, perhaps, but I'm in no position to strike the disinterested pose. Besides, if you remember, I never did go to swell the ranks of those who despise money."

Emma remembered. She was profoundly shocked, not because Grace accepted, but because Miss Thurloe, whoever she might be, offered it. Twelve guineas. On that sum she had had to live for ten weeks at Mrs. Flagg's. And this woman was willing to pay it every single week to gratify a whim, to buy the pleasures of an illness she had not got, to win the assurance that she would remain the centre of interest in her unhealthy little world. A sickness that was assumed. But was it? If—

"It's Miss Thurloe who—?"

"Wails and moans and makes the night hideous—yes. It is—it is." Grace ran her fingers up her face where the ebb and flow of firelight moved, and pushing them into the roots of her hair pressed it back tightly from her temples. "Oh, *let* me tell it my own way! Do you realize, I've never told this thing to anyone, not just as it happened, from the beginning? And I feel—I've felt I should go mad, *mad*, with having to put a good face on things—" She dropped her hands, hanging them limply between her knees, and looked at Emma with the ghost of a smile.

"I'm behaving very foolishly, Bet. It's been an upsetting day. That's why you weren't met. But I'm ashamed of myself and this—this hysteria. It shan't happen again. You're here now, to keep me from running off the rails. Start the good work straightaway. Ask me what you like, and I'll try to give you a coherent account of things."

Her voice was quiet, and she was making a not unsuccessful effort to appear calm. But Emma, who recalled the stirring of deep waters at Baden Square, guessed at the turmoil beneath.

"You've brooded on this too long, Grace," she said with a less timid air than she had shown before, and added, half to reassure herself, "We're not strangers, you and I. If we talk it over there may be some quite ordinary explanation of what has seemed to you abnormal. Now tell me—you mentioned two patients just now, who had stayed behind when the nursing home broke up. Who is the other one?"

Grace looked at her with evident surprise. "Old Miss Wand. But she has nothing to do with the story—except, she's been upset by Miss Thurloe's behaviour—symptoms—call it what you please, so I changed her room the day before yesterday over to my side of the house."

"This part, then—?"

"Is what I arranged should be left for Miss Thurloe and Miss Wand. You see, the place is too large for me. I'm left with only fourteen children and a very small staff. It's better from every point of view that we should all be together in one wing of the house, with the nursing home remnant suitably isolated here. Of course, when I found it was having a bad effect on Miss Wand's health I had to move her."

"Yes, I understand," Emma said dubiously, not altogether partial to the idea of sharing a wing with Miss Thurloe. "But is she—are we alone over here then?"

"No, no. The nurse sleeps here." Grace had defined her thought. "Why, Bet, I did it purposely—put you over here, I mean. You're not afraid of things. And what is wanted is an independent witness more or less constantly on the spot, whose hands are not tied, as mine are, by the responsibilities of a job. No matter how small a school is, there's no work on earth so exacting, especially when it's an understaffed boarding school like this. I *can't* be here, there and everywhere. I dare not take my eye off things for a moment to give attention to what's going on in another part of the house. If I do, something's sure to happen—as it did yesterday."

"Something to do with the girl who left this evening?" asked Emma, feeling that inquisitiveness was not only expected but encouraged.

"How did you know? Oh, she was going as you arrived. Yes. That was Linda Hart, one of my seniors. I expelled her this morning."

"Oh, dear." Emma was mildly shocked. Expulsion was still a serious step, she believed. "What had she done?"

"Visited a fortune-teller in the town, against explicit orders. She's been troublesome for some time, though. I was lucky to get rid of her so quickly, as her aunt, Lady Hart, is staying in Blandford at present, and sent the car for her. As a matter of fact, Miss Thurloe was at the bottom of this last offence of Linda's."

"How was that?"

"She—Miss Thurloe, I mean—is wrapped up in this crystal-gazer, or whatever it is he calls himself—the whole place has lost its senses over the man—and hung round him shamelessly until she got too ill to go out. Now it appears she's been using Linda as proxy to get what she wants."

"What does she want exactly?"

Grace shrugged contemptuously. "What we all want—knowledge of the future."

"How was Linda to help her to it?"

"By carrying small articles she had worn or handled for this man to—psychometrize. I believe that's the word. Nurse refused to do it. Very properly, I think."

"But a little tactless, perhaps," Emma ventured. "Nurses do have to compromise with conscience sometimes, in the interests of their patients."

"Well, Nurse Swain is a hardheaded northerner without an ounce of superfluous imagination. And Miss Thurloe—Miss Thurloe—"

"Yes? Tell me what's wrong."

"Miss Thurloe is being poisoned."

Chapter V

TELLING ABOUT——

"Either that," Grace added, "or she's doing it herself to attract attention and make up for what she's lost now the place is turned into a school and the doctors gone. But I don't think that's it."

The presentiments of the past week were crystallized for Emma into one sharp fear. Poison—the elusive, the damnable, the unforgivable. And Grace had asked for her help. "But a doctor is still in attendance, of course?" was all she could weakly say.

"Oh, yes. Both Miss Thurloe and Miss Wand were Dr. Fairman's patients. When Dr. Wick saw how matters stood with her partner she called in a G.P. from Bugle to help. Old Dr. Fielding it was. He took over the Fairman lot, but was soon left with only these two. When I came in three months ago he was still attending."

The implication was clear. "You mean he isn't now?"

"That's what I mean. Bet, it's part of the worry—fear, if you like. We got on well with Dr. Fielding. It seemed natural to call him in as school doctor since he was already visiting the house three times a week, sometimes four when Miss Thurloe was particularly jittery."

"She was afraid of something?"

"No, no. Not then. At least, yes—she was. The thing she's always afraid of. Death. Some days more than others. Then she would be afraid that the doctor's absence for two days together was a glaring instance of medical lack of interest in her case. And she'd ginger him up with angry or imploring telephone calls to keep him on the run."

"Well, well." But Emma did not sound surprised. Long servitude in families which could each claim at least one case of neurosis had made her familiar with the Thurloe tactics. "And was Dr. Fielding never unwilling to indulge such caprice?"

"My dear," Grace said, and sounded reproachful, "she is a very rich woman. She is therefore privileged to anticipate death and wallow in its torments just as often as she pleases. And she never keeps the doctor waiting for his money."

"Yet he lost her as a patient?"

"He couldn't help that. It was illness. By August he was too bad to carry on. They said a major operation would be necessary. He went away and a locum came in. Now it looks as if Dr. Fielding won't be coming back."

"You don't think he's likely to recover?"

"As far as this case goes he's as good as dead now," Grace said flippantly. "He'll never be equal to general practice again. And there's every chance that Dr. Bold—that's the locum—will take over permanently."

Emma gathered that this was an unpopular outlook. Dr. Bold, it seemed, was the not uncommon type of medical practitioner who owes his rise to the judicious throwing overboard of ballast in the form of a bedside manner—behaviour, oddly enough, less uncongenial to the patients themselves than it is to their friends. He had probably started with very little, anyway, and had seen its acquisition as a painful process for which Nature had not cut him out. Better be done with it early, and be damned to it—to the patients too. The masochistic creatures showed little resentment; indeed, they throve on the treatment, or lack of it. It was significant that Dr. Bold's practice gradually lost its general character and became particular—very particular. On a bedrock of conscious brutality and an artful appearance of neglect which never overstepped the mark, he gathered round him a fashionable and hypnotized clientele whose imaginations and purses were such as to suggest an amiable conspiracy on the part of their owners to keep the doctor in clover for the rest of his days. But if his patients approved, their relatives and servants did not. Those in no need of medical attention saw him without blinkers, and put a different construction on his ruthless jettison of the decencies.

"He's a frightful man," Grace went on. "An absolutely ferocious bully and the very antithesis of old Daddy Fielding—that's what the children called him, so you can guess what he's like—and yet in some diabolically clever way he always sees the red light in time and manages to stop short of the unforgivable. In his own hoggish fashion he actually toadies to these daft old women—Bugle's full of them these days, that's why he wants to settle here. He came for a holiday in the first place, but now he's had the run of Dr. Fielding's practice he can't resist these dotty dowagers and puling peeresses."

Even the subdued lamplight which treated Grace more kindly and shone too warmly on her own face could not hide from Emma the twist of the mouth feeling for the ugliest adjectives.

"Surely the change from Dr. Fielding to Dr. Bold has been a shock to Miss Thurloe?" she could not help remarking.

"My dear, of course. But only in an enjoyable sense. It's been thoroughly refreshing, and would have acted as a real tonic if only she weren't genuinely ill at last."

"But poison, Grace? Are you *quite* sure? I have heard—I believe there are things which simulate—"

"Not this time. Traces have been found. I know. Nurse knows. The doctor knows—but he won't talk, he won't confide in me. He lets me see plainly I don't belong, that it's nothing to do with me, that I'm a fool who must take the consequences of marrying a school to a nursing home. Utterly unlike Dr. Fielding, who consulted the interests of Makeways every time, for all his deference to the old lady."

"And what was his opinion of this—poisoning?" asked Emma,

who felt that the mere pronouncement of the word gave an air of unreality to the situation.

Grace gave her a quick look. "The occasion didn't arise for Dr. Fielding to have one. There was no suggestion of poison until after Dr. Bold's arrival."

Emma was astonished, she could not have said why. No dates had been imparted; she had unreasonably assumed that Dr. Fielding had turned over to his successor a patient already suffering the attentions of a poisoner. This was not the case.

"She was perfectly all right until about a week—say, ten days after the new doctor came in. Well, you know what I mean by all right. She was enduring all the agonies of her fictitious illness and torturing herself into half real hysteria over the departure of Dr. Fielding. Then, just as she was beginning to grovel delightedly to the new man this thing goes and happens. Right under the very nose and eyes of Dr. Bold—sharp eyes too."

"He's clever, then?" Grace's descriptive fervour had suggested bluster without brains.

"Oh, yes. Give the devil his due," Grace said magnanimously. "You mustn't get the idea he simply throws his weight about to hide his defects as a doctor. It's done, we know, but Bold's not the one to do it. His manner may be an obnoxious form of window dressing, but the goods are there all right. He's a very able man, I believe. You couldn't hoodwink him."

Yet somebody was doing it, Emma supposed. Somebody who had not thought it worth while to hoodwink Dr. Fielding? She was very tired. Her brain refused to function clearly. But even in this bemused condition she felt there was a profound significance in what Grace had just told her.

"You said just now," she reminded her, "that she might possibly be doing it herself, though that was unlikely. Doesn't it seem the most feasible line to work on, though?"

Grace shook her head. "She can't be. It's bound to suggest itself, of course, as an alternative one would gladly clutch at because nobody can bear to think a poisoner is at large. I mean, it's natural to think it at once, and *for* once—but it won't bear examination. I agree with the doctor there. It's simply out of character."

"But not impossible?" Emma probed.

"Well, put it like that—no, perhaps." But Grace was grudging. "What is? But you don't know her, Bet. Else you'd realize there's nothing genuinely suicidal about her—not, that is, in the protracted sense. I'm not saying she mightn't take an overdose of something in a momentary fit of depression or pique rather worse than usual, though I don't think she would. But this business has been going on for the past month and must be horribly painful. She'd never have the courage, whatever her game, to destroy herself slowly. She lives in terror of Death. She thinks she can buy him off by being ministered to in advance for diseases she'll never get. She'd never bring herself to watch his gradual approach, a little nearer every day. And that's what poisoning yourself over a long period means."

Emma nodded. She had again the irritating sense that something of special import had been said and had drifted, unheeded, past her foggy understanding. She found it impossible to give the kind of attention that would let her apply what she heard, and make it comprehensible. She was sluggish, inactive, the mere recipient of what Grace cared to give her. That was going to be of very little use to Grace. She was afraid she was making a poor impression.

"What poison is it?" she asked with an effort.

"Arsenic," Grace said. "As commonplace, and deadly, as that. I have an idea, though, it isn't the only one that's been tried. But Dr. Bold is too close to confirm this, and nurse seems as much in the dark as the rest of us. But arsenic's been found, in the tumbler by her bed, in her water bottle, in the remains of some milk she'd drunk, twice in coffee. Bet, if this got about outside Martinmas, Makeways—what's left of it—is finished!"

"Dear me, yes," Emma said. "How many people know?"

"Myself, the doctor, nurse—Miss Thurloe, of course. Nobody else certainly, but matron—the school matron, I mean—guesses something, I think."

She read again Emma's unspoken thought.

"The poisoner too."

Emma made a nervous gesture of assent. "How long has Nurse Swain been in charge?" The irrelevant words were no sooner out than she blushed for the suspicion they must carry.

"Three weeks," Grace said. "A week after these attempts began. One can be easy on that score. For the same reason, of course, one can exonerate her predecessor, since the poisoning went on after she'd been dismissed."

"Dismissed?"

"Oh, that was nothing. Miss Thurloe loved getting rid of people, and was still more in love with new brooms. Of course, in that first week when there were these alarming bouts of sickness and she was nearly off her head with fright, she had some excuse for wanting to replace the nurse. But apparently she's always been the same. By all account she was a thorn in the side of Dr. Wick and partner, always wanting the people who attended her changed for somebody else, and as like as not wanting the old ones back after a while."

"How do you manage about maids?" Emma asked. "Do the school maids wait on her?"

"Gracious, no. Mine look after Nurse Swain, that's all. The nurse does what's required for her patient. Before Dr. Fielding gave up, Miss Thurloe and Miss Wand shared a maid of their own, but after this started—poison, that's to say—Miss Thurloe packed her off in the general rumpus, without consulting Miss Wand. That might have made a further row if it weren't that the other old lady is disinclined to put up much resistance."

"Too old?" Emma prompted. "Or not so temperamental?"

"She's older than Miss Thurloe, certainly. But she has her own wilfulnesses. Oh, yes." Grace hesitated. "The fact is, she's properly ill. Not in the Thurloe style. Angina—and any undue excitement—" She left the remark unfinished.

"Then the doctor has her to attend, as well," Emma said.

"Yes. She was Dr. Fielding's patient. But there isn't a great deal one can do. She doesn't have a nurse. She hasn't to keep to her bed or anything like that. She's very little trouble." Grace glanced at the clock. "Bet, it's late. You should have gone to bed. But I feel so much lighter hearted. Tomorrow and tomorrow and tomorrow—you'll be here, seeing for yourself, standing by me, bringing a fresh outlook to bear on it all. My own thoughts can only work a treadmill."

She had risen and stretched out her hands to Emma, to withdraw them before they touched her. Her face was lit by the kind of sombre animation Emma remembered well, and she let her glance travel from the clock along the shelf and walls and round the room.

"You'll soon have this looking—oh, Charlotte Rosenheim's pictures!" She swooped on them, feasting her eyes on their naive charm. "They used to hang—no, wait, let me say. They used to face one coming in at the door of your room in Baden Square—at least, this one did—*that* was on the other side where the paper had faded with the damp and what remained of the garland pattern looked like rusty chains. Don't you remember, I used to call them the martyr's handcuffs? So she did—Mrs. Martyr, I mean—fetter us to her! I remember it all."

"You've an extraordinary memory," Emma said, awed. She too was standing, moved by the quick flood of excitement that had caught up the past like a ball and tossed it between them. "Fancy you remembering Lottchen's name—you never knew her! Why, only tonight I was thinking, she was more than twelve years before your time. How old—how terribly old I am—"

"Bet." Grace took her by the shoulders and pushed her towards the overmantel glass. Emma felt in her grip more than mock anger. "Look—look at yourself. You're confusing tiredness with age. In the morning things will be different. In the morning, after you've slept. Why, when we remember it all so clearly, should the past be the remote thing you'd make it?"

The almost pleading urgency of her tone surprised and disturbed Emma. It was evident that Grace was very near a breakdown. So desperate was she to establish some sort of security for herself amid the quicksands in which she floundered that she was not only prompt to see youth and vigour where she looked for help, but ready to challenge furiously a denial of those qualities. Wishful thinking, the moderns called it. A dangerous game, Emma reflected.

"But you can't telescope the past so easily, my dear," she said gently. "The water that's slipped under the bridges since those days—we must face facts."

She was unheard. Grace had wandered over to the dressing table and, with a low exclamation, snatched something from an obscure corner. She sat down hastily on the bed, clutching her find. Two bright patches of colour burned at last in her sallow cheeks. She smiled suddenly at Emma and spoke on a rising note, half laughter, half sob, waving the photograph at her.

"My final cue—what is it I say now? Tell-me-about—"

"Mary Shagreen."

Emma capped it neatly with a laugh. She was proud of her ability to match her memory with Grace's. If only Grace were a little less intense, she thought, the atmosphere would be lighter at this moment than at any since her arrival. The ice was broken. The magic name was still alive. She experienced a surge of affection for Grace Aram who, alone in her world, could still recall its properties.

"Ah, there's nothing left for me to tell," she said. "Only the old tales I told too many times."

"They were always new to me."

"And when you and I parted I never heard anything more of her."

"But I did."

"You?"

"I told you. In the letters I wrote from Lausanne. Bet, I must have."

Emma shook her head firmly. "Never a word."

"Oh—oh. How strange." Grace hesitated, face flushed, her eyes in their sunken orbits shining with the effort to recall. To Emma she looked the worn simulacrum of the child who had hung upon her stories all those years ago. She watched her lay the photograph on the bed and rub one finger slowly the length of its tarnished frame. "I can't think—are you quite sure I didn't?"

"Quite. It's not a thing I would be likely to forget. I have wanted many times to know what became of my aunt."

"I can't tell you that," Grace said quickly. "But I saw her—twice."

"Where?"

"Once at the Fête des Narcisses in Vernex, in June, twenty years ago. We were on the top row of the *estrade* in the burning sun, and she and her party sat below us, flirting enormous sunshades the colours of the rainbow. Decorated cars, massed with roses, were crawling round the arena. It was that stifling, lazy minute or two before the battle begins—the battle of the flowers. I can see it all now. We were bored and fidgety and, perched up there, tormented by the sun. We retaliated by tossing part of our ammunition in the form of confetti and blossoms—I expect we kept the serpentines for the real battle—on the heads below us. Some were annoyed, others laughed. Mary Shagreen laughed. It scattered down on her immense violet sunshade, and she turned and tilted her face up to us and laughed. A carnation hit her on the nose and confetti trickled down her neck—she still laughed. The girl next to me whispered, 'That's Mary Shagreen, the great dancer.' I didn't believe I'd heard aright. Then I did. The girl went on talking, but I don't know what she said. I wasn't on the *estrade* in Vernex on a flaming June afternoon. I was in Baden Square listening to you, and pretending, pretending, always *pretending* that the dazzling sunshine that lit those stories was streaming through our dark windows. I never even knew the shot that was the signal for the battle to begin had been fired—not till I was pushed almost headlong from bench to bench in the wild scramble the audience made to get down to the arena. Mary Shagreen had disappeared. But I still saw her upturned, impudent face laughing at us while she poked the purple parasol in somebody else's eye."

Emma saw it too. She knew those fêtes. She had watched the same drowsy flower-smothered processions winding through the summer afternoons in Montreux, Clarens, Territet, under its veil of warmth Lac Léman shimmering in sleep. She had known the moment when the crack burst to explode at once all that yawning indifference. Oh, the mad torrent that poured like an avalanche from the wooden tiers it leapt and kicked and sprawled over! Ah, the struggle in the streets, the tempest of flowers, the yards of coloured serpentine strangling one's neck, trapping legs and arms, the ceaseless confetti-fire of the cars, the ground ankle deep in "ammunition," the brilliant sun, the riot of reds, blues, yellow, green and orange! Then the lull at twilight, when the sky deepened and the lake cooled, and lights twinkled in the houses by the quay—when, except for guerilla warfare in the Grande Rue, a general armistice would be declared. Then the fireworks would sputter, and stars, huger and more fiery than those the heavens showed, blaze across their tranquil face. Ah, the gay peoples of Europe who had lost their gaiety…

All she said was, "It is exactly the setting I would have imagined for Mary Shagreen. I wonder you never told me. She must have been getting old even then."

"Sixty-one," Grace said triumphantly. "And as giddy as a girl. Now *don't* begin that all over again, Bet. She was the same age then as you are now."

"But how could you know?" Emma asked, astonished.

"You told me. Not that she was sixty-one, of course—we weren't together at the time. But you said how old she was in 1874 when she made her first appearance. I worked it out from that." She smiled. "You're right. What is there left you can tell me about Mary Shagreen? As far as biographical detail goes I'm better equipped than *Who's Who*."

"I believe you are," Emma said admiringly. But it was another emotion that moved her at thought of that singular devotion. Nothing brought home more sharply the isolation of Grace Aram's youth than this preoccupation with the career of a woman who had lived for her only in the words of another and in an upturned, laughing face in the sunlight of a Swiss holiday. "Where was it you saw her again?"

"One day, a few months later, we climbed from Glion to Rochers-de-Naye—an easy climb selected for demoiselles. We came back by another and longer route that took in the vineyards. And there, seated at a little table in the street of a village we passed through—I don't remember the name of it—was Mary Shagreen. A woman was with her, who looked like a maid, and a showy peasant you'd take for a guide—paying uxurious attention to Mary Shagreen. They were having a meal of grapes and *moût*—the maid wasn't. She was looking disapproval at the other two. The girl who had sat with me on the *estrade* in June wasn't there, and there was nobody I could speak to about Mary Shagreen. But her image went back with me. If I were to walk that dusty way again I should still see it."

Emma was silent. She wondered about the letters that had not been written. But even in the early days regularity had not been a characteristic of the correspondence; these encounters could have taken place in the silences between letters, and their importance been overlaid by later events when writing was picked up again. But was there anything to overlay for Grace the excitement of Mary Shagreen?

Grace did not seem to notice the silence. "How young," she said, and touched the glass of the photograph. "Haven't you anything of her when she was old?"

"No. How could I? We didn't see her again after she was thirty-five."

"She's more likely twenty-five here. But, yes—I do see the resemblance to the woman at the Fête des Narcisses."

She got up from the bed and returned the photograph to its place.

"Heigh-ho, the wind and the rain—I'm going to bed. You too, Bet—you're all in."

Chapter VI

THE HOUSE OF WOMEN

Prayers at Makeways were a hurried business of which everyone seemed defiantly ashamed. Their communal nature put them at once out of favour, of course; if only the proceeding had not taken up too much time Grace, Emma was sure, would have insisted on individual and self-chosen prayers and hymns. They were held, after breakfast and before the school timetable had been set in revolution for the day, in what had been the nursing home reception room, whose four French windows opened on the lawn east of the house where a tennis court had been marked out. To Emma their chief use this morning was to assemble under her eyes the entire household except Miss Thurloe, Miss Wand, Nurse Swain and the domestic staff.

She had waked early from uneasy sleep. As soon as Grace had left her last night she had taken the precaution of locking her door without questioning the instinct that impelled her. More purposeful had been her drawing of the blackout curtain when, lights out, she was ready for bed. There was a greater comfort to be derived from glimpses of the night sky than from the black box her room would be without it. But it was a consolation that did not extend beyond the first spell of wakefulness. She had soon fallen into that kind of slumber in which images rather than dreams flit, batlike, through the mind, some hastily, others in halting fashion. It was always the wrong ones that lingered. Among them was the angry face of Linda Hart, filled with a misery far exceeding that which she had surprised on it. It swelled to monstrous proportions, while the crying she had heard in the evening broke out again, turning, as the face vanished, to bursts of unnatural laughter. A crimson patch floated in front of her eyes, then dropped slowly to floor level, red as a lamp in the darkness—red as blood. When she had opened her eyes it was still there. For a minute she had lain in that petrified silence which hardly condones breathing for fear the vitality we permit ourselves should materialize nameless horrors too. Then she had seen it was no spilt blood, but a solitary ember in the heart of the dead fire glowing again in the cool pull of air at night. It stared back at her, unwinking, baleful. But, identified, it no longer disturbed her. What she had liked less was the feeling that the laughter heard in sleep was as real as the fiery glow. A thin cackle of it had been receding, she was sure, at the moment of consciousness. She felt a cold prickle spread over her skin. She was glad she had locked the door. There had been no more sleep for her till it was light. With the first wash of dawn in the room through a curling sea of September mist outside, she had fallen into an anxious doze, to wake unrefreshed two hours later to the doubtful pleasure of breakfast in bed. A glance in the hand mirror had done nothing to confirm Grace's faith in the rejuvenating force of the morning hours.

But if, she reflected, the purity of the light that had streamed into her bedroom and was now directing its shafts into the morning room below was cruel to herself, its treatment of everyone else was equally barbarous. Not everyone, perhaps; the smooth, blank, well-bred faces of the children gathered at the lower end of the room revealed nothing but the usual youthful insensibility. While Grace delivered her homily at the close of a short prayer, shorter hymn and no lesson reading, Emma found time to study them all. The briefest of general introductions to the teaching staff a quarter of an hour earlier had left her with a hazy recognition of individuals; but she thought she was sorting them out right now.

Grace, looking as hagridden as ever, sat at a table at the top of the room facing the assembled school, with the piano on her left and her staff ranged about her in a small semicircle. Emma, in a chair on the extreme right, had no trouble in observing everyone but the accompanist who, while she played, sat with her back squarely to her. There was something familiar about it, though, and Emma found her eyes drawn to her again and again; but it was not until Grace had begun her morning address and the girl turned on the stool to present a pudgy profile to the other mistresses that Emma saw who she was. There was no mistaking that small eye, large nose, and general air of unfeathered birdiness, with the sunlight betraying her daubed mouth. It was the watcher at The Teashop who had spied—that was the only term for it—on the departures from the Lanthorn.

Emma's discovery surprised her less than it might have done if she had not already recognized on Grace's right the second of the two women who had left the alley yesterday. This was the French mademoiselle who had declined to teach German. Lancret, Emma thought the name was. Her face was highly interesting without being attractive; neither aristocratic nor cultured, but full of the self-contained breeding of the French peasant, avid in a quiet way, unsentimental, even a little repellent if you cared more for warmth and mobility of feature. The black she was wearing was a poor foil to her lined, earthy skin. She stared before her with a look of stolid grief that saw neither the faces of the girls below nor the broad bands of sunlight swathing the room. It carried too that air of unsubmissive resignation which is the stamp of her race and class, and which serves to make impermanent its successive defeats.

Between the Frenchwoman and Grace a tall girl was seated, thin chested, with bright curly hair and a pale, clear skin touched vividly with pink. She was leaning forward with a look of eagerness, lips parted, hands clasped round her knee, the long wrists bare. Emma, who thought it was the English mistress, could not remember having caught her name.

On her own left, too near for close examination, was the matron, Nona Deakin, a large-boned, robust woman of fifty or so, with an apparent surplus of common sense and a healthy contempt for all forms of human activity not directly concerned with physical well-being. She had what is popularly termed a nice face, a disarming bluntness of speech that was faintly racy, no imagination, and the unfailing cheerfulness and pronounced lack of sympathy of one type of trained nurse. Emma could see without turning her head the square mannish hands laid palms down in her lap with the short bleached hairs on the backs of them.

There was nobody else. Including me, Emma thought, Grace's staff adds up to only five. Yet, inadequate though it might be for the school in its heyday, it did not seem too small for the handful confronting them this morning.

She turned her attention from mistresses to girls. Grace must have miscounted last night, or else she was still including the disgraced Linda in their number, for she could not make them more than thirteen now. Seven of them were certainly seniors, carrying *en masse* that forlorn air of adolescence which has actually done with school life but is as yet unacceptable anywhere else. Three were of an indeterminate age between twelve and fifteen, and the remaining three still more junior, small creatures of the nursery pet size of whom Emma had long ago had a surfeit.

None of them wore uniform. Everything of that sort was rigidly barred from Makeways, whose motto was, "I make my way in my way." Presumably it wasn't to be done in a gym slip or a hat with a band round it. Each girl was dressed in clothes of her own or her parents' choice. Each, so far as Emma could judge, looked neat and presentable enough, but she was almost startled to observe how lack of uniformity in dress failed nevertheless to endorse individuality. For the most part these children wore the same expressions of controlled boredom, silent criticism, acceptance of routine.

Why, thought Emma, they'd look exactly the same if they were all in the same cut and colour, school tie and black stockings—it's not clothes that count. Though, indeed, they might even look less stereotyped if only their frocks were of the same pattern, for then the eye wouldn't be distracted by clothing and would see more, perhaps, in their vapid, pretty faces. She felt she had made a discovery of some import, and could not help wondering how it was that the same idea had never dawned on Grace. If your aim is to develop individuality, then it is the individual that matters and not his framework. Uniformity in minor matters may even be an aid to a larger freedom.

Before she knew where she was the school had been dismissed and the mistresses were scuttling along the passages with a guilty air. Grace caught her up on her way to the staff timetable hanging outside the Common Room door.

"You're not teaching," she said. "I can save you the trouble of looking. Not till this afternoon. Miss Orpen is going to type you a list of your coachings for the week—it's only two girls, so they're really tutorials. They're infrequent, and will give you plenty of freedom for the main job."

Emma looked at her in dismay. "But, Grace, what is it? My main job, I mean? How can I throw light on what baffles you all? And how, in any case, shall I have the chance to do so? I can't meddle with a patient of Dr. Bold's. If he thinks things are seriously wrong he'll surely make it a—a police case."

She stammered a little at the epithet, but judged it best to speak plainly. If all she had heard were true, the doctor's forbearance was frankly puzzling.

Grace eyed her thoughtfully. "You're wondering, aren't you, why he doesn't have her removed? Well, the chief obstacle to that is Miss Thurloe herself. At the least hint of getting her out of Martinmas she throws blue hysterics. It's home to her, and beyond its door all the bogies in creation are in ambush—so she'd rather be poisoned in familiar surroundings than be taken away to die, if you get my meaning."

Emma was not sure that she did. It sounded both specious and callous. She still looked unconvinced, and Grace, anxious to press home her point, lowered her voice in deference to their semipublic rendezvous.

"And where would Makeways be if she had to be forcibly removed to hospital—a woman with a tongue nobody can quell? And the nurse leaving, and all? I may as well shut shop if that happens. Besides, once she's gone, what hope will there be of catching the poisoner?"

None, Emma agreed. But she was bewildered by the ethics which could justify jeopardizing Miss Thurloe's life almost to the extent of waiting on her death for the sake of trapping her murderer. Grace's state of mind seemed to her amply expressed by its startling inconsistencies. One moment she was sick with fright at the turn events might take, the next she was concurring heartily with the doctor's reluctance to remove the cause of her fear. Emma shook her head theoretically and, in metaphor, gave it up; but because her simple mind had always taken a lively interest in the vagaries of her fellows, the psychological issues at stake in Grace's problem suddenly infected her with warmer curiosity. And once she got really inquisitive only the tidied-up ends of a solution itself could appease her.

"What is it you want me to do?" she asked.

Grace squeezed her arm gratefully. "Not so very much after all. Keep your eyes open, and your ears. You can win confidence—"

(To betray it, Emma thought ruefully.)

"They'll expand with you—with me they're all back in their shells directly. The truth is, I don't get on well with people, no better now than I used to, else I'd have been able to keep my staff and children when the testing time came. And this is a case that needs talk and discussion—you know, the gossipy stuff that starts with Aunt Matty's canary and comes round to the last curate but one and why he really went away, my dear—"

(Grace thinks I've done nothing else for the past twenty years.)

"—and all the time you're imbibing and sifting and giving nothing away yourself."

"That won't be difficult," Emma said simply. "Giving nothing away, I mean. I don't know anything."

"Well, quite a bit, Bet," was Grace's cheerful rejoinder. She looked as if a load had been taken off her mind. "You know about the poison. That's something you share with me and the doctor and Nurse Swain—nobody else. And you mustn't breathe a word of it to anyone but me and nurse—better not to Bold, I think. Somebody else knows, of course. And that's where you come in. I want to know how the stuff is brought into the house."

Emma sighed. "I'll do my best, but you must be prepared for a poor one. You see, it won't be possible for me to get to know Miss Thurloe herself, will it? The doctor has surely taken the precaution of stopping visits?"

"Well, he has," Grace admitted. "Even I don't go near her now. Nurse does everything for her, and sleeps in the dressing room communicating with the door open. But it's all right. I've told her you've had a lot of experience with hypochondriacs—she hates 'em, by the way—and if you want to see Miss Thurloe you've nothing to do but make friends with Nurse Swain. It should be easy, especially as the old lady herself can't bear being shut away like this."

She went off without waiting for a reply, leaving Emma aghast. Lots of experience with hypochondriacs—so she had had, in a way, but not at all in the sense Nurse Swain would have taken it. Willy-nilly, she seemed committed to her course.

She moved off along the corridor in the opposite direction, resolved to explore a little. The house was rambling without being really large, an awkward structure that seemed to have sprung from a series of improvisations rather than from any architectural design. She came to a flight of dark, uncarpeted stairs flush with the end wall. They were lighted at the turn by a narrow closed window that framed a patch of brilliant sky and the whispering bough of a sycamore that scraped the glass with a meddlesome touch. Halfway up she heard a slapping noise, followed by a long sliding shuffle and, turning the corner, saw the matron, formidably starched, at the top of the stairs kneeling in front of an open linen cupboard checking her laundry.

She did not turn at her approach, only mumbled brightly with a pencil stuck at the side of her mouth, "Anybody want me?"

Emma apologized for her intrusion and did what she could to explain it.

"That's all right," Miss Deakin said. "Go where you like. Place takes a bit of getting used to, and will still more when the winter's closed in. These are the dorms up here, and a couple of staff bedrooms, and my own hangout."

She ticked a list of items rapidly, slapped the little book shut, tipped it into the basket and rose from her knees, shoving the empty basket in the bottom of the cupboard with her foot.

"*Yah!*" she exclaimed with violence, brushing furiously the top sheet of a pile. "Here it is, all over again! Look at it!"

Emma looked, and saw a mess of fine sawdust powdering the linen.

"Wood weevils," the matron said tersely. "Nasty little blighters. In the wood, and won't be got out. But what d'you expect? I tell Miss Aram the place is rotting about our ears." She wrinkled her eyes pleasantly at Emma, locked the cupboard doors and slipped the key into a capacious pocket. "But we must have it—no others would do, though we went over at least two other houses just as dead-an'-buried in the country as this, and guaranteed too against damp, woodlice, weevils, rats and silly old women!" She laughed. "You mustn't mind me—come see my room."

She propelled Emma along at a pace suggesting she came unwillingly. They hurried past closed doors and austerely stripped walls to a little room at the end of the passage. Emma was at home in it at once. She had entered hundreds of these snug, tasteless, overfurnished sitting rooms where framed and unframed photographs tumbled over one another or, curling at the corners, had to be propped in position with hair tidies and powder compacts and anything else to hand. It was not, perhaps, precisely the room she would have allotted Nona Deakin; but having seen it she was not much surprised. It was certain that the matron viewed without the least sentiment those hosts of toothy faces she would not for a moment have dispensed with.

"Nearly all my own stuff," she said with pride. "I don't like storing chattels, and this place anyway had hardly a stick in it when we took over—bar the Thurloe–Wand ménage." She grimaced tolerantly. "We've practically no equipment—and less sense, come to think of it. You'd say we were pretty well batty or thoroughly hard pinched, wouldn't you, to jump at a nursing home in the last stages of mental, moral and material decay?"

"Jump at it?" Emma echoed.

"That's what I said. Because that's what we did. There was every sort of snag about the other places, if you please, but *this* that was bristling with 'em—dear me, no! This got away with it—and us! And I may tell you we're paying a sight more here for the privilege of enjoying all the disadvantages than we were asked elsewhere for the—what-d'you-call-ems?—amenities."

Emma, overwhelmed, crossed to the window. It seemed not altogether loyal to Grace to go on listening. A bad bargain may have been struck; so far as she could see, it had. But, if so, she understood. Examining bedsitter after bedsitter in a dreary round of lodging houses she remembered how tired feet, aching head, a dulled critical sense, beaten and weary of the whole business, were only too apt to accept the last one with its fewer amenities, as the matron called them, simply because it promised the end of the journey.

"Was Martinmas the last house you saw over?" she asked.

"It was," Miss Deakin said emphatically, but still cheerful. The louder the complaint the happier she grew. "Doesn't it look like it? Go through the wood and pick up the crooked stick at last!"

She came behind Emma to look over her shoulder at the sparkling grass beneath. Her room was in the front, and there at the edge of the lawn the first autumn air was already crisping were huddled the sentinel trees that hid the lane from their eyes. Away to the right a solitary cedar spread its great flat hands above the grass that shone white with dew where the shadows lay. Here on two garden seats were the three youngest children being taught by the girl who had sat next to Grace at prayers.

"It will soon be too cold for lessons out," the matron remarked. "But September often lets you think it's a hangover from the summer term." She waved suddenly as the girl, glancing up, caught their eyes on her. "Nice gal, that."

Emma stepped back and sat down on a cretonne-covered couch indicated by Miss Deakin, who knelt to plug in a tiny electric fire. "I didn't catch everyone's name distinctly, I'm afraid. That is—?"

"Susan Pollard. We call her Susan—well, not the kids, of course. New this term." Miss Deakin moderated her singularly healthy tones. "Poor wench is T.B. Ought to be in a Swiss sanitarium if it wasn't for the war, and there being no money." She added hastily, "I don't mean there's any danger—nothing like that. She was discharged cured over two years ago from some such place in this country, but—" She assumed a shutdown look more eloquent than words.

Emma was amazed at the woman's indiscretions, which went beyond mere lack of reserve. Grace, she knew, would not thank her for feeling amazement and shock; it was just such tittle-tattle she was detailed to pick up. But the scrupulous reticence her own training had imposed upon her rebelled. Before she could turn the conversation the matron was at it again.

"Miss Thurloe quite took to Susan—when she was out and about, I mean. Of course, nobody's allowed near her now since she's worse"—she winked broadly at Emma—"but a month or two ago when she could still totter around, so to say, she made all the fuss in the world of Pollard."

Emma frowned. "But there wouldn't have been much opportunity at any time, would there, for intercourse between the school and the nursing home?"

"There isn't a nursing home," said the matron, pulling a shopping list from her pocket and scoring out old items while she scribbled fresh ones. "There's only a couple of old dames from the home that was, and two can't constitute a hospital, can they? Why, there's been plenty of chance for powwows if anybody wanted 'em—still is, for that matter. We all go to the same church, across the fields over there—Thurloe only missed last Sunday, and Miss Wand still goes in spite of her heart—and when the summer was younger they used to sit out on the lawn and one or other of the staff would chat with the old dears. Susan reminded Thurloe of a long lost relative—can you beat it?—and once that's happened it's all up, of course! We often tease her about it—well, not so much now, since the old lady's more or less isolated."

Emma, because she was interested, thought it time to change the subject. She did not want to appear unduly inquisitive at an early stage, though the matron's love of dispensing gossip safeguarded her in that respect. But one could not be too careful.

"Who is Miss Orpen?" she asked. "She is to let me have my timetable this afternoon, and I'm not sure that I know her, either."

"Music," was the cryptic reply. "She teaches it, plays for prayers and on any other occasion when a bit of thumping's the order of the day, and does secretarial work for the H.M. too." She beamed mischievously at Emma. "Incidentally, she hates poor old Mam'selle like poison, and as it's easy as kiss-my-hand to get a rise out of her—Mam'selle, I mean—" She rolled her eyes and shook her head with the born gossip's aim to get more read into her silence than she herself knows is there.

"That is Mam'selle Lancret?" Emma said. Here was her own particular mystery cropping up.

"Yes. She's been very low all term—last term, that is—France going under, and what not, you know—and flies off the handle at the least thing. Orpen is rather a little mess, I admit. Not that I've much patience with foreigners either, whoever they are, these days—you can't tell friend from foe, and that's a fact, so best not tell 'em anything is my motto!"

Which must, Emma thought, be a singularly exacting one to live up to, and perhaps accounted for the flood of mild scandal the matron was prepared to pour into the ears of her own countrywomen. She wanted to ask why it was Miss Orpen and Mam'selle were on bad terms, but the descent to the Avernus of private detection was not yet so precipitate that she could not restrain herself, though she did so with a sense of guilt towards Grace.

Instead she asked, "The staff here occasionally have a free afternoon, don't they, Miss Deakin—which can be spent outside?"

"Call me Nonny. Everyone else does. Yes, they do. You're not thinking, are you, you'll be hard done by here? We've only fourteen kids, you know, and loads of free time—all but the poor, racked matron, that goes without saying!" She winked expansively.

"There were only thirteen at prayers," Emma observed primly. "But I understand a girl was—expelled yesterday."

"So she was. But before that there were fifteen. The missing kid is in the san. Sick ward is a better name for it, I suppose, for we've only a couple of measly bedrooms to stick the sore throats and collywobbles in."

Emma wondered what the parents who were asked to open their purses so wide for the privilege of sending their children to Makeways would say if they could hear this.

"Nothing badly wrong, I hope?" she murmured.

"Nothing really. Only constipation and sleepwalking and a touch of hysteria—which seems to be catching in this benighted place."

To Emma they sounded formidable trio enough, but nothing short of leprosy looked like daunting Miss Deakin.

"I shall keep her under my eye for a few days," she went on. "This spot isn't healthy, you know. Oh, I don't mean the country exactly—though I'd have fewer trees while I was about it—but the house. A thoroughgoing morgue. Nursing home indeed—a snug little nest of knavery sponging on silly old boneheads! I wouldn't have worked in it for a thousand a year."

Emma believed her. It was more than likely that Martinmas would not have had her as a gift. Doctors Fairman and Wick had known up to a point on which side their bread was buttered, and sceptical nurses with an evident flair for quick convalescences had not figured in their scheme of things.

"Don't you think you might have been the right person for old Miss Thurloe?" she suggested with some duplicity, drawing a bow at a venture.

Miss Deakin gave her a sharp look, then laughed. "Never, my dear. She'd have poisoned me by now. Don't look so amazed—I'm not her cup of tea by a long chalk. I wouldn't have said Nurse Swain was either. Paranoia's her long suit—Thurloe's, I mean—not my line at all. I hate poking about in beastly mental cases that are half spoof anyway."

"But that—that's delusions—persecution mania," Emma stammered a little more eagerly than she had intended. "Surely if that were the case Miss Thurloe would insist on leaving Martinmas now?"

She flushed deeply as soon as she had spoken, remembering too late that the matron was supposed to know nothing about the poison. Miss Deakin was looking at her, surprised.

"Why now? Of course it's persecution mania—but by all account she's always suffered from it, harbouring suspicions right and left and sacking servants and nurses as lief look at them. Getting away with it too as long as the doctors were feathering their nest out of her. Why else do you think she packed the other nurse off a month or so back?"

The answer to that one was easy, but if she were to obey Grace it was not Emma's business to give it.

"What was she like?" she asked.

"Who—Edgeworth? Oh, the la-di-dah type—poker face, nothing to say, stood the old girl's cajolery and abuse without turning a hair. A bit wet, but quite good at her job, I should say. But, as you see, she had to go like the rest." She stopped, frowning. "You *have* come here to teach, haven't you?"

"Modern languages," Emma said brazenly. "French and German conversation."

"Oh." But Miss Deakin contrived to look doubtful. "Only you've nursed neurotics, haven't you? Swain says—"

She broke off to listen.

Emma opened her mouth to what piece of casuistry she did not exactly know, for before she could utter a syllable pandemonium broke out somewhere in the house.

It began with a roar that rose to shrill, sobbing screams. Metal clanged as if flung with force, doors opened and shut, voices rose on high, questioning notes, and were cut off by the closing of rooms or because they had got out of earshot. Still the piercing cries went on. Miss Deakin dived for the door and Emma followed her.

"Thurloe again," the matron, looking thoroughly happy, flung over her shoulder. "I'll say she's found the Shah of Persia under her bed this time, with a knife between his teeth—what ho!"

She thrust open a door down the passage and they came out into a shorter one that was almost a landing. There were lavatories on their right, and on the other side a little dark turn where was a door with a frosted glass transom.

"Short cut into Miss Thurloe's part—and yours," the matron explained, opening the door. They came into a bathroom where Mam'selle Lancret was drying her hands. Though the screams, subsiding now to wails and moaning, burst full upon them as they entered, the Frenchwoman wore the imperturbable look of the stone deaf. She passed them without a word and went out the way they had come. They crossed into a long, naked-looking corridor which Emma recognized at once. A few yards away was the shorter passage that led to her own room.

The matron hurried along to where Miss Thurloe trumpeted through an open door.

"Anything I can do?" she called in loud, bracing tones.

Emma kept close on her heels. Nobody else was about at the moment. Doctor's orders had evidently kept the stage clear. The matron, one presumed, was privileged when a crisis of this magnitude arose. Nothing venture, nothing win, anyway. If she herself were discovered she had sound excuse, for these were her own quarters.

Her first enthusiasm, however, was destined to be nipped in the bud. A tumbler, unbroken, lay on its side in the corridor in line with the door. Some way off was a thermos flask, shining like a good deed in a bleak, ungrateful world. On the threshold of the room a mess of some milky substance bespattered the wall close to the skirting.

Miss Deakin strode in, repeating, "Naughty, naughty," in a voice crammed with vitamins. Emma, stooping to pick up flask and tumbler, found herself gazing into a large bright room decked out expensively with every sort of fal-de-lal deemed essential to feminine comfort. A uniformed nurse, the same milky concoction spreading ruthless stains across her ample front, was trying to persuade her charge back to bed to the stubborn refrain, "The arrowroot was *per*fectly good—no poison gets into *my* arrowroot—the arrowroot was *per*—"

Miss Deakin cut short the praises of the arrowroot by seizing Miss Thurloe by the arm. Miss Thurloe immediately emitted a curdling screech. The nurse dropped her like a red-hot coal and, for the first time, noticed Emma who, hesitating, was lost. She advanced majestically on the door and shut it firmly in Emma's face.

Not exactly the right beginning, thought the exile, to making friends with Nurse Swain.

She stood foolishly clasping thermos and glass, staring at the door. Then she put them down by the lintel and made her way to her own room. Initial failure was hers, it was true, but not before she had caught a snapshot view of Miss Thurloe, a plump yet shrunken figure in a nightgown cluttered with ribbons and lace, tails of limp curly hair hanging about her babyish features, her mouth, wide with fear, the hideous square of Greek tragedy.

And something about the sight left her more puzzled than shocked.

Chapter VII

RATHER UNPROFESSIONAL

M iss Thurloe's latest upset had unexpected developments. Dr. Bold, arriving an hour later and examining her as best he could, pronounced in favour of poison. He imparted his suspicions to Grace Aram and Nurse Swain with less ambiguity and more rudely even than usual, and declared that a second nurse must be brought in to share the strain. Only he didn't put it quite so happily. She would take over duty in the day while Nurse Swain carried on at night instead of going to sleep. Nurse Swain heard him with mingled indignation and relief. She was moved to defend herself.

"There's never been any trouble after ten or so at night, doctor. You know that yourself. All these—these attacks come on by day. And if Miss Thurloe *was* to make a noise in the night I'd wake on the instant—yes, on the *instant*—and be there to attend to her."

"Off the point," snapped Bold. "Things have reached the pitch when she can't be left alone any hour of the day or night, and falling asleep for an hour is leaving her alone, isn't it? Carry on tonight, and I'll send another nurse in tomorrow—and you'll be able to take time off in the town and buy yourself a new hat!"

Nurse Swain, conscious that her face was at cross purposes with almost every kind of hat, matched his sarcasm with a glare of disapproval and watched him depart with the water bottle and samples of the arrowroot.

Grace, acutely worried, seriously considered closing the school. Then she remembered Miss Thurloe's twelve guineas, the presence of Emma, and the doctor's interest in the case as evidenced by the extra precautions he was prepared to take, cheered up a little and cancelled the staff meeting she had called to discuss it.

Repercussions in the kitchen, however, sent her spirits down to zero again. Two of the four maids, on hearing that a second nurse was due to arrive next day, promptly gave a week's notice, presenting a united and impregnable front to wrath, persuasion, and reasoning alike.

"These nurses aren't like human beings, madam. A cut above everybody, they think themselves. Never so much as a chat, and Miss Swain for ever using the cooking utensils without a with-your-leave or by-your-leave. They want the moon, they do. Sybil and me, we came to work at a school, not in an asylum."

That was that. The scullerymaid sulked furiously because twice in a week she had been sent for to clear up horrid messes of food flung in all directions by "the dotty old simpleton upstairs." Nurse Swain did ought to have done it herself, she did. Nurse Swain's excuse that she was too busy cleaning up the patient and herself to look after the corners, so to speak, was mere additional evidence of her hateful superiority complex. Worse, Nipper Simcox, the boots and only resident man in the establishment, who was rising fifteen and looked eleven and had had the distinction of working for Doctors Fairman and Wick, strolled into the kitchen to advertise his scorn of women with an invective not unworthy of John Knox, and succeeded in burning holes in the best drying cloth in a surreptitious attempt to smother in its fold the cigarette he should not have been smoking. He was enjoying an easy time under Miss Aram and, as a result, took the opportunity to air a great many more grievances than he had ever known were his. Cook, who quarrelled with her own sex on the slightest provocation and was equally quick to see red whenever she heard it defamed, was "that put about" after ejecting Nipper that she burned the curry, gave Miss

Orpen a severe attack of indigestion, and caused Mam'selle to sit glowering throughout lunch without eating a morsel, the while she passed silent but effective judgement on England's culinary habit of muddling through.

These livelier eruptions somewhat obscured Miss Wand's heart attack. Grace, investigating, found that the maid whose duty it was to take the old lady's meals to her had forgotten to see that she had handy the tabloids prescribed before lunch, and Miss Wand, distressed at the uproar, had failed to remind her.

"The whole place is set by the ears," Grace said to Emma, adding viciously, "all through that bedizened old horror. If I'm not careful I shall lose Nurse Swain now, and have two strangers about the place instead of one, as well as no servants."

But the new nurse came in next day and Nurse Swain did not go. Instead, she took the afternoon off to fortify her for the night hours, and surprised Emma, who was not teaching then, by asking if she would come and have tea with her in Bugle.

"I feel," she said, rather naively, "that I owe you something more than an apology for being so offhand and—yes, rude, yesterday. But I wasn't to know it was you, as Miss Aram hadn't had an opportunity of introducing us one to another—and you wouldn't believe how particular Dr. Bold has got about people with no business there going into Miss Thurloe's room."

She was still troubled by the same remorse two hours later over tea and cakes. Emma had made a private guess at her choice of café, plumping for Ye Nookye Neste, and was proved right.

"Silly of me not to guess it was you," nurse was saying as she poured herself a third cup, "but I don't mind admitting I was properly flummoxed—it was the worst shindy she's kicked up since I've been there. Letting Miss Deakin in was different, of course. The house is really in her charge, you might say, and being a nurse herself she's useful to have at hand when a spot of bother blows up."

Emma agreed. "I quite understand." She had already assured Nurse Swain of her powers of comprehension so many times that the words themselves had become an embarrassment to her.

She studied the nurse as, ignoring Emma for the moment, she buried her teeth with relish in a sickly iced wedge. A stockily built woman of moderate height, with broad, heavy features, small eyes and immensely wide nostrils, her lips had the thin, tucked-in look that stubborn people hope will be mistaken for resolution. Emma judged her unintelligent, mulish, and loquacious as soon as her stolidity had been melted by the right degree of flattery.

"Your duties with Miss Thurloe must be very exacting ones," she began. "I am sure they call for a great deal of tact and skill."

"They do that," Nurse Swain agreed. This was a refreshing change from Dr. Bold. "You've done some nursing yourself?"

"A little." Emma was prompt, though guarded.

"Well, then you'll know how it is with these mental cases—here today and gone tomorrow where their senses are concerned. It's an uphill fight." She sighed.

"Strictly speaking, Miss Thurloe is not exactly mental, is she?" Emma suggested.

"Borderline, my dear—borderline, and always toppling over the edge. It's beginning to get me down, I can tell you, and I haven't been with her a month yet. Time was I'd have said there was nothing could wear me down—but I've seen fit to believe otherwise in the last week or two."

Emma nodded. "That sort of case can be very tiresome, I know," and, skating hastily across the thin ice of personal experience, "particularly when you've to carry on single-handed for so long. You'll find things easier now."

Nurse Swain turned confidential with a rush. "I don't know about that. The truth is, and I don't mind telling you, I'm not at all accustomed to this type of patient. I was engaged all of a hurry like to fill the gap left by Nurse Edgeworth going off so quick, and if I'd known what I do now I'd have thought twice before acting. Anything to do with the body, now, and the ills that flesh is heir to, and Belinda Swain's your woman every time—a nice appendix mending slowly, or pneumonia on the road back to health but still a long way to go, that suits me. But this watchdog business on the deranged—" She shook her head solemnly.

Emma thought fast. Better move now while the iron was at least warm and the café still deserted.

"But Miss Thurloe's trouble isn't entirely delusion, is it?" she said, lowering her voice and speaking with an air of authority. She must give the impression of one who knew. All would be lost if Nurse Swain suspected she were merely an inquisitive old woman putting out feelers—which she reminded herself that she was. Professional etiquette, even in the absence of mental acumen, would keep the nurse silent then, she thought.

But Nurse Swain rose beautifully to the bait. She paused only to rake the café for possible eavesdroppers, then leaned her broad front across the table towards Emma. Her small eyes glinted.

"Then it's no news to you," she breathed huskily. "You can't think what a relief it is to me to know that, with only Miss Aram to talk to and the doctor as pleased as punch the longer he can manage to keep things up his sleeve. I haven't even been able so much as to mention it to Miss Deakin, who must think a great many things are funny. And all her experience too—it could've been a help. I never did hold with too much of this hush-hush—look where it gets you in politics, and the same with patients. Let a bit of air in on it, I say."

"That's very true," Emma conceded. "But in a case like this don't you think that secrecy helps one to get to the bottom of the mystery sooner?"

Nurse Swain leaned back and snorted. "There isn't any mystery."

"You mean—?" Emma hoped she looked knowing.

"She's doing it herself, of course. Now as to what the little game is, that I cannot say. But who can account for actions when there's softening of the brain sets in?"

"Of course," said Emma slowly, full of proper admiration for the perspicuity shown. "We must really believe then that she is attempting to—to take her own life?"

"Not a bit of it," was the surprising answer. "Doctor's right there—about her not being suicidal, and, really, the way she carries on sometimes about dying and such—it isn't Christian. Well, I mean to say, we've all got to come to it, and well—I mean to *say*—"

Emma produced some throaty little noises expressive of agreement, deprecation and recognition of the subject's solemnity. She put her head on one side and considered the nurse with eyes bright with flattery.

"There's a great deal in what you say. But if the object is not—er—death, what can it be to induce her to suffer so much pain and discomfort?"

"Ah-h." Nurse Swain dipped her bows to the table again. A smile widened her traplike mouth. "Now you've said it. Yes, indeed, you've put your finger right on it." She glanced round her again, uneasily. "This is strictly between you and me. I've never told Miss Aram—doctor's orders. The fact is, Miss Thurloe's never taken any poison at all—not after that first time in Nurse Edgeworth's last week."

"But," said Emma boldly, "it's been found several times since."

"Found? Of course it has been. And will be this time, you mark my words. But *she* doesn't have any of it—it's just found in things she's used when they were harmless, proving it's been put in afterwards. Doesn't that just show it's *her* doing it all?"

"But the sickness?" Emma urged.

"Self-induced. Lots of 'em know how to do it. Why, Miss Deakin says she's had kids in boarding schools in her time who knew how to bring it on so as to escape lessons they didn't like."

"Dear me," said Emma, whose experience rather surprisingly did not embrace this particular perfidy.

"And she's not always sick, either, only now and again. Most of the time it's screaming and carrying on you never saw, and shouting out she's poisoned and dying, and suchlike nonsense. What's more, three or four times since I've been here she's played us up like that and nothing in the way of poison was found anywhere at all! *I* say she forgot to plant it those times."

"What a queer thing the human heart is," Emma murmured, awed, and Nurse Swain, who had never made real contact with it, nodded profound assent.

"I'm rather perplexed about one thing," went on Emma, who was puzzled by a great deal. "Has Miss Thurloe suffered long from this persecution mania—the particular one of poisoning, I should say—or does it date from the actual taking of the poison before Nurse Edgeworth left?"

"That's right," Nurse Swain said ambiguously. "I understand—but, really, you don't rightly know what to believe with her old doctor away as well—stands to reason he understood her better than anybody else, *if* anybody at all does, which I must say I take leave to doubt—what I'm told is, she was always having mild attacks of paranoia, only then it took different forms, and sometimes she'd think she was being robbed, and sometimes slandered, and so on. And then she took this poison a month or so back, just after Dr. Bold took on the practice it was, and ever since then it's been poison and nothing else with her. It's my belief the old doctor's going turned her brain—just gave it the final push off, you might say."

"That's possible," Emma said. "If, as you say, Miss Thurloe has had nothing poisonous in her system since you've been there, why, I wonder, doesn't Dr. Bold let Miss Aram know? It would relieve her mind very much."

"Just what I said. But you daren't suggest a thing, of course. So bad-tempered, and not gentleman enough to have any real confidence in his nurse. I can't *say* why he wants Miss Aram left in the dark—but I can guess."

Emma, who could not, waited while Nurse Swain got her desired effect in a short silence.

"You see," she went on under her breath, "it's like this—if you had anybody like Miss Thurloe in your house and you found they weren't really ill at all but only keeping everybody on the run so as to get all the attention, and planting poison about and all the rest of it—wouldn't you get them out of your house in double-quick time?"

"I'd be tempted to," Emma said honestly.

"So would Miss Aram, I'll be bound. And the doctor mustn't let that happen."

"No?"

"No. Because Miss Thurloe won't be got out. She's lived at Martinmas sixteen years—think of it. And she'll go on living there till she dies. And of course Dr. Bold wouldn't be the one to see she goes."

"But he could insist in her own interests."

"He won't do that. She's a very worthwhile patient," Nurse Swain said primly.

Emma, who took her meaning, was unable to add what she herself knew, that Miss Aram found her also a worthwhile paying guest.

"Besides," the nurse added, "I know the doctor finds her case interesting. It's not often you come across such a funny persecution complex—"

"Indeed, no," Emma murmured with perfect sincerity.

"—and if he was to make her leave Martinmas he'd lose her as a patient; she's as good as said so. *She* means to stay because if she was to take up fresh quarters after all this time she'd never find anybody else to believe in her like the old ones did—hers isn't the sort of game you can start afresh in old age."

"Is Miss Thurloe a great age?" Emma asked.

"So-so. Eightyish, I'd say. Pretends to less, and apes the little girl at times."

They had finished tea by now, and at Emma's suggestion, decided to have a look at the town before getting the bus back. It was bright and pleasant in the streets, and after some lingering round shop windows, Nurse Swain evincing notable indifference to hats, they made their way to the small public gardens laid out on the crest of the hill on the opposite side to the older part of the town. These rose above meadows and river and the spacious prospect of rolling country beyond, and were filled with the vague, sweet scents of the four elements and the rustle of leaves already warming to the first approach of autumn. The wind blew cool, but they found a sheltered bench beneath a catalpa tree, and there disposed their modest purchases while they rested a few minutes to watch the glitter of the water below, its surface skimmed by the late swallows.

"Nice up here," Nurse Swain sighed, with a satisfaction she could not have explained to herself.

The last pram was being hurried off to tea. Emma's heart smote her at having to make use of such seclusion for further espionage. But there were questions she was burning to ask, though it was doubtful if a nurse of three weeks' standing would be able to answer them. She wondered how best to begin.

"Well, it's a very sad thing, I think—even rather a fearful thing," she said, her eyes on the golden distance, "to be left so much alone in one's old age. I expect it makes for eccentricity, helps to develop, I mean, the disagreeable side of our characters."

Nurse Swain wrinkled her large nostrils as if to say compassion was thrown away on its present object.

"That's how Miss Thurloe chose it should be," she said.

Emma sighed. "Well, it's a pity. A nice home with her own flesh and blood—what a lot it might have saved. Has she no relatives?"

"That's what the doctor wanted to know. Was nobody responsible for her? he said. It isn't right that an old lady with such dangerous tendencies should be left to handle her money herself—and such a pile of money too! Well, it seems she's got a sister up in Hartlepool, but she won't go near her—Miss Thurloe won't, that's to say—for fear the sister has designs upon her. There's nobody besides but the London lawyer that manages her affairs, and he keeps his distance as much as he can, by all account."

"So I suppose the sister she never sees will inherit all that wealth? It's to be hoped that better use will be made of it than at present. Perhaps she is married, with children?"

"That I couldn't say. But it's funny you should mention the money, and inheritance. There's days the old lady turns quite chatty, those times she isn't showing off her worst—and then it's always about what she got and what she's going to do with it that she talks. What she's *not* going to do with it, I ought to say—for she declares, of all things, that she's never made a will, and doesn't intend doing so, what's more. Says it shortens your days to do anything of the sort. Did you ever?"

"Very foolish," Emma agreed. "But not uncommon, I believe. No wonder there's such a lot of unnecessary litigation in the world."

"Good for the lawyers," said Nurse Swain tartly. "It wouldn't surprise me to hear they had a hand in it."

She yawned broadly, remarking, "I'm that sleepy since coming up country I don't know what to do with myself. Bridport's had me for the last four months, so maybe I miss the sea."

"You must take care," Emma said, "to get plenty of rest by day now that you're on nights. Have I kept you out too long, I wonder?"

The nurse shook her head. She looked resentful all at once.

"He ought to have asked *me* to go on in the day, and the new nurse by night. It's days Miss Thurloe is the most troublesome, and anybody used to her ought to be on the spot then. Every time there's been a row about the poison it's been in daylight hours. She'll be sleeping pretty well my hours on, now. Not that *I* mind a more restful arrangement."

It was, Emma perceived, exactly what she did mind. She knew that the doctor, dissatisfied with her supervision, had allotted her those periods of duty when his patient was least likely to create a disturbance. The train of thought she had started led Emma to her next query.

"It seems to me quite clever reasoning on your part," she began, "that arrives at the conclusion Miss Thurloe is pretending to poison herself. Indeed, if suicide is ruled out and only the dreadful alternative left, one would expect a much more determined assault on her that would include the administration of the poison as well as leaving it about the place. But I confess I'm still quite baffled by one thing—it doesn't appear to fit with your theory at all."

"What's that?" Nurse Swain said. "And it isn't theory, it's the truth. Nobody has any reason to wish harm to Miss Thurloe. She may be cranky and aggravating, but while she's alive—and only while she's alive, mind—the money she's so free with benefits Martinmas and everybody in it."

That was true. That was why it looked as if the poisoner were to be identified with nobody but Miss Thurloe herself. That, Emma thought, was perhaps how it was intended to look.

"What bothers me," she said, "is knowing how she can get hold of the poison at all."

"Me too," the nurse said snappishly, for she was sensitive on the point. "Anybody that *didn't* know would say I was neglecting my duty in the matter, and anybody that *did* know would say there's nothing to beat the craftiness of these mental cases—both for getting and concealing."

"That is well known," Emma admitted. "Have you been able to search her room?"

"Not to say search. It's harder than you think. She's not bed-ridden, you know, and the way she can hop in and out and start screaming if she thinks you're up to something she doesn't know about—well, you'd be surprised. You wouldn't say there was much wrong with her those times. No more there is, bar brain. Besides, look at the stuff she's got in that room—you'd have to get her out and have the place to yourself for a week before you'd expect anything to turn up. Whatnots, antimacassars, piles of frocks she'll never wear again. I've looked—when I could, and that's the most I can say."

Emma, remembering the clutter of furniture and gewgaws she had caught sight of in the moment before the old woman's bedroom had been shut against her, sympathized with this point of view. On the other hand, if the poison were somewhere in the room, it was, she thought, unlikely to be far out of reach of Miss Thurloe, who would need to make rapid incursions upon it at the rare moments she was left unguarded.

"Apart from where it's hidden," she said, "the source of supply is perplexing. Where would you say she could possibly obtain it?"

"I've thought about that a lot lately," Nurse Swain said, turning towards her with a determined air, "and I believe I've hit on a likely solution. Only it isn't the kind of thing you dare put into words without proof," she added regretfully, at once proceeding to give it as clear expression as possible.

"There's one of these low fortune-tellers in the town here, who reads hands and stares at a bit of glass and traces things in the sand, and puts down to the stars the things Providence wills, like Hitler and such—I've no patience with the rubbish. It seems he's a big person in his line—why ever's it allowed?—and was carrying on his trade by the seaside till the Jerries got too hot there and all the people went away. So he came inland a couple of months ago and set up here, and charges heavy for his lies and makes a lot of money out of silly, fanciful folk who ought to know better. Mostly women,

I'm ashamed to say." She sucked in her lips with disapproval. "The mistresses at Makeways are as bad as any. It disgusts Miss Aram. The French maddy-mazelle and Miss Aram's secretary, and Miss Deakin of all people, they say, are always running to him, and even that nice Miss Pollard, though she did laugh it off and say she always went to them just the once for the fun of the thing. Not the way I'd want to take my fun, thank you—making an exhibition of my private life to a creature like that."

"And you mean that Miss Thurloe too has consulted him?" Emma said patiently.

"I'm coming to that." Nurse Swain, who had plainly got into her stride, was not to be hurried. "They're all batty about the man—all except Miss Aram and me. Well, would you believe, Poppy—that's the girl in the scullery—went for a hand-reading a fortnight ago and didn't know his fee was such a whopper, or said she didn't, and found after she'd had it that she hadn't got the money to pay for it, and he told her it was all right, not to worry. Said there was no compulsion on clients to pay for that side of his work, and those that gave, gave freely. There's cheek for you. Nothing for nothing, I told her, but, bless you, she swears by him—all because he wouldn't take anything for telling her that she had a wonderful love nature and that Mr. Right was drawing near and would be here as soon as Jupiter had got the upper hand of one of the other stars; I'm sure I don't remember which—and it doesn't matter either. Nothing for nothing, that's what I told her."

She drew a deep breath and continued: "Plain idolatry, I call it. And even their names are pagan, aren't they? The planets, I mean. Not but what that isn't their fault. And those two girls that gave in their notice yesterday, that have looked down their noses at me ever since I came—they went to him round about the time Poppy did, and he looked in the crystal and told them they would shortly be leaving their present employment and would do well for themselves to seek a post away, in a northern city for preference. A lot of ice they'd cut up north, with their airs and graces! Of course, it was he who put the idea into their heads, as I told Miss Aram, and he ought to be sued for 'ticing away servants. You can be, you know."

"And Miss Thurloe?" Emma persisted bravely.

"Yes. Well, she was worse than any of them. So Miss Deakin told me. Till she got too frightened to go out of the house at all. She and Miss Wand both got the craze. They used to hire a car or a taxi and be driven to and fro between Bugle and Martinmas three and four times in the week. Miss Wand gave up, though—oh, a good while before Miss Thurloe. She said it was making Miss Thurloe jealous, and anyway she'd been to others like him in her time and the excitement always upset her heart, especially when the witch doctor—that's what she called him—was a good-looking man. These old ladies take the cake, don't they? And her Miss Thurloe's age, if she's a day."

"And what did Miss Thurloe do then, poor thing?" Emma asked, still clutching the thread of the narrative, and feeling that she was apostrophizing Cock Robin.

"Just what I'd have expected of her. Sly these mental folk are—up to every dodge. She hunted round to find somebody who would go visit the man for her."

"What would be the use of that?" Emma asked innocently. It did not always pay to admit previous knowledge. "Palmistry at a distance? Surely not!"

"No, no," Nurse Swain said, pleased to elucidate the matter. "Besides all the rest of it, he pretends to tell your fortune by the things you wear and handle. Mauls them over, and spins the same yarn as before. So Miss Thurloe got it into her head she'd have what was left of her fortune told that way—I can't think what new things the fellow found to say all the time, for up to the date of her collapse when Nurse Edgeworth left, Miss Deakin says she was getting practically daily forecasts. So the long and the short of it was, she made up her mind to send trinkets and a glove and a handkerchief—things like that—by anybody who'd take 'em for her. She actually wanted *me* to."

"You didn't, of course?"

Nurse Swain made a derisive sound. "Me? I'm not that sort. It's not my job to encourage what's going to disturb the balance of the mind still further. She made a fuss, but I stuck to my guns, and then she dropped all talk of it suddenly. That ought to've made me suspicious, but I didn't know her well and it didn't dawn on me till too late that she'd got hold of somebody else."

Emma was politely incredulous.

"Yes, she had—where there's a will, you know. She got round a girl named Hart—a pupil, that's to say, in the top form too—and Miss Aram found out and expelled her the day before yesterday. What do you think of that?"

"How naughty," Emma murmured. "But how was it managed? Surely it was difficult for Miss Thurloe to do any undetected business with a schoolgirl?"

"Well, no, it wasn't. The girl used to be drawn into talk with her sometimes when she was sitting out on the lawn—Miss Aram discouraged that sort of thing, but you can't keep tabs on the big girls all the time, and Miss Thurloe will chat to anybody she takes a fancy to. And then there's church. She only missed last Sunday, and the school attends the same services. So there's been plenty of opportunity one way and another."

Emma agreed. But what bearing had this upon the supply of poison at Miss Thurloe's disposal?

"Why, don't you see? I don't *say* there's anything in it, mind, but none of us can help our thoughts, and it just came over me that she *could* be getting the stuff from the fortune-teller through Linda Hart. If so, I wouldn't say for a moment the girl knew what she was conveying."

In spite of what Grace had said, Nurse Swain, for a woman of limited intelligence, took some daring imaginative flights. Emma expressed considerable surprise that was not altogether assumed. If by any chance the nurse were right, they were back again at their starting point, and this time with an additional motive to seek. Why exactly was Miss Thurloe doing it, and why was the psychometrist helping her?

"What does the man call himself?" she asked.

Nurse Swain puckered her brow. "Now, what would it be? The times I've heard it said, too. The 'Great' something-or-other, I do believe. A fancy title, anyway—ashamed to use his right one, I'll be bound. Yes, that's it—the Great Ambrosio. Seems it's what he was known by years ago when he used to be employed by some travelling show or other."

"And he's here in the town? I wonder," said Emma indiscreetly, "where?"

The nurse gave her a sharp glance. "Don't say you're thinking of going there! *I* don't know at what address he practises his frauds, and if I did I wouldn't tell."

Emma blushed, and assured her that such was not her intention.

They were back at Martinmas shortly before seven. Nurse Swain, who took over at nine, went off to have a bath. The place was quiet. Miss Orpen and three of the seniors were knocking a ball about on the east court. Emma climbed the old stairs past the linen cupboard on her way to her room by the shortcut the matron had shown her. From the dormitory on the left came sounds indicating that Nonny was putting the babies to bed to the accompaniment of the Three Little Pigs, which lent itself admirably to the hundred percent gusto of her voice. A bubble of laughter burst into an excited treble piping, "*We*'re the little pi-igs, an' Nonny's the Big Bad Wolf!"

Outside the door that led past lavatories and bathroom into her own and Miss Thurloe's corridor Emma paused for a second. She thought someone had spoken her name. She could not be sure, nor did she know from what direction the sound had reached her. It was mere fancy, perhaps. She pushed open the door and went down the little passage into the dark entry by the bathroom. The drawback to this as a lazy cut to her own room was the possibility that someone was having a bath, in which case the door would be bolted against her.

It was open, however. She walked in, only to pull up short on the threshold. There was someone here; crouching on the floor, her back towards Emma, half supported by a chair, groaning horribly at intervals, her hands pressed to her stomach.

Emma's heart leaped, then beat suffocatingly fast. She ran forward and stooped over the kneeling figure. It lifted a pale, drawn face, beaded with perspiration. It was Susan Pollard.

There was no recognition in her eyes, but her first words belied them.

"Oh… Miss—Betony. I think—I think I'm—dying."

Chapter VIII

THE WITCHING HOUR

"What was she doing there at all?" Grace asked sternly. "Those lavatories are for the dormitory corridor. The bathroom is in the east wing which has nothing to do with the school, and is for the use of yourself and the nurses. Miss Thurloe has her own bathroom."

"Nurse Swain didn't take her bath there this evening," Emma said. She did not think it necessary to mention their encounter with the French mistress the morning they had hurried through to Miss Thurloe.

"No. She prefers the one the mistresses use next to the dorms because the water's hotter, she says. I've no objection. But from now on the door accessible to the dormitory corridor will be kept locked. No matter what Nonny says, that room is *not* a public route to Miss Thurloe's quarters, nor was it ever intended for people to pop in and out there to wash their hands."

"I'm sorry," Emma said. "It was used quite naturally by Miss Deakin and myself yesterday because we were close by when Miss Thurloe's cries startled us, but I ought to have realized those were exceptional circumstances."

"It's not your fault," Grace said, mollified. "As things turned out it's lucky you chose that way, or the girl wouldn't have been found till later. But I'm surprised at Susan. It's right out of her way. As soon as she's able to talk I shall want an explanation."

*

The clock on the mantelpiece chimed midnight. As the tinkling died away Susan Pollard opened her eyes and looked drowsily out of the shadows in which the bed lay. A reading lamp burned on the dressing table, and beside it, in a low chair, sat Nona Deakin writing a letter, head bent over the pad propped on her knee. When the clock finished striking, the scratch of her pen on paper sounded noisy.

The girl in bed lay on her back without moving, her eyes turning slowly from object to object in the dim light. It was good of Nonny to sit up with her. Thank God, the ebb and flow of pain that had plunged her into a well of fear was gone now; she was comfortable, though weak, so weak that it was too much of an effort to lift a hand to put the hair out of her eyes.

How many hours ago was it since the doctor had stood there, running practised eye and hand over her, barking hoarse commands at the others? Memory echoed the disjointed phrases—"Peritonitis? No—appendix sound—is she a gastric subject?"

She recalled the ring of faces that had swum in and out of vision as her senses, flagging with pain, revived as the nausea passed. Nona Deakin, brisk and unruffled, the little new nurse, Collins, who had handed Miss Thurloe over to the night nurse and delayed her own departure in case she were needed, Miss Aram, white-faced and anxious, the maid who had brought in the hot-water bottles, frightened—yes, and behind the fear, sullen, as if she were sorry she had ever set foot in Martinmas and were counting the days till she could shake its dust from her feet.

Were those her own feelings too? With the term so young, and so little yet achieved of all she had planned? She did not know. She was too weak to think. Arriving like that at the beginning of the holidays had been unwise, perhaps, but it had seemed best at the time; she had been able to make herself useful with the children who had not gone home, she had got to know the old ladies. Miss Thurloe—Miss Thurloe—there was something—something half remembered.

Susan turned her head from side to side, then, with the sudden alarm of the partially asleep, fixed her eyes on the washstand. Thence they travelled slowly to where the matron still sat scribbling. Did Nonny suspect? Was it possible that she was here to—?

She opened her lips to speak. It hardly seemed worth the effort, though, of exerting her lungs to take the preliminary breath. Before she could do so sleep had overwhelmed all her senses.

Nona Deakin dashed off the last words of her letter and appended a fine sprawling signature. She always felt better after writing her name like that. She flattered herself it acted like a tonic on the recipient too. It made her know that she was still a person of consequence in spite of being buried alive in this last-place-on-earth where there would never be any appreciation of real ability. What a fool she had been to toe the line meekly, and for the sake of a tuppenny-ha'penny job accept with a shrug all those defects that cramped her style at every turn. Soon, before they knew where they were, autumn would be upon them, shrouded fields, damp, ugly mists winding the house in a burial sheet, the terrible feeling of isolation the approach of winter in the country brings to the town-bred whose efficiency, to remain unimpaired, asks for constant stimulation.

She ought to go while the going was still good. Soon it wouldn't be good at all. She would do better in munitions, making bombs. Making bombs! Making bombs. She wouldn't be bad at that. She laughed shortly and glanced at the bed. She did not want to wake its occupant. It was all right, the girl slept placidly, almost without breathing, lying on her back with something of the calm finality of the dead. Her face, still flushed, wore a look of extraordinary innocence. No wonder that Thurloe had been taken with it; that pearly rose and white belonged to the sixties and seventies that were a more living reality to the old lady than was the present day.

She stretched out a hand to the dressing table and fingered a little tortoiseshell bonbonnière in gold piqué; a pretty thing, not without value, that had belonged to Miss Thurloe. She had bestowed it on Susan in one of those gushes of affection that had been so noticeable a few weeks ago. Here too was a gold chain for the neck, its pendant a cluster of ivy-strangled hearts set with garnets; old-fashioned, unsuitable, but acceptance of it had not seemed to embarrass the girl.

She got up quietly and, with another glance at the bed, moved across to the washstand which she studied critically for a few seconds. Then, wrapping her handkerchief carefully round the neck of the water bottle, she picked it up, tilting the spoonful of water that lay in the bottom. She did not take it away to refill it, however; instead, she placed it gently on the floor in a secure and inconspicuous position in the angle formed by wardrobe and wall. It would not get knocked over there, and when her vigil was done she could remove it at leisure. As she raised herself after setting it down, the wardrobe mirror gave back her reflection.

She was smiling broadly at herself with a firm display of teeth.

The portable on the table gave the signal for 12 P.M. a little hoarsely. Lilian Orpen, who had got into bed five minutes before, took up her watch and set the hands for midnight. She wound it, replaced it on the table, and lay down, only to pull herself up on her elbow almost immediately and switch off the news. It was simply a hash-up of the nine o'clock which she had heard when everybody else was wondering if Susan Pollard would live or die. She had other things to wonder about—to worry about, she might have said, if she had not believed that with properly played cards success was within grasp.

She had lost twice at the game. She was thirty-three. She dared not consider failure this time. What had he said? That he would be leaving Bugle before Christmas and trying his fortunes in a larger town. After all, what scope could a little place like this offer for psychiatry, clairvoyance, psychometry, on the scale that he could dispense it? Most likely, hustled away from the seaside, he had settled temporarily in the most convenient spot; certainly he seemed never to lack clients.

That was not to be wondered at. The man—it was almost profane to label him so humbly—the man and his power were alike miraculous. What was it he had hinted at? A temple and a cult, a magic that should disturb a wider circle than the cluster of devotees in Bugle. When he had established himself in permanent quarters somewhere on the fringe of a great city where there were people who really understood these things, then he would exercise his arts as the Master whom he served intended that they should be exercised.

He had confided in her, trusted to her faith and devotion to their common cause not to disclose his intention before he was ready. She would be silent. She could hold her tongue. Rewards awaited loyal servitors. In the temple there would be an altar, rites, acolytes in attendance. Women would not be excluded from their number.

The Great Ambrosio—how beautiful it was—how it resounded—though that was not what she privately styled him. To her he was the Master, just as to him the Master was that Other whom he adored in secret and one day would proclaim. But Ambrosio was splendid too... Am-bro-si-o... how the syllables slipped like honey round the tongue.

She ticked the months off on her fingers. Three to Christmas. Before then she must have won him. For the first time she was not angling for money. There were things in life that thrilled more sharply. The man himself, the secrets to which he would introduce her, the unholy quest that should end in the materialization of the Master himself, Ambrosio's Master, within the design of the pentagram. But first, and last, the man. She sighed ecstatically.

If only the Frenchwoman did not queer her pitch. How she loathed her—the stringy hag. Always there, always making appointments, hanging on him, cadging free periods to run into Bugle, pushing, edging, fighting for attention. It was behaviour for which there was only one interpretation. And the creature was of Gallic blood, and even more desperate at fifty than one felt at thirty-three.

She wished she could hex her. She wished she could consult the Master about it without betraying the jealousy that stirred her blood to trembling malice. She wished she had an image of the woman she could torture with pins and knives, burn slowly at the fire. She believed the woman was hexing on her own account. She herself had had greater difficulty than usual in the last week to get into the presence of Ambrosio; when she had contrived to see him he had appeared preoccupied, distant, even cold. She had suffered mental agony. It might be nothing, but she dared not chance it. She must work harder than ever to get him within the next month or two. Was it perhaps, after all, that remembering she was the poorly paid secretary of a headmistress whose school was fast sinking under her he had turned his eyes in another direction? The cult would need financial support. The French were noted for their acquisitive genius. Lancret might have a hoard snugly laid by in this country. The powers of darkness grant that all she had was invested in France, and all lost...

She thought of the two old women from the nursing home, burdened with wealth—the one old woman who had pestered the Master almost beyond endurance. Well, she at least was out of the running now. She should stay out too.

She longed to inspect the Frenchwoman's room. She was sure she would find in it an image of herself, defaced, mutilated, outraged. The idea did not altogether repel her. It was good to know that you lived in the thoughts of others, if only as an object of intense odium, that you were a torment to your enemies...

She snapped off the light and lay back, staring into the darkness, smiling.

*

In a small bedroom in the west wing looking out on kitchen garden and garage, two candles burned while the day passed quietly over into another. To a visitor the room, without pictures, flowers, comfort of any kind, would have struck bare. To its occupant the bleak four walls enclosed the only refuge the world afforded. Here she could legitimately lock her door and escape into herself.

On a table at the south end of the room a silver crucifix stood, resting against the wall. Beside it was a blue and white porcelain stoup for holy water. In front stood a *prie-dieu*. For the rest, there was a bed, its harsh iron frame softened a little by a lavender silk coverlet thrown over it, a small deal washstand behind its screen, a chair, a dressing table, and a squat wardrobe with a damaged lock. There was a moderately good rug on the floor and a threadbare mat by the bed. It was actually a maid's room, for Martinmas had kept a larger domestic staff than Makeways could afford. But Mlle. Lancret was poor, plain, middle-aged, she was paid a low salary, rarely complained, and did not belong to the class which calls for consideration when creature comforts are to be dispensed.

Julie Lancret knelt on the *prie-dieu*, a faded striped dressing gown draping her gaunt figure, her hair trailing unbecoming wisps about her shoulders. Wax from the candles ran down the metal sticks.

She was a long time about her prayers, which mingled oddly with a host of ungoverned thoughts and images. She saw again with the painful clarity of the past weeks the old white house in Normandy in the windless hollow behind the cliffs. Her old mother was there, a widow since Second Ypres, which had taken her brother Henri too, and her sister Marie-Josephine, a widow since the first bitter days of the Marne. And where Marie's son was, who had never seen his father nor his father's grave, only the good God knew. She besought Him now, with lids firmly closed and lips that betrayed no tremor, to preserve Nicolas from the clutches of Death and his lackey, the Boche, who took for themselves the male Lancrets and left only women and young girls to spin out life without them.

Again, unbidden in an agonizing moment of illumination she saw her own daughter's face—Yves, born of the tender folly of a summer in Paris twenty-one years ago, when the people she knew and understood were lighthearted and light-headed with the passing away for ever and for ever of *la guerre*. For ever and for ever. She lifted her eyes in desperate question.

Behind the house was an orchard where the unpruned trees were heady with flowers in the spring. Yves, taught by big cousin Nicolas to climb their writhing limbs, had sat in the Aprils of childhood watching the world through their curdled foam of blossom. There it was that she and Henri and Marie-Josephine had played their games in remoter Aprils. A sudden absurd picture flashed across, obscuring the others, of Mignon, the old speckled hen, clucking on a high, fretful note to the seven ducklings she had mothered, as they disported themselves in the pool at the bottom. There the road wound past, shaded by bosky elms; and beyond, under a sky ribbed with dawn or burning like a lantern, were the plumy colza fields, soft and luminous in the light of other days.

Normandy... France... home, her people, her heart. On them all had closed the long, cruel silence like the effacing fall of snow. No word reached her. No longer could she get the money to her mother and Yves, the half of her salary that had gone twice each term until now. Instead, she was spending the money that was theirs trafficking with strange powers, because in desperation she had thought they might vouchsafe a word of comfort when God was silent. They had not answered yet.

She crossed herself, folding bony hands upon her breast. It was only a word she asked for, only one word to break the dumb conspiracy that had netted them all—Yves, Marie-Josephine, her old mother, Nicolas, herself.

She was losing grip. Her work was going to pieces. If she did not pull herself together Miss Aram would be tired of her soon. She would send her going. There were so few children, the school could not afford drones. Children and staff alike seemed to have receded from her this term; even their voices were far away at times. She never thought about them, could not remember their names. She was sure that they never thought about her either. What did these English know or care or understand, with their grey water always around them?

"*Yves, chérie... et maman...*" She covered her face with her hands, the tails of iron-grey hair hanging forward to touch the sloping back of the *prie-dieu*.

"*Notre Père... que votre volonté soit fait... pardonnez-nous nos offences...*"

Pardonnez-nous nos offences... But would He forgive, *le bon Dieu*? Had He forgiven? Was not Yves herself for whom she prayed reckoned one of her sins? And what of her appeals to the Evil One, who made no reply?

Pardonnez-nous nos offences. There was only One who understood. She must leave it to the good God Himself.

Nurse Swain closed the book she had been reading, tucked it at the back of her chair and picked up her knitting. Better go on with the yellow jumper than waste time reading trash. Yellow was a nice colour for the autumn, though now she'd started she wasn't sure it was really *her* colour. Oh, well. As a rule she liked a good love story, plenty of misunderstandings, and nothing sad in the end. But this was all my eye. Old ladies in real life didn't leave their fortunes to their nurses to console them for broken hearts. No, indeed. All they actually did was to show marked lack of appreciation while they kept your nose to the grindstone, get rid of you—look at the way Edgeworth was treated—the first time they had a sick turn that really frightened them, and end up by leaving all they'd got to a Cats' Home. Or else behave like Miss Thurloe and swear they'd never make a will at all.

She lowered the lamp in case even a subdued glow might disturb the old lady. The last thing she wanted at this hour was one of those screaming bouts. There was the hall clock striking midnight. She got up and went quietly to open the door to let in the sound more clearly. When the last stroke ebbed away she shut it again. It was nice to hear a voice, if it was only the clock's. Silly of her, but she'd never cared much for night duty. It was an unsociable time with nobody to chat to, and the silence getting thicker and thicker. A bit of harmless gossip did wonders to kill time. This Miss Betony now, she wasn't one of these touch-me-nots like the rest of the staff. Funny what a good opinion schoolmistresses had of themselves. She'd heard the same said of nurses, but it wasn't true. Funny thing for that girl to have such a bad gastric turn tonight. Gastritis was a rotten thing, and the cooking here wasn't of the best—only what you'd expect, of course, from those uppish madams in the kitchen.

She glanced at the face on the pillow, flabby with the laxity of age, petulance and soft living. The little slack lips drooped into cheeks that had once been plump and perhaps charming, and were now merely formless and pouchy. The small, gross hands that by day were crusted with rings gripped the sheet where it was folded across her breast. From beneath the cap she wore little escaping strands of hair of a pale brown hardly touched with grey moved lightly to the rise and fall of her sleeping breath. She had the look of defenceless innocence common to youth and old age.

"Ah, my lady," Nurse Swain said softly, clicking her needles with a steady rhythm, "you look as if butter wouldn't melt in your mouth, don't you? But what we'd like to know is how you get up to your tricks—and when—and why!"

She yawned involuntarily, and felt sudden alarm. It would never do to get sleepy now, even though she was unable to remember a night since she had come when Miss Thurloe had seriously disturbed her slumber. The old lady was a notoriously good sleeper. She dared not risk it, however. The electric fire warmed the room well, that was what was doing it. But she loved a warm atmosphere. Presently she would make herself some coffee, in the dressing room where she had slept other nights. Meantime, the intricate pattern of the jumper ought to keep her awake.

She knitted on, thinking how strange it was she should have been so sleepy almost the whole time since coming to Martinmas.

The figure in bed stirred. It spoke, in gasps beneath its breath. "Yes—yes—yes—pour it out, my dear—pour it all away!"

Nurse Swain jerked herself up and stared hard at Miss Thurloe. She looked next, she could not have said why, at the water bottle, a new one, full to the neck. Nobody had used it since she had refilled it tonight. As the fluttering tones faded, she leaned her head back for a few minutes to rest her eyes from the knitting. Before she could have counted twenty her head was nodding in sleep.

She was still sleeping an hour later. She did not wake when the door opened.

Across the landing from Julie Lancret's room and down two steps a bedroom door stood ajar. The little old woman in nightgown and wrapper inside the room moved over to shut it. That door had a nasty trick of sliding inwards without a sound, and extending invitation to who knows what. The past itself might come gliding in one day—or night. But which?

At thought of being able to select one out of a number of pasts, Miss Wand giggled. It made her look suddenly happy and ageless; only she was always forgetting a minute later why she had felt happy just then. It was the same absence of mind that sent her flitting across to the chiffonier to try pulling out an imaginary drawer in the belief that it was the bureau she was used to. Of course, this was the other room, her new one. Belated recognition of the fact pulled her up sharp twenty times a day. She wondered why they had bothered to move her. Mistaken kindness on Miss—what was her name?—Aram's part, for she was used to Miss Thurloe's carryings-on after twelve years, and even though these were more vehement than usual she had not complained. They had judged it wise, however, to give her a room in the west wing. Until now she had never occupied any but the old one all the years she had lived in Martinmas, and it was not easy to adjust oneself to entirely new surroundings.

Not that she had put up much opposition to the change; opposition even of the most trivial kind brought on a deathly fatigue nowadays. Besides, she had always been one to greet the unknown with a cheer. It hadn't always paid, naturally, but it had never failed to give a spice to life. And now she was installed over here, with Miss Aram close by, and on the other side of the landing a dreary-looking Frenchwoman who did not look as if naughty stories would amuse her. But you never knew. That was part of life's spice. You could but try.

She had more awkward stairs to climb now, but, as Miss Aram had explained, summer was nearly over and she would have to keep to her room more in any case, and she was so much nearer the servants it saved a lot of trouble. That was a consideration, of course. She had never liked to give trouble. And servants were kittle cattle—think of Bertha Glass, their own maid for years, going off without even saying good-bye, just because she had at last taken offence at some remark of Miss Thurloe's who had been consistently offending her for years! Not to speak of Nurse Edgeworth who had been so good to them, overlooking the temperamental oddities some might have resented. Life without those two was lonely at times.

This present illness of Miss Thurloe's was a little puzzling when she thought about it at all. It seemed as if she were being isolated over there in the denuded east wing. Was it mental trouble, perhaps? As long as she had known her she had been autocratic and wilful, pampered and moody, an exhibitionist because she lacked experience. She had tried to draw the doctor out on the subject, but he had not responded. A self-important little man who mistook rudeness for authority, his manner the antithesis to Dr. Fielding's leisured sociability. His visits too were both flying and infrequent, even yesterday when she had had another spasm; and whenever he looked in he seemed preoccupied with something else of more urgent interest than this silly old heart she had worked too hard.

Well, Miss Thurloe was no concern of hers.

She sat down in front of the dressing-table mirror and, taking up an old silver-backed brush, began to brush her hair. There wasn't much of it left now, but she was glad that what there was shone bright. It was good to go down with flying colours. Not that she felt like going down just yet. If she remembered to treat her heart respectfully there would be a few years left to her still. And life was sweet, though the sweetest were gone. There had been one nasty turn a few days before Dr. Fielding had gone away, rather different though from the pain of *angina pectoris* she had learned to dread. But it had not recurred.

There was that door open again. She said a naughty word and got up to close it. As she turned back, the tall cheval-glass opposite reflected her image. That was one of the things she did not like about the room; whoever entered was caught in the glass and disconcerted at being met by himself. It swung loosely too, and without warning plunged you forward, legs ridiculously telescoped, or else carried you, chest out, with a majordomo's dignity. And the slight angle at which it was placed set yourself watching yourself while you lay in bed. Miss Wand, with a mischievous grimace, thought that in one's eighty-second year that was rather hitting below the belt. She would have it moved. But the maids came rarely, and were not very obliging. She drew a finger across the chiffonier and left a clear track on the coated surface. They did not even bother to dust.

The little French watch decorated in enamel that was one of her treasures ticked away inaudibly on the dressing table. She saw that the hands pointed to twelve o'clock. If she did not get into bed soon the school matron—whose name she was always forgetting—would be looking in, to scold her with the hearty playfulness she thought old ladies appreciated. The poor dear...

Miss Wand pulled a face at the cheval-glass, and then examined with critical detachment the small, withered features gazing at themselves.

"You were always rather like a monkey, my dear," she whispered, "and you're like one still."

She pirouetted shakily, and kicked her slippers into the air, one after the other, the mirror repeating the insouciance.

Was that the matron she heard moving? Perhaps not. She wasn't used to the sounds in these quarters. She climbed carefully into bed and turned off the light before settling down to feigned sleep.

She had no mind tonight to indulge in baby talk with an unsatisfied spinster who had never grown up beyond the hockey field stage. She supposed spinsters had their uses, but after living in the house with them for three months it was hard to see what these were.

Grace Aram put out her own light as the wireless signal reached her from Lilian Orpen's room. She rattled the blackout curtain aside and snapped up the blind, pushing the casement out as far as it would go to draw the cold night air into her lungs.

Only a light wind moved over the face of the sleeping country. Garden, paddock and orchard, the meadows beyond whose path led to the church of St. Martin-by-the-Brook, lay indistinguishable in the darkness. No breath rose or fell in that motionless, shadowy world, or so it seemed to her—nothing but the almost inaudible sigh of wind. It was deathly. That meant like death. And Death had brooded too long now over this house, playing with it, feigning action, committing indignities, hinting at frightfulness. It could not go on much longer...

She leaned on the window and took a deep draught of the tangy air. It tasted like Switzerland, like the mountains and lakes and narrow gorges. She drew back and closed the window. It was bad to review the past. There was nothing to do but go on from the present, resolved and unrepentant, making past errors a lesson for turning the potentialities of the future to certain advantage for oneself.

One thing she had made up her mind to do. She would get Miss Thurloe out of the house.

After saying good-night to Grace, Emma took a long time getting to bed. Training and temperament alike had taught her never to hurry the act of undressing, nor scamp the smallest detail.

For all that, she was tired tonight after a day which had ended with Susan Pollard's curious seizure. In the light of recent events she was not prepared at once to accept it as normal sickness. And she was as puzzled as Grace to know what had brought the girl to the east wing.

Listening too was an exacting job—especially when you listened so as to apply the knowledge gained to the problem at hand—and Nurse Swain's rambling confidences were not particularly easy to follow. It was clear, however, that, misjudging the course paranoia was likely to run, she believed Miss Thurloe to be the author of the alleged attacks upon herself. But if Miss Thurloe were really the victim of persecution complex, and planting evidence of attempts at murder for want of an actual persecutor, Emma found herself unable to square with the fact the terror that possessed the old woman. The oblong mouth, the glaring eyes, the pitiful moans—if they were assumed as part of the "let's pretend" the woman was a consummate actress. But not even an actress, especially a spoilt one more than eighty years old, could sustain the game successfully for several weeks. The fear was real therefore. But nobody would fear the consequences of a fraud he was himself perpetrating, when consequences of a harmful nature were not intended. Miss Thurloe, the author, could stay her hand and spare Miss Thurloe, the victim, at any moment she liked. Therefore Miss Thurloe was not responsible for these attacks upon her. Therefore somebody else was at the bottom of them. Therefore murder was intended.

To Emma it was so logical a sequence that she was astonished Nurse Swain had not worked it out for herself. On reflection, though, it seemed to her that the nurse had merely borrowed the doctor's views and made them her own. If that were so, it was still more surprising. In spite of Grace's extravagant claim for her, Emma was neither nurse nor doctor, but the absurdity of a persecution complex functioning in the way attributed to Miss Thurloe's struck her at once. It was incredible that it had not struck Dr. Bold long ago.

The nice balance of her judgement, however, refused to admit that all the available evidence pointed to an unknown murderer. There were objections even to that theory. No feature of the case was at present more peculiar in Emma's eyes than the conspicuous lack of success attendant on these attempts to poison Miss Thurloe. With the stuff so skilfully planted and the identity of the poisoner so ably concealed, it was frankly unbelievable that murder itself should be bungled time after time. As it was, the old woman appeared to bear a charmed life; and in a situation like the present one that hypothesis was inadmissible. Yet, rack her brains as she might, Emma could find no excuse for a murderer who tried, tried, tried again, and never did succeed. Suicide, murder with an individual motive, homicidal mania, attempts on the part of a neurotic old woman to give the impression of a murderer at large—the bottom fell out of them all on examination. It had not yet dawned on Emma that there was another theory which fitted all the facts.

As she plaited her hair, the clock on the landing whirred, and struck twelve. Another day—it was Saturday. There were no classes and she was free to use the whole day as she pleased. Her plan was ready. Nurse Swain had given her the idea, though she could not wholly subscribe to the nurse's implied suspicions. It was still possible, however, that a clue, a hint, the merest whisper of what was going on inside Martinmas, might be picked up outside. A fortune-teller lived in Bugle with whom Martinmas had strange, excited and—yes, forbidden dealings. Emma made up her mind to consult him too. It was a decision, she thought, of which Grace would approve; she would tell her, of course. She knew neither his address nor his consulting hours, but it was more than likely that Grace could tell her both. In any case she would find out without much difficulty. It would not be the first time that, with a more credulous motive than now, she had secretly taken the road to Endor.

She got up and went over to the wardrobe to get a bottle of eau-de-cologne she had bought in the town that day. It was still in a pocket of the coat she had worn, she remembered. She opened the door, and then stood, her hand on the latch, frowning. Something was wrong—different. The wardrobe was tidy, frocks and coats on their hangers, a scarf for the colder days on its hook. But she was urgently aware of something missing. That was it—on the shelf above, the shallow brown cardboard box she had put there when she unpacked. It contained only oddments, ribbons, ties, an old pair of gloves, shabby but usable things she had not cared to dispense with. Since the Wednesday evening of her arrival it had been up on the shelf, and every time she had opened the wardrobe door the legend across the end of it had caught her eye—"Freshly Cut Flowers," with the Channel Island address beneath. Long ago it had held narcissi, and for sentimental reasons as well as for its useful shape she had kept the box. It was still there, but the familiar words, never thought about so long as they stared at her, were not. The box had been turned round and pushed to the back of the shelf.

As soon as she had made this discovery, Emma tried to recall whether she had herself taken the box down and replaced it the other way round. It was dangerous to jump to hasty conclusions. But on reflection she was quite sure. She had not touched it since placing it there more than two days ago; what was more, it could not have been handled earlier than her last visit to the wardrobe, or else the heavy black type would have been missed then. When had she been last to the wardrobe? After summoning Grace and the matron to Susan Pollard—when she had slipped into her room for a minute to take off her hat and coat. It was just possible, of course, that in the agitation of the moment she had overlooked the changed position of the box.

She lifted it down and, removing the lid, looked inside. The rather confused appearance of the contents might have been due merely to shaking on the journey. Anyway, in such a medley it would hardly be possible at once to say that this or that had been tampered with, or was missing.

Without moving she let her gaze wander round the room. At first glance it looked much as usual. But she was leaving nothing to chance. Her dozen or so books on the bureau were tidy, but there was something peculiar about them. Emma was sensitive about books. She believed that their arrangement on a shelf should accord with their temperaments and characters, and that, as in human relationships, only mutual irritation was induced by stressing incompatibility. So what was *The Mistress of Shenstone* doing next to *Commercial Book-Keeping for the Student*, and *The Tailor of Gloucester*, threadbare now from his many readings that had delighted Emma more than they had generations of polite listeners, shoulder to shoulder with Mr. Pendlebury's excellent *Arithmetic*? The maid perhaps had disarranged them, dusting. But up to date the room had received scant attention, and books were commonly the last things meddled with.

Besides, here on the floor were the pressed pansies she had kept for years in *The Complete Poems of Rosamund Marriott Watson*. They stuck a little to the leaves, and to dislodge them one would have to shake the book vigorously.

An idea struck her, and she went across to the bed, stooping to draw out the suitcase. It was not there. She found it a moment later pushed up towards the head of the bed, its handle swung round against the wall. That again might have been the maid. On the other hand, it might equally well have been an impatient reply to finding the case locked. For, Emma congratulated herself, the key was on her person. *Wings of Friendship* in mind, she had taken the precaution of removing it from the lock.

On a sudden impulse she pulled out the top drawer of the chest of drawers—and remained staring. Up to now she had felt only uneasy; this removed her last doubt. The contents of the drawer were not exactly tumbled perhaps, but they had been thoroughly rummaged. She was certain, with the unshakeable conviction that only the scrupulously tidy dare have, that nothing here had been left in this condition by her own hands. She pushed the drawer home, opening each of the other two in quick succession. They told the same tale. Somebody had been in her room, methodically searching it.

Searching for what? Emma sat on the end of the bed and posed the question to the room. Whose interest, suspicions perhaps, had she managed to arouse in the short space of two days? What had she got that could possibly excite anybody to a feverish hunt?

Neither memory nor imagination suggested an answer. Her possessions were spare, old-fashioned, obvious. There was none to know the truth of her presence at Martinmas, unless residence in the east wing had alarmed someone. If so, alarm could be felt by only one person, the one responsible for the attacks on Miss Thurloe.

She sighed, and decided to go to bed. Any meticulous examination of her things in quest of missing property must be left till morning.

She would lock her door again; it might be as well, too, to keep it locked by day, during absences.

Her head ached, recalling to mind why she had gone to the wardrobe just now. She returned, and felt in the pockets of the coat she had worn into Bugle the afternoon before. The bottle was there. As her fingers closed round it they fastened, too, on a piece of paper. Conscious of having made no shopping list or anything of that sort, Emma drew it out, wondering idly what she had left lying there. It was a moderately large cutting, snipped with scissors, from the advertisement pages of a local newspaper. The bold, simple type announced:

THE GREAT AMBROSIO
Psychiatrist, Clairvoyant & Psychometrist

6 THANKFUL COURT
LANTHORN, BUGLE

Consultations daily, 11 A.M. to 6 P.M.
Other times by appointment.

Someone else, it seemed, was not averse to her visiting the wizard of Bugle.

Chapter IX

A QUESTION OF BOTTLES

"That's brave of you," Grace said unexpectedly. But she sounded doubtful, though her eyes were excited. "You might pick up something, of course. Don't tell anybody else, though, Bet, because I've been so hard on the Ambrosio fans they might get the idea there was something funny going on if they heard you were off to have your fortune told too, before you'd time to settle in!"

Emma, who wanted silence in any case, promised to keep the visit secret.

"And put it off till afternoon," Grace said. "I'm going into town then to see about new maids. I'll get the car out, and Orpen will drive us in."

That was after breakfast and an hour before Dr. Bold was due. When he came in Emma was in her room, checking the contents of drawers and bureau against yesterday's marauder. At eleven o'clock there was a tap on her door. She raised a flushed face from inspection of a stubbornly sliding drawer and called "Come in!" Grace came in, looking with some surprise at her posture.

"Lost something?" she asked, but did not wait for an answer. She had the taut look that worried Emma.

"I've been talking to Bold." She caught Emma's wrist as she got to her feet. "The arrowroot's been analysed, and is as good as ever nurse said it was. But there had been arsenic in the water bottle she'd used. There was only about a spoonful of water left anyway, but it was as full of poison as—"

She did not finish, but stared hopelessly at Emma.

"That's not all. Nurse Swain swears she filled the bottle herself that night, and says neither she nor Miss Thurloe drank from it before Miss Thurloe fell asleep—there's nothing but her own memory to support this, of course, but if it's true I suggest that whoever's trying to kill the old lady poured the rest of the water away later in an attempt to hide what they'd done."

"But," said Emma tentatively, "wouldn't the bottle have been empty in that case? The only safe course would be to throw out *all* that was left."

"That's what the doctor says—and wash the bottle out afterwards too, in his opinion. I say there wouldn't have been time. But he declares that if there was time to tamper with the thing at all before it got into the analyst's hands, there was time to do it properly. It doesn't follow—but arguing with him's useless. He always takes the prejudicial standpoint. But I'd like—how I'd like to know what's really in his mind."

It struck Emma that the disclosure of quite a number of minds would not be at all a bad thing. She said so.

"I know," said Grace. "It's ghastly. And now Nurse Swain says when she handed over to Nurse Collins this morning the bottle that was full last night was again empty! She had none herself and is quite sure that the old lady slept soundly all night—was still sleeping, in fact, when the day nurse came on."

"I don't understand it at all," Emma said truthfully. "If the water goes somebody must surely drink it. Unless the bottle runs out," she added with a gleam of mischief. "That's only my nonsense. Has—has Miss Thurloe shown any alarming symptoms yet?"

"Not yet. But if I know anything about her it won't be long— she'll start screaming soon."

"Did Dr. Bold take that bottle away too?"

"With glee. He's the only one who seems to be enjoying the affair. Bet, I don't care what they say, I shall get Thurloe out. I'm not bound by any specific clause in the contract to keep her indefinitely, and if I were, I think circumstances like these would absolve me. There's no consideration that weighs against the risk of having her murdered under my nose—besides, who knows who will be the next victim? She'll have frightful hysterics, of course, when she knows I really mean it, but better that whirlwind once for all than this sickening repetition of fears."

Emma nodded. "You would have been wise to do it a month ago."

"You know why I didn't."

"I know, Grace. But if you depend on Miss Thurloe to keep Makeways going through its bad times, and anything happens to her while she is here, the consequences to the school will be even more unpleasant than having to close down through lack of funds, won't they?"

"Of course. That's why I'm going to take the longer view and get rid of her."

"How is Miss Pollard?" Emma put in.

"Asking for you."

"For me?"

"Yes. She says she was on her way to you yesterday evening when she was taken ill, not knowing you'd gone out."

"I wonder what she wanted. May I see her now?"

"When you like. She's much better, but the doctor advises a few days in bed." She hesitated. "Bet, go warily. Remember we move blindfold in this business. It's not only you who have a room over here. Don't misunderstand me—but it's possible for a visitor to Miss Thurloe, who isn't allowed visitors, to pretend when caught out that she was going to visit *you*. No, I insinuate nothing—because I was going to add, if that were so, there may be a perfectly innocent explanation. Before Miss Thurloe became more or less inaccessible nobody in the school saw her more frequently than Susan. And the girl has been worried over these queer turns of hers, I know. So it wouldn't be unnatural—"

"I understand."

Grace went to the door. Before going out she said abruptly, "I trust your discretion, Bet."

Susan Pollard's room was warm and sunny when Emma got there five minutes later. The girl was alone, propped up on pillows, with eyes too large and bright and a hectic flush on her cheeks.

"I'm so glad to see you, Miss Betony," she said simply. "Please sit down if you can spare a few minutes—no, not that knobbly chair— the other one. I—I wanted to apologize for being such a nuisance yesterday, and to thank you for coming to the rescue."

Emma smiled. "It wasn't really like that, you know. I happened along by chance."

"A lucky one for me. Did I frighten you?"

"Oh, yes. But I didn't dare spend the time indulging in shock."

They both laughed. Emma was conscious of an uneasiness on Susan Pollard's part that made her uneasy too. The girl was frowning, smiling, clipping her remarks, giving the impression that she was thinking of something else. She wound a corner of the sheet tightly round her finger, unwound it, started over again, and all the while watched Emma with a brilliant gaze.

Emma spoke of this and that, of the quiet of the country round Martinmas, of the sensitivity of the body to weather conditions at the turn of the seasons when hot days and cold nights alternate, of the wisdom of taking things quietly for a time.

"Wasn't there something you were coming to see me about before you were taken sick?" she asked gently at last, when beating about the bush failed to produce anything.

"It wasn't important," Susan said on a quick, high note. "I only mentioned it just now because Miss Aram wondered why I was in the east wing at that hour. You see, I had no idea you'd gone into Bugle, and not finding you elsewhere I made for your room."

"I see. What was it I could have done for you if you'd found me there?"

"It's really a trifling business. You know the two girls who do languages with you—Jean Cavell and Nancy Bates. Jean learns violin with me—yes, my job's English, but I help Miss Orpen with the music—I was wondering if you'd much mind changing your Monday morning class with them for my afternoon period with Jean. You and I are free in each other's teaching hours that day, and Nancy too has nothing that first hour after lunch. Miss Aram allows the staff to swap periods for their mutual satisfaction when this can easily be arranged—and Jean cuts right into my only free afternoon of the week. Do you mind?"

"Not at all," Emma said, surprised. She was about to add that her own timetable held so many gaps that adjustment at any point might readily be made, when she remembered that it would be better not to arouse curiosity about her apparently idle position at Makeways. Instead she observed, "It won't apply to this Monday, though, because you mustn't get up till later in the week."

"Well, no—though really I feel all right again. Thank you very much for changing. As a matter of fact, I came along last night about it because it was this Monday I had in mind. I've a friend in Blandford just now, and I'd hoped to run over for the afternoon and, if you'd consented to swap teaching periods, was meaning to ring her up to fix things."

"She'll perhaps be there another Monday," Emma said.

"Oh, I think so. Anyway, it's not important."

She drew a quick breath and said with a rush, "That's not really what's worrying me. Do you know, my mind's a blank for the time I was ill yesterday? I want so much to know one thing—where was it you found me, Miss Betony?"

"*Where?*" Emma echoed, stupidly, she feared. "But you know where, my dear. You've been explaining it to Miss Aram. In the east wing, of course."

"I know. That's what Miss Aram said. But, I mean—which room?"

"Oh." Emma recovered herself. "In the bathroom. The one just off the dormitory corridor. It's not to be used as a shortcut any more, I understand, and that door will be kept locked."

Susan Pollard leaned back with a sigh, pressing her shoulders luxuriantly into the pillows. "That's all right, then. I don't remember anything properly, you see—not till I was here in bed. Nonny hasn't been back since the doctor left, and I was asleep till he came, so I couldn't ask her anything—it was Miss Aram who told me you had been the one to find me. And I was horribly afraid of what you would be thinking."

"About what?"

"I was afraid I'd been taken ill in your room."

Emma's heart missed a beat. She had a sudden vision of rummaged drawers and the box turned round in the wardrobe. Meeting the girl's candid gaze she was annoyed to know it was herself, not Susan, who blushed.

"But you didn't succeed in reaching it," she pointed out.

"Oh, but I did. As you found me in the bathroom I must have managed to get back so far before collapsing. But I'd been to your room, and knocked. When there was no answer I opened the door a little way and looked inside to make sure. That was when the first wave of pain passed over me. I do remember that. I remember leaning against the door, fighting the sickness, knowing that I'd got to struggle on somehow and sit down. I don't remember anything else—that's why I was afraid I'd fallen down in your room."

Emma reassured her, and was herself gratified at the relief in the girl's eyes.

"Have you any ideas about the cause of your sickness?" she asked.

"The doctor wanted to know the same thing. No, not really. I told him I ate scarcely any lunch. I've been a bit off colour for a week or so—nothing like this, though."

"What did you do after lunch?"

"Just after? I was teaching later. Until a quarter past two I was here in my bedroom, mending a stocking and looking over the provisional cast I drew up for a little play the babies want to do in the garden before the fine weather goes."

"And what then?"

Susan accepted her curiosity quite naturally. "I took a junior class till three o'clock, then seniors, and got in a short music lesson before tea."

"And did you eat or drink anything during the afternoon—before tea, I mean?"

"Not eat. I drank—freely." She glanced swiftly at the door, and away again. It was closed. No sound from outside reached them. "Miss Betony, I can't help thinking—I wonder—it's silly of me—I express myself badly, but draughts of cold water taken copiously on an empty stomach could upset one, possibly, couldn't they?"

"Possibly," Emma agreed. "Do you believe that yourself?"

Susan lowered her eyes and stared down at the sheet. "I—don't know," she said. "I can tell you what I did. My bottle here was almost full, and I drank all the water before going into school. If you remember, there wasn't much to go round at lunch, and I was thirsty."

Emma remembered. At this inattentive stage it was not to be expected that the kitchen would remedy the defect in time, and lunch had been over without a fresh supply of water appearing on the table.

"I thought it tasted nasty," Susan went on. "But I've thought that about things lately, and put it down to not feeling too spry. When tea came, I didn't want any. Actually I was beginning to feel groggy then, though there was nothing definite to complain of. I drank some tea, but I didn't eat anything."

Emma asked her if she knew how long before she was found the illness had started.

"It was just after six I decided to look for you in your room. It came on almost directly."

These were important facts, Emma was sure. She went over in her mind odd scraps of information picked up from time to time from newspaper reports of arsenic mysteries. An empty stomach—delayed action of the poison—arsenic in liquid form.

She said nothing to Susan, but left wondering how much the girl herself suspected. There were other things too that called for speculation. Where was the water bottle from which Susan had drunk? A quick survey as she went out failed to note it. What a lot of water bottles there are in this affair, she thought. Such an innocuous article too.

And what was this about Blandford? Elsewhere lately she had heard it mentioned—when and in what connection? After puzzling for a few minutes it came to her. It was to Blandford Linda Hart had gone on Wednesday evening. It was possible she was still there. And, sharing as they had shared a certain degree of intimacy with Miss Thurloe, it was not difficult to see in Linda the friend with whom Susan had hoped to spend Monday afternoon. Was it safe to infer that Miss Thurloe might be the object of the visit? Emma only hoped she was not seeing too much.

Of one thing she was sure, and the certainty pleased her immensely though it left the mystery uncleared. The girl's worried references to her presence on the threshold of Emma's room might have been made, it was true, with a sense of guilt; if, indeed, she were the person who had searched her belongings and had subsequently suffered amnesia through falling ill at the time, she might well have argued that a show of frankness would be the best policy. Her inquiry as to where Emma had found her would have confirmed Grace's worst suspicions. Grace would probably have guessed that Miss Thurloe's apartments were in Susan's mind. Emma herself, if she had not got something up her sleeve, might have entertained misgivings.

But from a discovery made in her room last night she had the best of reasons for knowing that it was not Susan Pollard who had paid a secret visit there.

Chapter X

THE GREAT AMBROSIO

The car stopped in the parking place just off the public library. Grace had business and shopping she thought would take her something over an hour. Miss Orpen was going to the library to change her book and was then having her hair washed and set, a nice long job for which Emma was supremely grateful. It put her comfortably out of the way for the afternoon and reduced the possibility of her spying on the Lanthorn.

"When and where shall I pick you up, Miss Betony?" she asked, holding her with a frosty eye.

I wonder if she suspects where I'm bound for, Emma thought, and was annoyed to find herself colouring guiltily. Aloud, she said, "Here, I think—about—about—"

"I know," Grace interrupted. "When we do get an afternoon off there's no need to cut it short and cling together half the time. What about meeting here at half-past four and having tea somewhere, and till then going our own sweet ways?"

They agreed, Emma heartily, because it spared her, as Grace had intended it should, concocting the length of time she was likely to be absent. She nodded to them and slipped round the corner of a hat shop window, where, under cover of examining the latest creations, she could watch Miss Orpen's safe departure. Grace was already walking away briskly, and when she had seen the last of the secretary's not very shapely back disappear through the library doors, she wasted no more time but hurried across the hilly High Street and in another minute arrived at the Lanthorn turning.

There was not much sun this afternoon, only a warmish, quiet hush with a premature hint of October mist. She turned in at the entry expecting she hardly knew what. In so narrow a thoroughfare there was no separate roadway and path, only cracked flags stretching lopsidedly from one side to the other, twisting, dodging, diving suddenly under little archways that mocked the sound of one's footsteps. Grass sprouted in odd corners, human dwellings in still odder sprang suddenly into view, flanked here with a water butt, dressed there with flower boxes. Cats with a lean and roving air sunned themselves on sloping tiles, where sparrows hopped at a respectful distance; unwashed children slipped past or played their secretive games on doorsteps and stones, sparing her a fleeting, uncommunicative glance. Of other people there was scarcely a sign, though once she passed a pawnshop, its balls glinting warmly in a shadowy recess, and again, up two steps worn into saucerlike depressions, a little dark crooked shop with bulging leaden panes, where an antiquarian bookseller moved among his wares.

I must go there one day, Emma told herself, passing with reluctance the dimly seen groups in old calf, and tumbled copies in a tub in the doorway.

Now, however, her objective was Thankful Court, which she was afraid she might have overlooked in spite of care in threading the maze. She had walked slowly, savouring the names on corner and arch—The Holes, Willywood's Rents, Correction Street, Pennyquick Row. She had not seen the police station yet, but she did not think she was far from a main street. Now and again the rumble of traffic seemed close at hand and in front of her, though the High Street lay behind; and once, in a gap between two tenements, she caught the distant flash of a passing omnibus.

A chimneysweep, black of face and with the tools of his trade, came round the corner, whistling. Emma was pleased to see him, for she had begun to feel she had strayed into a goblin world avoided by mortals.

"You're there, ma'am," he said in reply to her inquiry, and jerked a thumb over his shoulder. "I've just come outa Thankful Court."

She thought he gave her a curious look. She walked under an old square arch and came out into a small courtyard, bounded on three sides by tall, crumbling buildings, and on the fourth by the archway and a humble tavern bearing the legend "Fox and Grapes" on a sign so faded that the fox, presumably from envy, had turned as green as the once-purple vine. So far as she could see, the place was a cul-de-sac, but when she had looked again she noticed a gap in an angle at the bottom and another lane, narrower even than those she had already passed, squeezing its way out.

What a maze the whole place was—and in the palmy days what a paradise for tourists and artists. Actually it was now only a tortuous mass of decay, its frailties condoned because they were old and had once been sightly.

Emma retreated for a moment to the shelter of the arch for fear the bleary eyes of the houses were more lively than she supposed. She wished she could see Number 6 at once without having to parade the yard looking for it. Her luck was in, however. As she pondered there came the patter of bare feet behind her, and two little girls, red and blown, darted by, playing tag.

"Which is Number 6 in this Court?" Emma called, and at the sudden raising of her voice they pulled up short. The more enterprising of the two struck the other triumphantly and they were off again, but not before the one in front, cupping her mouth, had yelled back, "The pet shop!"

Emma advanced, in some trepidation. What was she coming to next? The fourteenth-century houses swelled grotesquely in their upper storeys like the bows of a sailing ship, with tiny windows a man would be unable to get his head out of. The ground floors were withdrawn, hard to distinguish, like a face under beetling brows. But halfway down the left-hand side Emma saw the animal shop.

There were mice in the window, and something she thought was a cavy, and on a shelf above a long cage with little crimson-throated birds whose name she did not know. The door stood wide, and as she went in a squirrel rattled the wires of his house close at her elbow; something else crooned at her with a horrible, soft, imbecile note, and there was an African parrot, scarlet and grey, head downwards in a domed cage.

The shop was small, sanded, moderately clean and full of an odour compounded of animal, grain, sawdust, warmth, old straw and lack of air. It was almost bisected by a short, broad counter piled high at one end with boxes and packets of various foods, on top of which sat a monkey absorbed in its toilet. From all sides rustles and thuds and slithering noises came to her ears, and from somewhere above her head a thin, sibilant note rose, cutting the air with the piercing quality of a bat's scream before fading away. In the silence that followed the parrot gurgled, and then said in a hushed voice, "Who's there? Who's there? Who's there, I say?"

Emma shivered slightly, with pricking skin. She felt as if scores of unseen eyes, bright and disinterested, watched her. There was nobody in the shop, but she thought she heard a movement above, and across a slip of passage with a dark shaft at the side where stairs must rise, she supposed, a parlour door stood open. She was afraid to tap her foot or rap the counter as she might have done in any ordinary shop, lest she conjure up a genie better left unsummoned.

A door shut somewhere out at the back. There was a slow shuffling sound, and a thin old man with ragged hair that almost touched his stooping shoulders came out of the parlour and advanced into the shop, peering hard into the gloom. He said in a weak, testy voice, "I told you he was engaged."

"I don't think——" Emma began, when all at once he leaned on the counter and thrust his head out towards her, tortoise fashion.

"I beg your pardon, madam. I took you for the lady who went up just now. You are the lady who has an appointment with Mr. Ambrose?"

"Oh, no," Emma said hastily. Her attention was drawn to the monkey, who swung himself off the boxes and whipped up the old man's arm to his neck, where he clung gibbering excitedly and working his eyebrows up and down at her.

At the same time the stairs creaked, and a stout young woman, wearing hat and coat and carrying an ostentatious-looking handbag, appeared behind the old man. She uttered a shrill, disgusted cry at sight of the monkey and put herself clumsily, though with commendable speed, on Emma's side of the counter.

"Quite right," she said with a touch of asperity. "Engaged for the afternoon—and me with only the Saturday I can get into the town at all. I didn't see another client up there, neither."

"Good-day," the old man said pointedly.

The woman stared from him to Emma, then flounced to the door.

"Good-day to *you*," she said, and pulled her skirt away from the parrot's cage with exaggerated caution.

The parrot uttered a derisive whistle, beautifully modulated.

Emma looked anxiously at the old man. "I'm afraid I've made a mistake then," she said. "I did not know Mr. Ambrose was engaged just now." She took from her bag the cutting announcing the fortune-teller's business hours, and held it out. "You see, it says eleven to six—I've come within the times named."

The old man glanced at the paper without taking it. He showed no interest in her or her business, and caressed the monkey while he spoke.

"That is correct, madam. Will you please go up? Turn right at the top and knock on the door facing you. It's probable you are the lady Mr. Ambrose is expecting—if not, he will tell you himself that he is engaged."

"But I can't be," Emma said, vexed and bewildered. Having delivered himself of these enigmatic remarks, the old man took no further notice of her, but shuffled over to a cage in the corner and, squatting down while the monkey bounded over his back, began discoursing intimately with a marmoset.

Emma decided to go upstairs. The situation was intriguing, and even if a mistake had been made and Ambrosio was expecting a client at this hour, she might at least appease her curiosity in part by a glimpse of his abode.

She moved round the counter on to a piece of matting between shop and parlour doors, turning left to a stair so black that only the bottom treads were visible. In passing she looked in at the open parlour door. A piano stood against the wall. On top of it, on a litter of music, sat a mongoose, watching her with clear, unblinking eyes.

When she had mounted the stairs she came to a landing with immense naked beams stained black overhead and, on the right, two deep steps up to a door partially concealed by a curtain. There was no knocker. She rapped twice with her knuckles. In a moment a voice called, "Enter," and she heard a soft unhurried noise.

Ashamed though she was to confess it, Emma went in with her heart in her mouth. Though sensitive and normally superstitious, she was not as a rule susceptible to atmosphere to a disturbing degree; but, with her hand on the knob, something queer about this dark small landing made itself felt. She consoled herself with the reminder that to a visit of this kind the pet shop was a bad prelude for the nerves.

It was a little square room she came into, roofed by the same huge beams and sagging ceiling. A window opposite the door, larger than the mere porthole apertures in the front of the house, stood open a few inches to admit what air there was in the Lanthorn. A decaying wainscot ran round the room, visible, however, only on the left, where the wall above showed wide cracks in the buff distemper and supported a single picture. The other three walls were covered entirely from top to bottom with heavy black velvet curtains that hung in great folds like lustrous carving and, by concealing their background, gave a curious perspective to the room, suggestive of some mysterious and unseen hinterland. Flush with the window frame on either side the curtains fell, even the wall space between window and ceiling being carefully covered with more folded velvet, so that the square of light appeared far more dazzling than it would otherwise have done.

Emma was taken aback at finding nobody in the room. So, the curtains concealed either a door into a second room or a recess large enough to receive a man. She did not much care for either notion, conceiving of few things more unpleasant than that of being stared at by an unseen watcher. And what other object could there be for disappearing at her entry?

The only furniture to be seen was a small table in the centre covered with a black baize cloth, on which stood a tumbler of water and a writing pad, the cover folded back and some pencilled words scribbled in a fine hand on the top sheet, two office chairs and, beneath the window, an oblong shape smothered in black velvet that suggested a chest. Emma had watched in her time a number of magicians at their parlour tricks, but never in a room so simply and effectively contrived as this one.

She sat down on the nearest chair, her back partly to the door, partly to the undraped wall. It was, she felt, the only safe position she could take up. She put her bag on the table and clasped her hands lightly upon it. She hoped she looked calm and collected in the accepted spinsterish fashion, though she was really feeling vexed, flustered, off her guard. The cool little remarks she had prepared for her first encounter with Ambrosio were all gone; she could only sit there, waiting with a sense of apprehension for the appearance of the man she had come to see.

She might as well utilize the time in observation of her surroundings. She must be careful, though. She herself was under observation. Eyes more devastatingly bright than any she had left downstairs followed, she felt, every movement. Care must be taken, therefore, to steer a moderate course between excessive inquisitiveness and too great a show of indifference. Some natural curiosity was only to be expected in the circumstances.

She let her eyes wander over the black curtains, her mind busy trying to locate the door or niche they must cover. She could detect no bulge anywhere; nor was a door set in window wall or the opposite one by which the stairs ran, for in neither of these could it lead to a room. As it was not behind her, where no velvet hung, that left only the wall in front. A recess, of course, might be anywhere covered by the curtains.

She looked down at the table, and away again, avoiding the writing pad. Her glance wandered to the floor, and was arrested by marks she could faintly discern on the stained unpolished boards between table and window. She frowned, leaning a little sideways to see better. Were not women expected to pry, anyway?

The marks, almost erased now and covering a fairly wide space, had been made with chalk. In places, she thought, the lines ran together, forming points. She got the impression of a star.

She remembered the picture behind her and peeped over her shoulder to look at it. What she saw made her twist round in the chair to get a complete view, regardless of spying eyes. A coarse canvas, some two feet in width by three to four long, was nailed at the corners to a panel of wood slightly larger than itself. It did not hang, but was posed on the ledge of the wainscot. Across the bottom edge a strip of brown cardboard, looking out of place, was pinned.

The artist, whoever he might be, had applied his brush with brutal vigour. The background, occupying the central and upper portions of the canvas, depicted a leafy grove, the trees seen through wreathing coils of mist or smoke, Emma was not sure which. The limbs of the trees, twisted and misshapen, were mingled unpleasantly with other limbs. Between the foliage flesh gleamed, disporting itself in dances and revels only to be guessed at, and faces, half formed or merely suggested by the brush, peeped lasciviously. At the heart of the grove a red light burned, flinging up a lurid reflection that steeped the top of the picture in a rosy glow.

But this was of secondary interest. It was the foreground of the painting that compelled attention and gave significance to its wanton setting.

With all the skill at his command the artist had striven to execute the face of an unearthly being. It stared from out the canvas with the features of a young man, the grove and its evil congregation a nimbus for the beautiful yellow hair. Emma noticed how a sweep of the brush had given circular form to treetops and vapour and the motions of the revellers, so that they curved about his head like a halo round a saint's. But here was nothing holy. The face was white, the clear-cut, unimpassioned mouth scarlet, the eyes, a shade too large, blue and unfathomable as the remoter seas, glowed beneath slanting brows with a strange mingling of lust and melancholy. There was, thought Emma, an awful expression in them of hope abandoned, and yet a look of triumph too that forbade compassion. She could not withdraw her own eyes, and when she did, to discern the small, slightly pointed ears, and gentle curve of the jaw, it was to return to that hot, slumbering gaze as if hypnotized.

Such vitality as expressed itself in action and movement sprang from the background of the picture. The head was immobile, with a stony purity of line. Yet Emma was aware that the power informing those other figures lay in this static portrait, that all their vile sportiveness derived from its force alone. She felt herself in the presence of something intolerably wicked and obscene.

"How do you like it?" a quiet voice said.

She turned, controlling an impulse to be quick. On the other side of the table a man stood, his hand gripping the back of the vacant chair. His chin depressed, he looked down at her gravely.

Emma's instantaneous impression was of a being of superhuman stature—later she discovered that though he was indeed very tall his height was not so great as she had supposed, and remembered that at this first encounter she had been seated. His garb made a single brilliant splash of colour in that funereal room. Beneath a black gown of severely academic cut which hung in straight folds from shoulder to ankle, he wore a full-sleeved scarlet blouse, zip-fastened to the neck, black trousers, and on his feet pumps. His clean-shaven face was very pale, or else pallor was accentuated by the red and black costume, his hair a glistening iron-grey; his blue eyes were brilliant and cold beneath strong silvery-black brows that looked as if in youth they had been several shades darker than his hair. In the rather hollow cheeks, lean jaw, yet full lines of the mouth that might in different circumstances be generous or brutal, there was a disturbing blend of asceticism and passion. Emma thought him the handsomest man she had ever seen.

"You admire my picture?" he repeated softly, and drawing out the chair sat down, laying his large thin hands flat on the table.

Something warned Emma that she stood on the brink of an important decision. She was free, if she chose, to be frank with this man, present herself to him as she really was and as she really thought, and be prepared to see her chances of divining Miss Thurloe's mystery slipping away; or she might play a part, appear to him as she appeared to so many others, a rather foolish spinster of no account, with an epicene mind and a talent for self-deception. There was the chance it would catch him off his guard. She knew, however, too much of life, not to be aware that among crystal-gazers and those with kindred gifts might be found some whose powers were, at least, inexplicable. It might well be that the Great Ambrosio would know her for what she was in spite of a pose. But if he did not? If he were merely a charlatan? It was on that assumption that she must act.

"It's *wonderful*," she breathed, lifting her eyes to his. "I've never seen anything like it, ever." This was the simple truth, but is one of those things which can be variously understood. "Who—who is the artist?"

"I painted it myself." He was looking at her, his head a little on one side, with a warm, immediate interest that she found appealing. It made her feel that she was the only client he had ever wanted or waited to see.

"Oh—but how clever of you—Mr.—Mr.—"

"Ambrose will be best," he said in the same gentle, casual tone. "Where I come from my patrons like the touch of mystery— Edward Ambrose has not the same panacea for their ills as the Great Ambrosio"—his lip curled slightly in contempt—"and so one keeps it up. Do you know who he was, this Ambrosio?"

Emma, surprised, shook her head. "No, indeed, I supposed it was simply a—a professional name."

Curiously, he did not reply. Instead he lifted his gaze to the picture, and his face grew stern. Emma thought suddenly of a copy of *The Vigil* hanging above the sideboard in Mrs. Flagg's dining room. But though profile and reverence were perhaps reminiscent, these were not the crusader's eyes and mouth.

"What does it mean?" she asked, drawing a quick breath. "Who is the subject of the portrait? What *perfect* colours! And what are they doing behind him? Is it all symbolic?"

He looked back at her, his features relaxing. "To say who he is, and how he comes to be part of that rather grotesque company, and what it all means, would be a difficult and involved tale at present.

The world—the untaught, infant world—is not ready for his story yet. So I may not weary your ears with it. But, yes—we will call it a symbol. That was a happy thought you had. It is, if you like, a symbol of power—power largely untapped, power lying within each one of us, strong and beautiful potentialities we dare not longer ignore." His voice, which had risen on the last phrases to a sonorous pitch, dropped again to conversational level. "But I bore you."

"Oh, *no*," Emma fluttered, at pains to look bewildered. "It's marvellous—so interesting—so—so—almost *frightening*, one might say. Then it would be correct, would it not, to call it a futurist work of art?"

"Futurist indeed," said the Great Ambrosio, and laughed on a short, deep note.

"But don't you think," Emma suggested timidly, "the piece of cardboard along the lower edge—it rather catches the eye and spoils the effect, doesn't it?"

He looked at her sharply. "The modesty of the artist," he smiled. "But we waste time—or, rather, you do. *I* can only be grateful for the interest shown in my poor skill."

Emma blushed. "I came—I thought—a hand reading—"

"With pleasure." But a mask seemed to shut off his real face. He looked suddenly tired. "You would like the crystal too? It is often more interesting, and more immediately helpful."

"Yes—I think I would, please." The crystal had never failed to excite her.

She pushed her handbag and gloves further off, extending her hands towards him, palms up and relaxed so that the lines showed deep. He did not touch them, but first looked at her.

"You are experienced in having your hand read." It was a statement, not a query.

"Oh, yes," Emma said, and laughed nervously. "Have I—is there a professional touch about me?"

"Quite. You make the palms slightly concave without being told. Most people hold them taut, and thus smooth out the scoring of the lines which tell the story."

Emma hoped she was not being too intelligent. To offset such a mischance she inquired innocently which precisely were the lines of head, heart and life, confessing that she had never been able to distinguish between them.

He studied her with a faint frown that politeness just saved from incredulity. She wondered then if she were being too stupid. What an exhausting game pretence was... He pointed out the lines, not on her own hand but on his, as if he were still reluctant to touch her.

"And here are the mounts—that of Apollo bumpy for me, Jupiter your own most highly developed one, showing a deep sense of religion—not necessarily orthodox."

He stopped exhibiting his own palm, supported his clasped hands on the table and studied hers with an impassive expression. He was silent so long that Emma wondered if he were making use of the time following his own train of thought rather than conning the story of her life. The motionless lids looking as if carved in ivory, the lines of the mouth, betrayed nothing. She let her eyes wander, but the picture was behind her and, except for the few articles on the table, there was nothing to distract attention from the matter in hand. It was a setting obviously designed to promote that cleansing of the mind, the elimination of superfluous thought, psychiatrists aim to produce.

Her gaze fell on the open pad at Ambrosio's elbow. She looked at the lightly scribbled words, first idly, then frowning. Just as, upside down, their meaning began to register itself on her brain, Ambrosio spoke.

"In a moment when I tell you what your hands have told me, do not interrupt. Do not affirm this, deny that, when I pause in my remarks. Some you will have visited"—his voice took on an arrogant edge—"halt for that very reason, to pick up the 'Yes' and 'No' the client inevitably murmurs. How much do the shells of those small words contain—what cannot be their interpretation! In 'Yes' and 'No' you possibly lay bare your life, knowledge of which the *pretender* to knowledge lacks, and which he must pick up somehow if he is to make an impression. *I* do not acquire information in that fashion. So please be silent."

This was a technique new to Emma, familiar with those time-dishonoured methods by which the oracle first extracted from its questioner the truth which it doled back at a price. The audacity which cut the ground from under one's feet by reminder of this device won her admiration. She said nothing.

When next he spoke he turned his eyes towards the window.

"You have had a difficult life so far as the mere purpose of keeping oneself alive goes—especially in its later phases. Quite recently— within the last month, it appears—you had to decide between two courses of action, both to some extent fraught with peril. Upon your choice your whole future hung. You made it, and are at present working out your destiny on those lines. The next six months are the most important of your life. Until now women have been largely instrumental in shaping and reshaping your career—from this time on a masculine influence will be dominant. When you begin to feel the impact of this man's personality you should yield to it. I say, more strongly, you must. Your own happiness, and the future happiness of others depends on your willing cooperation with this person—*this is very important*." He examined his nails, not a muscle of his face moving nor any real interest in what he was saying apparent.

"I am emphatic on this point because your own character may be an obstacle to the fulfilment of what is planned for you. In ordinary relationships, you see, you appear extremely—flexible. Actually this is not the case. So long as your dealings are with relatively unimportant matters, so long will you appear submissive and, because you rarely have to grapple with anything that is *not* unimportant, this compliance is taken to be the key to your personality. It is not the key. You have great powers of resistance, a core of stubbornness against which you are prepared to see many things—yes, and people—break. Once your sense of duty is roused you are ready to deny yourself and others that self-expression which may seem to violate what you believe right. Notice I say *you*. For you are one of those potentially dangerous people who set up an ethical standard for universal application—not admitting that others may have their own standards, though different from yours. Do you understand?"

"I—I think so," said Emma, who began to see herself as a tough proposition and her role stripped from her before she had time to assume it. "It means I'm pigheaded—I've been told so before."

He gestured lightly with his hand. "You rob my reading of its niceties. That blunt term suggests nothing pleasant—and there is something charming and right about the way in which you stick to your guns. But in the contingency foreshadowed here"—he tapped his own palm for hers—"resistance is shown to be harmful. You will do well to accept what comes—then there will be happiness."

Emma was flustered. "But—but then—there must be an indication—" She grew pink. "I mean, my hand shows, does it, that I am going to feel that this influence *is* wrong—I shall *want* to withstand it?"

"No, no," he said gently, but to her astonishment there were small beads of moisture on his forehead. "Not necessarily. But here in the hand, you understand, is character. For all who learn to read, it is writ plain. And your character suggests that you *may* reject a great offer of happiness. Don't—that's all."

"One wouldn't want to," Emma said simply. "But happiness comes in strange guises sometimes. How shall I know that all is for the best?"

"Details are not revealed—the crystal may help us. But I think there will be little chance of making a mistake when the time comes. A proposition will be made to you in the simplest terms."

"Which I should at once accept?"

"If you would be happy."

"'Ever afterwards,'" Emma finished softly, and uttered a little laugh at his look of surprise. "Isn't that the way we were taught to round it off?"

"Certainly." He sounded cold, and began at once to serve the palmist's usual stock-in-trade. For the next ten minutes he treated mechanically and, Emma had to admit, with accuracy, of her health, wealth and occupation.

"Nor can I hold out any hope of improvement in your material position—it would be only an illusory dream. You will always be comparatively poor. But," he looked suddenly into her eyes with a return of the intimate interest he had shown at first, adding tenderly, "we who are poor have little to fear. Love, friendship, all our human relationships are unmotivated by the money interest. We are richer than the rich who are unable to distinguish themselves from their possessions because they do not know what distinction others make for them." He studied the cloth spread over the table. "You will always be loved for yourself alone."

"Dear me," said Emma, breaking in upon the solemnity with a titter, "I should hope so. Indeed, I never thought of it any other way."

He did not answer. She moved her elbow so that it pushed her bag a couple of inches nearer the edge of the table. It caught the tumbler and tipped it over. The water gushed freely over the black cloth.

"Oh—I *am* so sorry!" she cried, dabbing ineffectually with her handkerchief at the widening pool. "*How* clumsy of me—how very, *very* clumsy."

He assured her it was nothing, removing glass and writing block while Emma retrieved her own possessions. Picking up the wet cloth he took it over to the window, which he opened wide and, after glancing down, shook the cloth out of it. For the first time Emma was able to observe him in action. He moved swiftly, with a light catlike spring, on the balls of his toes.

Instead of coming back to the table he closed the casement and, setting tumbler, pad and cloth on top of the draped chest, drew the velvet folds on either side of the window more closely together. When he had done, only a strip of light a few inches wide shone through, where before the window had shown clear.

"Too much light is unkind to the crystal," he explained, returning and deftly arranging the cloth, with the pad, now closed, at his elbow, and the empty glass beside it. "We will consult it next."

He went back to the chest under the window. As he swept off the covering and raised the lid, Emma was unpleasantly aware of the character of the room, by wholesome daylight only dimly apprehended, now creeping about her in full tide. Light was suspended like a sword against the blackness it could not dispel. The deliberate blackness, thought Emma, for there was nothing of the night about this velvet-smothered gloom. Deliberate... a choice of dark instead of light. She did not dare to glance round at the picture.

Ambrosio placed the crystal, covered with a black cloth, in front of him on the table. He did not uncover it immediately, but spread his hands lightly over the cloth, his fingers hanging over the curve of it. In that heavy twilight face and hands glimmered strangely white, and gave a fixity to his gaze.

"You are much troubled at present," he said in a low voice. "Isn't that so?"

"Yes," Emma admitted. She plunged on, "The—the illness of a friend. I am living in a house where there is grave illness."

He shook his head slowly. "You vex yourself unnecessarily. All will come right. Do not let an apparently serious situation deceive you into taking steps you might regret."

Emma, who had only the vaguest ideas herself of what her next step was to be, thought it peculiar advice. It was not, perhaps, too fanciful to see in it a hint of menace. "There's not much I can do, alas," she said. In the hope of disturbing him she was suddenly inspired to add, "The doctor has her case well in hand, and there are two nurses now, day and night."

"And not even they will be able to kill her since she is destined to recover," he observed. She got the impression that he was laughing at her. "You, and others in your house, are worrying about nothing. Death will visit the house—I see his coming—but his visit will be in the ordinary course of his travels, not the violent entry expected of him."

Emma opened her lips to speak, thought better of it, and remained silent.

Ambrosio whipped the cloth from the crystal. In the cavernous room, caught by the single ray of light, it shone with a soft, welling glow. Emma had seen many in her time, but not one so large as this. Ambrosio took it lovingly in his hands, curving his fingers round the smooth base, rotating it gently. He himself sat out of the line of the window, merged in shadow. His face was hardly more than a blur in the darkness, but the thin bar of light focused sharply on the hands gave them a preternatural whiteness and put a fire in the heart of the crystal.

Ambrosio held it out to her. "Hold it for a few minutes, will you? Don't think about it."

Emma took it, cupping her hands as she had seen him do. It was heavy, its coldness painful. He gave her no chance to examine it, but engaged her at once in easy conversation of a detached nature. He was right, Emma saw, in drawing a distinction between himself and those of his profession who sucked the minds of their clients. He was careful to avoid any reference to matters which would have provided him with clues.

When he was ready he received the crystal back in silence, sitting a few moments without saying anything, head bent and eyes fixed on the globe. His voice, when at length he began to speak, held a strange note. To Emma it seemed as if he were communing with himself or with an unseen companion in a fourth-dimensional world of which she was not an inhabitant.

"Here are rooms—many rooms—and a confusion of ways between them. There is one room in particular to which all these ways lead. It is cluttered, inartistic—but in it dwells a mind that colours it... I see unfolded there the pageant of a life wielding a strange power over other lives—a power long, delicate, subtle, not directly felt, unintentionally working for evil—for what men call evil. For evil and good are nothing in themselves, they are only instrumental to the full life, to power, power—*power*..."

His voice had fallen to a thick whisper. Emma felt uncomfortable, cold. She shifted a little in the chair, which creaked embarrassingly. It did not disturb Ambrosio.

"Darkness—then darkness—and death—to open for others the gate to life. I see a procession leaving the house, standing stones, a wind blowing the trees and grasses... You are not of the company grouped there—yet you are present. Your eyes see all that passes... then again swirling blackness, a cloud that must pass before we see further. It goes—here is a tall grey building beside water, running water... here..." He faltered. He rotated the crystal. Emma heard him breathing. "Here is something—*hostile*," he whispered, "something I cannot understand—you are hurrying towards this building—this building in another city—there is no time to lose. The earth covers all, but you—you—*you*—" His voice rose to a cry that seemed wrenched from him. Emma, frightened of the whole business, heard in it the echo of a bitter frustration she could not explain.

Ambrosio was leaning back in his chair, not touching the crystal that reposed on its tumbled wrapping on the table. She felt him watching her.

"Was it interesting?" he asked softly. "When the picture dissolves, I do not remember." He laughed on a low, friendly note. "The oath of Hippocrates—it is not necessary to us clairvoyants. If we are the real ones the vision melts, and with it all secrets evaporate... *Was I interesting?* Sometimes I am only incoherent."

"I didn't quite understand," Emma said with a tremulous air not all affected. She clasped her hands. "But it was—oh, *wonderfully* interesting. Though I think—I thought things sounded rather gloomy for me."

"For *you?*" he said sharply. It was odd, she thought, to emphasize the pronoun. "It need not be. In your own will lies the remedy. Hand and crystal alike utter the same thing—keep watch on yourself. Don't take the independent line. Yield to the persuasion of others."

"Yes, I see."

"Would you like to look?" He pushed the crystal across. "Do as you saw me do—warm it with your hands. Let your being flow into it—but not your thoughts. As far as you can, keep your mind a blank, relax physically and—don't be afraid. Remember that whatever you see—and I can promise nothing—it is more likely to be in the nature of a warning than inevitable destiny. On our own plane it is customary for caution to precede punishment—and the powers we only dimly apprehend will be no less merciful."

Emma clasped the crystal, fondling it in the approved manner. On similar occasions before she had seen nothing, or at most strange fires she had taken for light refraction. Without looking up she was aware of Ambrosio rising, towering above her and the table. She heard a long, low mutter like an intonation. From the tail of her eye she saw the darkness move. It was the sleeves of his gown, she knew, lifting with the spread of a bat's wings, as the hands groped in the air above her.

She dared not look up. She could not. She had committed herself to this, and she would go through with it. Until now she had not realized how cold, as well as stuffy, the room was. It should have been warm, she supposed, smothered in arras and the window shut. But it wasn't. It was clammy, like a well, or—a charnel house. She shivered…

She was doing all the wrong things, busying herself with thoughts of her environment, speculating on what Ambrosio was about. No wonder that the crystal made no response. She stared, but there was nothing but a pool at the heart of it, burning now red, now golden, now grey flushed with pink. It was beautiful, fascinating, but she had desired a picture…

Something was happening—not to the room, not to the crystal. The crystal, she thought, swelled to an immense ball of pulsing fire, a luminous globe which caught up into itself all the light that filtered into that swamp of blackness. It shrank, sinking, its fires quenched, until it was a piece of common glass, until it had diminished to pin-point size. It began again, swelling, ebbing…

Nothing was happening there. What was happening to herself. It was happening outside the room. She was running, with the stumbling, painful, unprogressive run of dreams. Her feet were trapped, immovable, yet her lungs laboured, and time's sands were running out. Somewhere in front salvation loomed—"beside running water," she heard herself repeat. Struggling back to consciousness of the room, the crystal cold as ice between her hands, one last blinding flash tore past her vision, and she saw a squat, square tower that looked familiar.

Before she knew where she was blinking in a rush of daylight. Ambrosio had gone over to the window, swept back the curtains, and opened wide the casement. A current of blessed air flowed in. Emma, who was perfectly all right except for feeling a little dazed, seized the opportunity she had planned to make.

She gave a weak cry, drooping against the table, and exclaimed, "Oh, dear—I'm sorry—a passing faintness. I shall be all right—in a minute—a little water. Could you get me a little water, please?"

At her sound of dismay Ambrosio had turned. He muttered something and hurried forward. His hand reached for the tumbler when, remembering it was empty, he picked it up with an impatient gesture and slipped over to the velvet-draped wall opposite the picture. Pushing aside one of the heavy folds, he disappeared behind it, but this time Emma heard distinctly a door being opened.

She wasted no time. Gone in an instant was the wilting pose. Her heart beat suffocatingly in her throat. It was not the faint—her generation had known how to simulate swooning, and if she had not indulged in the practice herself she had been witness to it more than once. She prided herself that in Ambrosio's eyes her collapse was genuine. What frightened her was the risk she ran of being watched even now. She must be quick.

She put out a hand and pulled the writing block towards her. There was something she had to confirm before Ambrosio got back. She pushed the cover up with trembling fingers and stared eagerly at the brief scribble. She was right. Here it was. Without a moment's hesitation and not a prick of conscience she tore the sheet straight off. The hard rip it made turned her cold with fear. But she had it. She flapped the cover over again and pushed the pad back to its original position on Ambrosio's right. Then she sank down on her chair, a good deal nearer fainting than she had been just now, and, lifting her bag from the table, stuffed the sheet of paper in without stopping to fold it. There was not time to close the bag before Ambrosio was back in the room. He saw her fumbling for a handkerchief which, found, she raised to her eyes and mouth.

He was at once solicitous and gentle. But his hovering presence as he handed the water to her, and the flapping gown, made her think of a predatory bird preparing to swoop.

"The revelations," he said, "were probably too much for you. You must tell me some other time what you saw."

"Oh, not very much. It wasn't that," Emma murmured truthfully, more thankful than she had supposed at having the water to drink, and congratulating herself on the whiteness of her cheeks. "It was the dark, I think—that, and the—the close atmosphere."

"Ah, yes. The dark." His voice was soft as he took the glass from her. "The darkness we have not yet learned to understand... when power is set free."

She stood up shakily and opened her bag. "I—don't know," she began, and murmured with a vague air, "Your professional fee—"

He looked down at her, aloof as a god. "The question does not arise. Not at a first consultation. You will return—and then again. Afterwards it is for you to decide."

She fluttered protestingly, but he paid no attention. He was smiling down at her, his white face a mask. With her eyes raised timidly to his and the colour beginning to tinge her cheeks again, Emma, who was astonishing herself afresh every minute, felt that she had passed with credit her examination in the role of the Trusting Spinster. When he went over to the picture and began removing the pins from the strip of cardboard effacing its base, she thought distinction might be a more correct label for her prowess.

"There's no reason why you shouldn't share the artist's secret," he said with an air of indulgence, and pulled away the cardboard.

In scarlet the well-spaced letters, two inches tall, flamed at her: A B A D D O N.

The red beat upon her eyes. There was always a pulsating quality about the colour from which one shrank. She stood her ground, keeping her face under control, and surpassed herself at once.

"What a very bold signature the artist has!" she exclaimed archly.

Ambrosio said nothing. Glancing at him she saw that his face was alight with a strange excitement. He had forgotten her. He had removed the covering strip under a secret compulsion, simply to gratify his own passion, and because in his eyes she was a person of no account.

The next minute he was ushering her, all courtesy, to the door. His manner was tender, attentive without familiarity.

"You will come again—soon? The crystal is all whims, moody as a lady." He laughed caressingly. "It can change from day to day, perhaps even hourly."

"Oh, yes," Emma said in a low voice, with what she hoped was the right degree of eagerness. "Indeed, I shall come again. You—your generous reading today—I—" she stammered, embarrassed.

He was holding the door open. He bent and patted her wrist. It was the first time he had touched her since she had come.

"There must be no talk of that between you and me," he said with a nicely contrived touch of daring.

Emma's heart beat faster. She was anxious to be gone, acutely conscious as she was of the crumpled paper in her bag, filched from the writing block.

"You are not afraid of the animals downstairs?" he was asking. "Some of my clients are nervous."

"No, not really," Emma said with a doubtful air. "They're none of them *dangerous*, are they?"

"A few snakes, I believe. But the old fellow secures them properly."

She shuddered. "Oh, I hope so. Snakes are so—so *creepy*, don't you think? I find them *quite* repulsive."

He handed her down the steps on to the landing, solicitous, smiling.

"I'm not sure that they don't add to my prestige. They're oracular creatures, you know."

He stood on the step of the open room while she groped for the handrail that ran down one side of the stairs where all was so dark, and felt gingerly for the top tread.

As she moved cautiously down, something, she could not have said what, made her glance back for an instant.

The Great Ambrosio was still standing on the threshold. But now he was looking at her with an expression of violent distaste on his face.

Chapter XI

A WIND IS RAISED

On the night that brought in Michaelmas the wind rose, surging and complaining about the scattered parish of St. Martin-by-the-Brook. Martinmas, with its higgledy-piggledy passages and sudden architectural excursions into wings and corner-pieces, was loudly resentful of the visit. Doors creaked in protracted agony or uttered soft little thuds still more unnerving, chimneys boomed, windows were rapped by imperious, unfleshly hands, the corridors breathed long gentle sighs, mats lifted, beating tattoos upon the floor, the sycamore at the stairs window whined against the glass.

"Gives me the heebies, that it does," Nurse Swain muttered, impatient at the long night hours ahead. It was no sedative for the nerves when Miss Thurloe woke suddenly and made an angry noise like a cat.

In the corridors, past dormitories and sick ward, Nona Deakin made her nightly round, buffeted by draughts as she stuck her head round doors and called genial good-nights, her mind at work wondering if Dr. Bold were as smart as they said he was. Well, she had given him a chance to prove it...

Susan Pollard, her light burning, stretched out a hand to the water bottle by the bed. This wasn't the one she'd had yesterday. A pulse in her throat beat wildly... The wind, sweeping along the passage, sent a low, intimate whistle through the keyhole. She drew back her hand without pouring any water.

In the dormitories the children turned and twisted, stuffed the clothes round their ears, grunted peevishly at the dull, receding grumbles outside. The more wakeful thought or whispered inaudible good-byes to tennis and picnics and lessons under the cedar, and fell asleep counting the remaining Saturdays till they broke up for Christmas.

Not Dolly Finch, the sleepwalker, though, who stared wide awake into the solitude of the san. The feeble nightlight made it, if anything, more eerie. She hated the bumpy wind, the squeaks and raps and horrible sliding sounds. Things whispering—close behind your head. What was it she'd heard Miss Orpen telling the Sixth in July when there was a thunderstorm and the wind blew great guns all night? She'd said that witches were abroad when the wind rose... that they could raise the wind... that wind always meant bad things—bad spirits... Witches—witchcraft—the old woman in the east wing. She was going to scream—she knew she was. She caught the sheet, pushed it hard into her mouth, bit on it. Over the edge peeped her smooth, blanched face.

It was not the wind that frightened Emma, though it tugged at her blackout curtain and sent slow, shivering gusts down the chimney. Its assaults on the house even set the bureau rocking a little now and again. She knew what that was, and would have slept in spite of it. Yet she was afraid with a deep, cold fear.

For the second time since coming to Martinmas she saw herself a thread in the pattern weaving there. The first time had been when her room was searched, with what purpose she could not tell, and the cutting advertising the Great Ambrosio, slipped into her pocket. The next was in Ambrosio's room when a few letters and figures on a writing pad had caught her eye. What she had risked to get hold of them! And now possessing them was an embarrassment, since it meant a further risk in revisiting the fortune-teller. It was unlikely that he would not have missed the leaf from his block. And once the absence of the memoranda was noted, he could not be long in putting a name to the thief.

Even that, however, was a small and intermittent fear beside the curious, nameless one that had crawled out of her discovery. The implications of having taken the paper were less important than the implications of having found it. Yet she was ashamed, as well as fearful, of her suspicions. There must be an explanation other than the one that stabbed at her through the restless night. But when she tried to make coherent a new theory, what it involved amounted to almost the same thing, set her mind in a whirl and brought her full circle to the beginning again.

Sunday came in grey and blustering. It started inauspiciously with an altercation between Grace and Miss Wand which promised to develop out of all proportion to its importance. Nona Deakin, exuding the satisfaction that wrangles not one's own frequently inspire, told Emma all about it after breakfast.

"Did you hear the fireworks this morning?" she inquired with a broad wink.

"No, I didn't," Emma said in innocent surprise. She was undecided as to whether, in spite of a poor night, she had slept through a daylight raid on Bugle and its environs, or had missed a premature display by the boarders who felt November still a long way off. "Where? Who was doing it?"

The matron chuckled. "Purely domestic ones, my dear. Miss Aram and little old Wand. I don't know why they should both get so het up, though. Over going to church, too. It's been hammer and tongs and all the other fire-irons."

"Oh, dear," Emma said, commendably incurious. "Well, it didn't get to my ears. My room is rather shut away, you know, and the west wing a long way off."

"Of course—and you've your own racket here. I know," Nonny said grimly. "But we aren't all little birds in their nests over *there*, either. Not by a long chalk. There's little Wandy thinking she's fit as a fiddle again, though her heart did let her down on Thursday. She wants to go to church this morning, and Miss Aram won't let her risk it—an uphill field path, you know, and this gale blowing from the wrong direction."

"It doesn't seem sensible to attempt it. Isn't there any other way to church except over the fields?"

"Round by the road—but it's three times as long. The old dear could never do that."

"A car?" Emma suggested, a good enough churchwoman herself to sympathize with Miss Wand's frustrated desires.

"My *dear*," Nonny said, shocked. "And petrol what it is—and Miss Wand what *she* is..."

Emma had an uneasy feeling that she was mocking someone by quotation. "What *is* she then," she said sturdily, "except a sick old lady?"

The matron had the grace to look abashed. "I didn't mean to put it like that," she said. "She's a funny old dear in lots of ways—a bit childish an' all that, but all these old women who have outlived their proper span are a bit trembly in the top storey. No, all I meant was—*she* wouldn't hire a car, or pay for the school petrol. The trouble with her is she's mean. Not like Thurloe."

"Oh. But then, may not that trouble be rather different from what it seems? Perhaps she's not like Miss Thurloe in that respect because she's not rich like her."

"Even richer, Miss Aram says. No, it's just what's in the blood—can-the-leopard-change-his-spots business. Loads and loads of it wouldn't make Miss Wand more openhanded as long as she was born stingy. It's just plain nature. And that's why Thurloe pays twelve guineas a week and why Wandy asked when we took over if her three might be reduced to two-ten in view of the changes in the house. Aram was batty to have agreed—the poor little frump may not be so exacting as Thurloe, but she's a big responsibility, mind. But she's like that—the H.M., I mean—softy when it comes to the point, and lets herself be got round by any designing madam, young or old."

Emma, though she had not met Miss Wand, was nevertheless unable to see her in this role. Nor, remembering the prompt dismissal of Linda Hart, did she consider Grace as malleable as all that.

"Miss Aram won't regret kindness," she said.

"But she has—regretted it often, where both of them are concerned. She said to me a week ago—it would be a day or two before you came—that she wished she could give Miss Wand notice to quit. I said, you mean Thurloe, and she said, no, Wandy. I shouldn't feel responsible for her then, she said, with the other old woman carrying on like she does. I said, well, why not? And what do you think she said to that?"

Emma shook her head in the manner provoked by this inane question.

"Said she couldn't do it—she remembered too well herself the awful feeling of not being wanted in the house where she lived as a youngster. I've no room for sentiment. I said, whatever's that to do with the present case? The old are insensitive to that sort of thing, however much it flicks you on the raw in your green days."

"I honour her for it," Emma said primly. "This has been the only home Miss Wand's known for years before Miss Aram entered it."

Nonny shrugged. "It's not going to be much longer, by all account."

"Oh—why?"

"Miss Wand's done the deed herself. Raised the devil and said she's going—hello, where *did* you spring from?"

Grace had come up, dressed ready for church. She was calm and collected, but Emma thought she looked rather hard at Nona Deakin.

"Who's going? You, I hope, Nonny—churchwards with the children. And you, with me, won't you, Bet?"

"Yes, I didn't know it was late," said Emma, and "Miss Wand," said Nonny, together.

"Oh, that," Grace said. "Well, it's all for the best. It's a tremendous relief—her going, I mean. Though I'd rather for her own sake she'd kept cool about it. All I was doing was underlining Dr. Bold's instructions—complete rest, no stairs, and so on. As one can't be aerially transported to St. Martin's, I consider churchgoing included in the forbidden activities."

"Wish it was in mine," said Nonny wickedly, and departed to collect her charges.

"I didn't realize," Emma said, "that you would be glad if Miss Wand left."

"You wouldn't—Miss Thurloe's so much the greater anxiety that I've not time really to think much about Miss Wand. But it's not too good, you know, to feel responsible for somebody suffering with heart trouble—especially a frightfully parsimonious old woman like Wandy. We all like her more or less—she's amusing, and never *tries* to give trouble like Thurloe. But she's by way of being a dead loss to Makeways, and after more than four months of the two of them, Bet, I've reached breaking point. I've simply got to cut it all out and let them both go."

"A little hard when you've reached the eighties, isn't it?" Emma murmured.

"So I thought. I did nothing in the matter, but now that Miss Wand's voiced it herself I'm certainly not going to be the one to dissuade her from it. I only hope she won't have changed her mind by tomorrow—probably not, though. In that sense she's not as mercurial as Thurloe. The way she flew at me—I was thoroughly scared of what it would do to her heart. I called Nonny in case she collapsed then and there. And in the end we walked out on her because even our efforts to soothe her were misinterpreted. But I sent one of the maids up just now to see she was still all right. She says we're merely trying to boss—well, after all, it is my house, and she and Thurloe are only here on sufferance."

Emma shook her head. "What a pity, Grace, your choice lighted on Martinmas!"

"I know," Grace said savagely. "Well, it did—it's no use bemoaning past mistakes. Come on, Bet, hurry—we shall be late."

"I shall make *you* late," said Emma. "Don't wait for me. I know—I'll miss Matins and come on to communion at 11:30. I can use the first hour when you're all gone—"

"Oh, *no*, Bet—you must come *now*. I need you. It's all been horribly upsetting. You can't stick behind with Wandy and Thurloe and Susan and the nurses. Now hurry—we'll be gone in a few minutes."

Grace was speaking with the vehemence Emma was used to by now. She made no more demur—indeed, it was not a matter of particular moment to her whether she attended both services or not—and went off to her room to get ready. Thither Grace followed, sitting on the bed and watching her hungrily.

The field walk to church took ten minutes, along a path that Emma would not have called hilly, though she reminded herself that the least incline might tax a weak heart. Under a sky of blurred, racing clouds, the wind blew strong across the open turf. Grace's company kept Emma's mind from circling the hopeless track it had pursued through the night. Here, in the open, Grace clinging to her with an insistence she felt pathetic, all her surmises were invested with unreality. Her spirits rose at the feeling that to Grace she represented all that was stable among the quicksands in which they moved.

Morning service in the little church that was largely filled by Makeways staff and children was undistinguished for Emma except for one disturbing moment. And that had really not been during the service, but before they reached the churchyard. At sight of the stumpy, thickset tower at the west end, she had been carried back to yesterday and the ugly shapeless fears that Grace's trust in her had gone far to quench.

For this was the tower of her vision in Ambrosio's room—seen with the blinding clarity a lightning flash reveals, when she was coming to her senses, the crystal between her hands. It must be—it is, she thought, the tower I caught a glimpse of through the hedge the evening I walked up from the station. That would account for it, perhaps. Seen but not thought of again, it had nevertheless been registered on the brain—or whatever it was, Emma supposed vaguely, that stored the pictures of a lifetime—and hung out again on view for the second or two she had taken to return from that queer little hypnotic trance. The crystal, she had been told, treated one to these throwbacks as often as it produced an unrecorded vision. There too in the burial ground were the trees, limes and chestnuts and beeches, the limes already leafless, the others tossing their first gold and copper, soughing and swaying in their top branches. She was childishly relieved at so early and innocuous a fulfilment of at least part of the crystal's prophecy. The tall grey building and the running water, not in the picture at present, would probably turn out to be just as meaningless—that is, if they appeared at all.

In the afternoon Grace, complaining of a headache, went to lie down. Alone, Emma felt again an agony of doubt. This emotional seesaw worried her; it was puerile to let suspicion be allayed by company and conversation, and to have it flood in on one again as soon as one was solitary. She retired to her room and began to jot down at haphazard a number of apparently unrelated features of what she imagined in alarm a reporter might dub "The Affair at Martinmas." But when she saw what she had written, such a miserable sense of guilt overcame her that she scribbled it all out and began again.

The sound of voices below drew her to the window. Julie Lancret was marshalling the boarders for their Sunday afternoon walk. There they were, all odd shapes and sizes and colours, doing their best to uphold the school motto and avoid even the semblance of a crocodile. They moved off through garden and paddock, out of sight, Mam'selle's uncompromising figure bringing up the rear. By her side walked a short, stolid, pale child Emma had not seen before.

Their going somehow emptied the house. It seemed sucked of sound and movement. The matron, she knew, was writing letters in her sitting room. Lilian Orpen was paying Susan a visit. Nurse Collins was reading to a wholly inattentive Miss Thurloe, while in the adjoining dressing room Nurse Swain tried to satisfy her abnormal craving for sleep. Emma applied herself to her task, and a few minutes later looked at what she had written.

1. Dr. Fielding fell sick and gave up his practice suddenly.
2. Miss Thurloe was all right (*i.e.* she betrayed none of her present symptoms) while Dr. Fielding was in attendance.
3. Dr. Bold took over the practice. Dr. Bold is young, and reputed to be clever and ruthless.
4. It was generally known that Miss Thurloe suffered from mild paranoia.
5. Miss Thurloe had her first attack of poisoning not much more than a week after Dr. Bold came in.
6. Arsenic was found after the first attack.
7. Whenever arsenic has been found it is always present in the *dregs* of food or, more often, drink. The natural inference is that somebody has eaten or drunk the article in question, and left a teaspoonful or so in the bottom of the vessel.
8. Nurse Swain alleges that Miss Thurloe never takes poison now, though traces of it are found. She screams out about being poisoned, and then poison is discovered. Sometimes she screams and no poison is found.
9. Miss Thurloe is always *going to be murdered*, but is never murdered. Why not? (This sounds heartless, but is really

the most puzzling point of all. If she is doing it herself to attract attention and sympathy, the question is answered, of course. But if this is so, *why is she terrified?*)

10. If murder is intended, what can be the motive for murdering Miss Thurloe? Money? Her death will benefit nobody, it is said, but an unknown sister at the other end of England. Her life, on the other hand, is of obvious and continued benefit to Makeways and, since their employment depends on the prosperity of Makeways, to everyone in it. Personal hate? Weak. *Very* weak, because everyone in the house, except Miss Wand, was a stranger to Miss T. four months ago, and under present domestic arrangements can be completely segregated from her if she is a cause of annoyance to them.

11. Miss Thurloe is reported to have dismissed Nurse Edgeworth and Bertha Glass, maid to herself and Miss Wand, within a few days of each other. The maid was not replaced.

12. Miss Thurloe is fond of Susan Pollard, who is said to remind her of a "long lost relative."

13. Susan Pollard has a friend in Blandford.

14. Linda Hart, who visited the fortune-teller on Miss T.'s behalf, left Martinmas for Blandford.

15. Susan was taken ill on Friday evening with alarming symptoms resembling gastritis.

16. My room was searched during Friday evening. (Why not earlier when I was in Bugle with Nurse Swain in the afternoon? Because when I popped into my room ten minutes *after* Susan was taken ill, to remove hat and coat and hang them in the wardrobe, the box on the shelf had *not* been moved. I am positive of this.)

17. It was not Susan Pollard who searched my room. (Why not? See 16. But there is further evidence to support this. The slip

of paper advertising Ambrosio was in the pocket of the coat I wore into Bugle. I did not take off this coat till Susan had been got to bed. She was much too ill—and under too constant an observation—to have tried anything like slipping it in herself. Did somebody else take advantage of the confusion round Susan and put it there? No. Because (*a*) I was never close enough to anyone but Susan and Nurse Collins until *after* I had removed the coat, though I summoned Grace and Nonny before going to my room; (*b*) the Ambrosio cutting was *underneath* both my handkerchief and the bottle of scent, so that I should most certainly have felt a hand introducing it to my pocket.)

18. On returning to Susan's room I found Grace, Nonny and a maid there waiting for the doctor for whom Grace had telephoned. I stayed in Susan's room until he came, as I knew he would want to question me. The only person besides myself who stayed the whole time until Dr. Bold arrived was the matron. The others—Grace, the maid bringing hot water, Nurse Swain before going on duty, Nurse Collins when she came off duty—visited Susan's room at various times during that period of waiting and afterwards. Any one of these, also Miss Orpen and Mademoiselle and the other servants, had ample opportunity for examining my room in my absence. (In the above list of "suspects" (!) I suppose I ought to include both Miss Thurloe and Miss Wand! It is most improbable, however, that Miss T. was the guilty party, since she was constantly under observation by one or other of the nurses during the time in question.)

    N.B.—As it would be fantastic to suggest that two people visited my room independently of one another, I am assuming that the one who planted Ambrosio's advert was the one who rummaged my drawers and moved the box in the wardrobe, etc. I have shown above that the only two people who cannot have done this are Susan Pollard and Nona Deakin—with Miss T. as a possible third.

19. Susan has probably drunk poison. (*N.B.* what she told me about her eating and drinking on Friday, and the water bottle.) The doctor should be able to confirm this on his next visit.

20. Nurse Swain, on her own admission, is always sleepy at Martinmas. It is not usual for her to be sleepy in other places.

21. Why did Ambrosio (*a*) make the notes I saw on his pad? The question ought rather to be: *How* could Ambrosio have made the notes on his pad? (There seems to be only one answer, and I am afraid to give it.)

> (*b*) show strain when he was trying to impress on me the necessity of yielding to circumstance in the form of the person who is coming into my life?
>
> (*c*) suddenly turn frigid when I used the phrase "ever afterwards" about the happiness in store for me?
>
> (*d*) suggest that death in the house where I am living is expected to come violently and not as a natural event? Nobody had mentioned the possibility of violent death. (Does this mean that Miss T. is going to die, and her death appear natural? Impossible after all that has happened.)
>
> (*e*) reply so queerly with, "for *you*?" when I said I thought the crystal revealed a rather gloomy picture for me? Who else could it be but me?
>
> (*f*) look at me with loathing as I went down the stairs?
> *N.B.* (*a*), (*b*), (*d*) and (*e*) might be answered on the ground that Ambrosio is a genuine clairvoyant. I do not think this is the answer. And I am sure that anyone who was present at yesterday's seance would not think so either.

Emma pushed it from her, unsatisfied. She would never make a detective. And perhaps her more valuable observations, after all, were those she had felt obliged to scratch out.

On second thoughts she picked up the paper and, drawing her suitcase from under the bed, locked it up securely inside, together with those other compromising documents, the August and September numbers of *Wings of Friendship*.

Chapter XII

DEATH IS QUIET

The wind that had dropped in the evening rose again at night. Emma woke in the dark and listened to it gathering strength beyond the barrows and the downs and all the hidden country between Martinmas and the sea.

The sea… Whimby and the Pact-and-Picture Club; Ambrosio, giving up his practice in Brighton to settle in the obscure corner of a little town like Bugle; older, cleaner, more enchanting visions— the indolent sway of the Adriatic on the beaches below Rimini; passing the Balearic Islands on a June morning in the voyage from Gibraltar to Genoa; further off still, paddle steamers, striped awnings, shrimps and buckets, herself a little girl with her frock stuffed into her knickers, beating the wet, soggy, delightful sand into a batter with the flat of her spade. Far away and long ago… only it didn't seem to be either tonight. The past was not done with. It was never finished. Of that she was sure. Hers was here, close at hand, urgent, a warm, breathing, palpitating presence more real than anything that was happening in the house this week, today, now. More real—and more important. That was absurd, of course. But its insistence made her sit up in bed and feel a tingling anxiety to be occupied somehow, somewhere, in a manner she felt was imperative but could not define.

She got out of bed to adjust the blackout before switching on the lamp to see what time it was. It was twenty minutes to three on Monday morning.

Her hands were trembling. It might be the wind that quickened her blood to this strange excitement. She did not know. The house was quiet. There was only the roistering gale that punctuated its thunders with determined assaults on it. One clap after another shook her window and set the bureau quivering. It was a badly posed piece of furniture and wanted something underneath the back foot to stop the rocking motion when pressure was applied in front.

She looked round. Nothing was at hand except the matchbox in her candlestick. There were three or four matches left, she remembered; she would get a new box tomorrow and put them in it. She tilted them out and, taking the empty box, crushed and flattened it and went on her knees by the bureau to push it under the defective leg.

It was disconcerting to find so much dust, even though you were aware of slapdash attention from the maids. Her fingers encountered soft, fluffy wads of it. They touched something else—something stiff and shiny, and doubled across the middle. Somebody else had been bothered by the insecurity of the bureau, and had given it this for support. She pulled it out, blew the dust from it, straightened out the bend.

It was a picture, a photograph. But the light over here was poor. Emma carried it over to the lamp to examine it properly. The sepias, more than half a century old, she judged, were so badly faded it was almost impossible to discern features. Almost, not quite. She could see that the face was a girl's. It looked impish, unsmiling. There was a faint mockery that was even familiar; but she could not be sure, for where the mouth should have been ran the crack made by folding. Smaller cracks radiated from it, but top and bottom the picture was undamaged, and across the right-hand corner, where neck and shoulder met, and a single curl, once shining, caressed the smooth flesh, a message had been written. It was not easy to read by lamplight. Only the one word, "Love," was clear. By morning light, perhaps, the ghost of her who had given her picture with love, would come to life again.

When she got back into bed something elusive nagged at her, like a dream that is lost. Perhaps that was it—she had waked just now from a dream she could not recall.

There was plenty beside to remember, though. Yesterday's fears and suspicions jostled one another in her mind, and she felt a rush of contrition for all the things she had not told Grace. It was partly Grace's own fault, of course. She had been surprisingly incurious. Though it had been impossible at tea on Saturday, with Lilian Orpen there, to discuss her visit to Ambrosio, she had imagined how impatiently Grace must be awaiting a word in private. But when the opportunity came she had not invited confidence. On the contrary, absorption in private worries showed as an indifference that made it easy for Emma to give a censored account of the interview. It was not that she wanted to practise deception, but after discovering the jottings Ambrosio had made on the pad she was inclined to treat with the greatest reserve an episode she did not yet understand. She was moving cautiously too in the matter of her proposed visit to Miss Thurloe. Since Nurse Collins had arrived to take over duty by day, it would have to be a night call, and Emma felt reluctant at the thought of being smuggled in at some questionable hour in face of the doctor's orders. And there was now the possibility, she reminded herself, that by consenting to meet Miss Thurloe she was falling into a trap set for her. It was an idea that made her heart beat quickly, not so much from fear, as because she realized at last how suspicious she had grown.

She slipped further down in bed, nodding. She settled herself, drawing the clothes about her again. After another resounding thump, the wind left the house alone for a minute or two, retiring, it seemed to her, to an immense distance, whence its rolling drums might even have a slumberous effect.

They must have done so, for, without any prelude of conscious thought, she would have said, she was at once entangled in a ridiculous dream, in which Miss Thurloe, twirling a vast purple parasol, bobbed and leered at her, her face turning as she watched to the mask of terror she had caught sight of from the bedroom door. The queer, repulsive mouth opened in a scream that tore past her ears. "I'm coming—I'm coming!" Emma cried, and woke herself, trembling, half out of bed, breathless, gasping brokenly in what she had thought was a shout, "Wait—oh, *wait*—I'm coming!" As she put her feet to the floor, struggling between waking and sleep, a second scream ripped out, and then a third that sank to gurgling sobs, to rise to another shriek—and another—and another. Then she knew that the first one had been real.

The next few minutes were for Emma a nightmare from which it seemed impossible to detach anything coherent. Yet, later, it had to be done, when it became known what issues depended on the movements of people that night. Snatching up a dressing gown and pushing her cold feet into slippers, she ran from her room without turning on the light, down the passage, and into the main corridor where she could see light shining through Miss Thurloe's open door and could hear a voice pleading, urging, insisting, and getting no reply. All the while somebody went on screaming, but not in this wing, not on this floor even, not up here. It was from downstairs the piercing, at last bestial, notes of it rose. Doors banged, feet pounded, voices muffled or shrill babbled inquiries that never got answered. The house, dead and hollow so short a time ago, was suddenly a boiling pot. Only the wind, unequal to the contest, had subsided to jealous, protesting mutters.

Out of breath, Emma found herself peering fearfully in at Miss Thurloe's door. In the room were Grace and Nurse Swain—nobody else. Grace was wearing a dressing gown over pyjamas. It was she Emma had heard talking. She was still talking—bending over the chair in which the nurse lay sprawled, shaking, encouraging, trying to lift her. She turned a white face to Emma, the eyes enormous. The movement of her body disclosed that other face—the queerly coloured face of Nurse Swain, her mouth hanging open, slow noisy breaths coming out of it.

"Bet," Grace cried hoarsely, "go and look for Thurloe—she's gone—get Nonny—get anybody—tell them to stop her screaming—*stop her screaming*. Nurse Swain has drugged herself, and if I know anything about it she's dying on our hands!"

But it was not Nurse Swain who died, nor Miss Thurloe.

When the horrors of the night melted to blessed day, and there was time to remember those who had had no part in them, they went to Miss Wand's room. Death, as the Great Ambrosio foretold, had come to Martinmas. Even the particulars of the prediction seemed not to have been overlooked. For the certificate which Dr. Bold delivered the following evening declared that he had come in the natural course of things.

Chapter XIII

A FACE IN THE GLASS

Later, memory touched to brilliance individual pictures of the night's events. To Emma at the time they had flashed by, unrelated and menacing; she had felt herself struggling in the obscurities of some ugly phantasmagoria. But when it became necessary to reproduce them, not once but several times, she surprised herself with the clarity and ease of her telling. Fear and despair and, in the fullness of knowledge, remorse might gnaw at her, but they did not make her falter in her tale.

She remembered them too in chronological order...

First was Nonny, striding down the passage to Miss Thurloe's room, a coat flung capewise over her dressing gown, an electric torch burning in her hand, as she waved it at Emma, illuminating odd bits of her—cropped hair blown back like a Mænad's in the draught, the thin stripes of her pyjamas, the large, muscular hands, the face unsentimental and wearing always a superficial geniality... but not now, Emma thought, not now... and, for an instant before the matron snapped out her own light and turned on the dim bulbs in the passage, a sudden disturbing gleam of eyeballs that made her look frightened.

"What's wrong?" She clapped fists to her ears, the torch sticking up like the weapon of a unicorn, and pulled a hideous face. "That screaming—that *screaming*—why the heck can't somebody stop it?"

"Nurse Swain—Miss Aram can't rouse her—Miss Thurloe is gone." Emma, pointing behind her, hurried by.

"What, *dead?*" matron cried in a hearty voice that douted every other sound.

"No—no," Emma called, wagging her head vehemently over her shoulder and feeling all at once as if she and Nonny were partners in some ludicrous game. "She's lost!"

"And why *not?*" Nonny retorted viciously. "Why can't we lose 'em all, I'd like to know? Best news I've heard this many a long day. If it comes to that, I *have* lost somebody—Dolly Finch out of the san., the bounder—sleepwalking again!" She swung into Miss Thurloe's room.

Emma broke into a run, her heart thudding. The moment she got to the top of the stairs that would take her down to the hall, and had switched on the light, the screaming stopped. She was so unprepared for the silence that plunged over them like a wave, dropped like a theatre curtain, for the hideous clamour to stop like the turning off of a tap, like... she groped for a simile to express the blessed sense of relief... like a tooth ceasing to ache after hours of torment, that her knees felt weak. She leaned on a rail at the head of the stairs and took a deep breath to steady herself before descending. In the distance, among the dormitories, there was a cloudy buzz of talk that reached her like nothing so much as the confused murmur of a dovecote. Its blurred, gregarious quality was balm to the nerves. She poised her foot to go down, and at once all the lights went out.

The blackness behind and in front was so intense after the blaze flooding the stairs that it was all she could do to stop herself plunging headlong. She leaned hard on the wall for a second or two, her eyes closed. It was then she heard somebody below her, breathing hard.

Emma, conscious that moment and for as long as she was to remember it, of the primitive fear that possessed her, always insisted that the only reason she did not retreat to the shelter of the corridor was a still wilder repugnance she had for turning her back on the stairs. There were ten steps down, she remembered, then a narrow landing on which two could comfortably pass, and then a longer flight to the ground floor. Whoever was below her, waited on the landing.

She took a step forward, swaying her foot a little, feeling for the tread. Her right hand gripped the rail and slid down it jerkily, with her left she clutched the dressing gown at her throat. She went steadily down in the smothering darkness, and as she went forced herself to speak aloud.

"Miss Thurloe," she said softly, "Miss Thurloe… it's all right… I'm coming."

It did not occur to her till afterwards that she had used the language of her dream.

Nor, until she came to the landing, had she thought of giving her name. As her foot left the bottom tread, she stretched both arms before her, groping.

"It's only I—it's I, Miss Betony…"

It was only then she remembered that Miss Thurloe did not know Miss Betony.

The unseen figure on the landing, which had held its breath since she started to come down, let it out now in a deep, shaky sigh. Emma's fingers felt and fastened on the slightly rough texture of a sleeve and the bone beneath it. This isn't Miss Thurloe, she thought with certainty, and as if at a signal there came a loud whisper, "*Mon Dieu*—and I thought—what did I not think? It is Lancret, Mees Betony. I was coming *up* ze stairs, you on'erstan', when, pouf—the lights are out. I hear one move—one breathing—a hand on ze wall. I cannot move."

"I too," Emma whispered. Darkness imposes an odd restraint. "I heard *you* breathing. I was afraid it was—you were—"

But of what had she been afraid? Of whom? She felt herself on the edge of hysteria. A gust of laughter she knew to be unseemly welled up in her, though she did not let it escape. But she could not help shaking a little with suppressed mirth at the thought of two elderly women—to be honest, one of them was an old woman—standing still and sick with fear of one another at a few yards' distance.

"What is de matter?" Julie Lancret muttered, feeling the arm on hers quiver.

"Nothing." Emma had herself in hand again. "Where is Miss Thurloe?"

"I do not know. I t'ought, per-haps, she had come up here. I came down ze ozzer stairs. When I get into ze 'all ze screaming stop. It is Mees Aram I seek—I go to her room jus' now, but her bed—it has not been slept in."

"She's all right," Emma said quickly. "She and Nonny are doing what they can for Nurse Swain."

She explained, still in whispers, the nurse's condition. The two women fumbled their way down to the bottom, mutual confidence growing with talk and the touch of arm on arm.

At the foot of the stairs they turned left into the main passage that ran parallel with the front of the house. Halfway down, and opening off the hall, was a small room that served Grace as office, where the telephone was installed. A light shining through the door left ajar made a yellow wedge on the black corridor floor.

Like cheese, Emma thought with sudden incongruity. Aloud she said, "Where's the switch for this passage? I'm sure we can get a light. There's nothing really wrong, with the office light burning. Those stair lights and the corridors too can be manipulated from upstairs, so that the last people to go to bed, like Miss Aram and matron, can go up in the light and turn them out. Somebody up there has done it—one of the children perhaps."

Mam'selle nodded. "I know—it is here, no—here." She rubbed her hand over the wall, and clicked the switch down. They blinked in the dazzling rush of light. A voice, low but audible, reached their ears from the office. There was the sound of the receiver being replaced, the light in the room went out, and a figure appeared in the doorway.

"Hello," said Susan Pollard uncomfortably.

She stared defensively from one to the other. A heavy quilted dressing gown was wrapped tightly round her, the swansdown at the throat no whiter than her white face. Her eyes shone large and brilliant, her hair against the dark background of the office gleamed with a luminous quality like a halo of misty light. A halo. Emma thought involuntarily of Ambrosio's picture with its nimbus of wicked yellow hair.

"I was ringing up the doctor," Susan said. She said it defiantly, as though they had accused her. She explained unnecessarily. "Miss Aram sent me. He's coming directly. Has Miss Thurloe been found?"

"No," said Mam'selle, and, "No," said Emma.

They made a strange group, Emma thought, the young woman, straight and taut, outwardly at least self-possessed, the two older ones confronting her with their bewildered, defenceless air. If for an instant Susan had seen herself as the accused, her manner had undergone a subtle transition to that of the accuser.

On the silence that enveloped them the clock in the hall chimed the half-hour. The clear impersonal notes lifted the strain.

"Half-past four," Susan said and, again unasked, "Those awful screams woke me at twenty past." She walked past them, challenging denial. "I shall search the downstairs rooms."

"That end, then," Emma suggested, pointing the way she and Mam'selle had come. "We'll take this."

She wanted to ask the girl about her health, to try to dissuade her from wandering about the passages at this cold hour. But she was visited in time by a presentiment that solicitude would be misinterpreted.

They separated, Susan Pollard going into the drawing room on the left, where she could be heard softly calling Miss Thurloe's name. Emma, with Mam'selle at her side, continued down the corridor. Upstairs, disorderly noises had broken out again, setting the nerves on edge with the suggestion of activities more purposeful than one's own. They irritated Emma so much that she broke away to hurry across the hall and unbar the front door which was thumping uneasily. The idea that somebody might have escaped the back way and got round here to the front encouraged her to take a look abroad. But there was nobody in the porch. Only a damp, gusty air blew over the lawn and set the cedar creaking to a mournful tune. As the darkness thinned to eyes grown accustomed to it, she managed to pick out the black huddle of trees at the bottom.

"You catch your deat'," Lancret murmured lugubriously, and Emma came in and shut and bolted the door again.

Mam'selle had gone into the little schoolroom on the right of the porch. She did not put on the light here because the blinds were up and the dimly lucent night, invading it, washed it to a wan semblance of what it looked by day.

"Nobody there," Emma said, adding inconsequently, "I'm glad the doctor's on his way."

Mam'selle grunted. She looked and sounded fatigued, and eyed Emma with the kind of disfavour that carries no personal bias.

"*Le médecin?* Oh—*là*! But it is not usual to address him as 'my dear'—even in England, *hein?*"

There was no spite behind the words, only a vast indifference. Emma said nothing. She too had heard Susan Pollard's closing words at the telephone.

They pressed on to the bottom of the passage where the stairs ran up to the dormitories, opening doors, poking heads round, calling, coaxing, inviting Miss Thurloe to show herself, flashing lights on and off where the blinds were down, where the windows appeared as ghostly squares trying to penetrate the gloom of rooms that, familiar by day, resembled now only distant relatives of themselves. All the while the queer rumpus was in progress above. It was as if some spectral removers were at work, turning the whole furniture upside down in a determined effort to unearth Miss Thurloe.

"We shall do no good down here," Emma said, beginning to shiver. "I've an idea there's nobody in charge of the boarders and they're just up to high jinks. I wonder where Susan is. I—"

She was talking to air. Mam'selle had already gone. She opened the door of the common room which she had just closed, and gave a glance round the music room next door. Lancret was in neither. Probably had the same idea as me, Emma decided, and gone upstairs. She prepared to follow.

It was forbidden to carry a light of any kind up these stairs because the sycamore window, awkwardly placed, did not lend itself to blackout. As further precaution Emma turned off the light at the end of the passage before going up.

"Put out the light, and then, put out the light," she whispered. It looked as if what remained of the night would be spent in literal interpretation of it.

Before she had got to the bend by the window a patter of light feet rushed down upon her from above. Emma drew aside hastily to avoid being knocked backwards as a flying white figure bounded towards her. The dormitory corridor was in darkness, so that she could only guess it was one of the children. She caught her by both arms and held her wriggling and squealing, not with fear, it seemed, but with excitement and the bubbling gratification at a chance to spread it.

"*Crumbs!*" gasped the prisoner, "*how* you frightened me... *who*... how... *where's* Miss Aram, please?"

"Who is it?" Emma demanded.

"Cicely—oh—aoh—"

The name conveyed nothing to her captor. Uncovered pyjamas and bare feet told another story. Emma lugged her upstairs to the tune of grunts and peevish resistance.

"Let me go—*let* me go—you—you—you don't under*stand*! Let me *go*, I say! Who *are* you, *any*way—I've got to find Miss *Aram*—the *house* is on fire!"

"You wicked girl," Emma said stoutly, and administered a resounding slap of the good, old-fashioned kind in what might be called the good, old-fashioned place. Among all the noises of strife and anguish that had torn it, such a sound had never before rung through the independence-loving kingdom of Makeways. The promptitude of the delivery was so startling, indeed, that Cicely subsided at once, padding along beside Emma with heaving breast and stricken tongue.

"Now, which is your dormitory?" Emma asked, greatly encouraged. Other heads were popping out and being withdrawn to the accompaniment of rustles and giggles.

"Here," Cicely said in a savagely subdued voice. "All *right*—if you *won't* believe me"—the menace melted to a protracted wail, "we shall *all* be burnt in our *be-eds!*"

More heads, the pummel of naked feet on boards, mock lamentations, a burst of tittering from the other side of the first door that stood open a foot, and then, to Emma's heartfelt relief, a familiar, robust voice.

"You *miserable* wretches—back to your beds!" And there was Nonny, heading them into their respective folds like a forthright dog. "*What's* all this nonsense about being burnt in them, I'd like to know? Who's been stealing matches, the fiend? Now then, own up!"

Outside, Emma listened to the virtuous chorus. "No, Nonny—it wasn't *us*—Nonny, it *isn't*—really an' truly we haven't done *any*-thing—Bingo, you pig, that was *ages* ago—well, Nonny, I mean to *say*—Nonny, it's Miss Orpen—her room's on fire! *Honestly*—we *wouldn't* say it—Margaret smelt it when she was looking for Dolly—"

Nonny slammed the door on their morbid glee and herself inside. Emma waited in a pother of doubt. It might be, probably was, only a puerile joke; nobody else was raising the cry that never goes unheard. She, in any case, had no notion where the secretary slept.

Nonny flung out of the room. "Don't let me hear another word from you tonight." She clapped the door smartly and seized Emma's arm.

"Better not leave it to chance," she said between breaths, breaking into a run and forcing Emma to the same pace. "Maybe—little imbeciles've got hold of right end of stick—for once. Say—seniors knocked on Orpen's door in a too conscientious—search for Finch—got no answer—smelt burning—Margaret—usually sensible kid—says really noxious burning—bit like tar, only nastier. Hadn't got pluck to open door and take a look-see—Orpen puts the wind up 'em, you know… here we are, *and* my holy Aunt Jemima, what's up now?"

There was an altercation ahead of them in a little passage down which she hurried Emma. What has happened to us all, Emma thought—scurrying hither and thither with as little direction as mice when the wainscot's pulled down about their ears, the whole place agog, each unprofitable journey ending in a clash like this? One might almost believe an evil spell had been cast upon the house. The next minute she had cause to renew her conviction.

An open door was banged in their faces as they drew near. Voices raised in a torrent of voluble discord were shut off without being extinguished. Emma had already recognized Mam'selle's.

Nonny rapped sharply. "Smell it?" she said to Emma, wrinkling her nose in disgust. It had been only a perfunctory tap and, without waiting for an answer, she opened the door and went in. Emma stood on the threshold, grateful for the first time that night for the chill in the air that braved, if it could not quench, the impurities of Lilian Orpen's room.

"What the devil's burning here?" Nonny ignored the quarrel going on under her nose. She screwed and puckered and tilted that expressive organ again, in the unselfconscious manner of a dog.

Indeed, it was alarming. Emma saw a small room, the window unbecomingly swathed in a voluminous dark curtain. At the moment it was filled with an acrid black smoke that hung about assuming shapes and slyly transforming them, as she had seen a London particular do. The smell was vile and choking, hot as steamy resin. Behind the smutty veil of it faces glared at one another in hate and tongues grew shrill. Lilian Orpen, in a scarlet dressing gown, looked like a viper about to strike Mam'selle who, gripping some sort of garment in her hands, waved it in her face and poured out on her a torrent of French.

"Miss Deakin," the secretary said with frigid restraint, "you mistake my room for a dormitory, I think. I am not to account to intruders for its character."

"Oh, come off it," Nonny said rudely. "Don't talk like a book at me—my poor little brain won't stand it. Here's you and Mam'selle capering about in a belching furnace, and half the school running wild in the belief the house is burning over their heads—I'll jolly well say an account of some sort is due!"

"*Eh bien*," Julie Lancret cried, shaking with passion, "it ees *I* who will account it!" With the loosing of rage her command of English slipped. "*Les enfants*—zay tell me ze 'ouse burn! But it isn't *so-o*! She light candles to ze Evil One! She steal my cloze zat she may burn ze soul from me!" She flapped the chemise in Emma's face. The wan light burning in the room drove its monstrous shadow up the ceiling, so that the sleeves shot up like the ears of some gigantic ass. The tails of her hair swept round her cheeks. She pushed them aside with a veiny, calloused hand. "Look over zair—look for yourselves!"

"She's crazy," Orpen said with cold venom, "just stark. She doesn't know what she's talking about. *I* can't help it if you mixed her things up with mine when you gave out the laundry. I've never seen the — article before."

But Nonny and Emma were both looking behind her.

The dressing table had been cleared of its usual freight. It stood stripped but for a black cloth, at either end of which rose two squat candles in brass sconces. Their peculiarity was not in their presence but in their composition. They were of some black malodorous substance, thick and greasy, that burned with a dull slatish-coloured flame. Between them was a shallow copper pan not unlike one of a grocer's pair of scales. Something had recently been burned in it, for the bottom was covered with what might have been bone ash and another more slimy deposit. Emma saw that this was the source of the smoke that filled the room and clawed at their throats. She looked again at the candles, misshapen, ugly, bulging, the substance that composed them slipping in hot gouts down the sticks and oozing on to the cloth.

"Pitch," she said on a high note that surprised herself.

"Which defiles by being touched," Nonny finished sententiously. She switched on the light in the room and, striding over to them, blew both candles out. The reek of them drove her back, a hand to her mouth.

Orpen turned on her with the fury of a cat in defence of its young. "What is it to you, the colour of the candles I choose to burn? Is it any more harmful than turning the school upside down and joining a pack of bedlamites in a manhunt? Get out of my room. All of you. *Get*—"

"There, there, there," Nonny soothed with a maddening air of calm. "Take it easy, Orpen. Miss Thurloe isn't a man, she's a woman, dear—and nobody cares what colour your candles are, nor your eyes—though why you can't get proper wax ones while you're at it—candles, I mean. But *this*"—she tapped the dressing table, "is school property, and the beastly stuff is messing up everything. Now be a good girl and clear away the silly caboodle, and get to bed. It's going on for five, and we've all had as much as we can stand."

"She ees *not* a good girl," Lancret cried in a deep voice. "She pray *au diable*! And I… *Mon Dieu—mon Dieu—*"

"Get *out*," Lilian Orpen shrieked and, twisting round, caught up one of the candlesticks. Nonny seized her wrist and doubled it back.

Emma took Mam'selle by the elbow and steered her outside. She went willingly enough, her rage spent, the rumpled chemise held against her face like an immense handkerchief, its sleeves hanging limply down with a ridiculous air of resignation.

"As for the shimmy," Nonny, practical to the last, called after them, "you'll identify it by the name tab—if it is yours. And we'll all have a nice cup of tea by and by."

Emma could hear her expostulating with Orpen in the tone she employed for Dolly Finch. The next minute she had joined them in the passage.

"Pestilential piece of goods, eh?" she said good-humouredly. "*What* a tea-party!" She yawned with abandon and cast a doubtful look at Mam'selle's rigid back. Emma shook her head and fell behind a pace, keeping Nonny beside her. The matron assumed the popular conception of a knowing look, compressing her lips, rolling her eyes, and exhibiting a general appearance of imbecility. Mam'selle, stalking ahead in stolid silence, made her way to her room.

Orpen's excursion into the macabre, whatever her doubtful experiment, was the last ugly episode of the night. Miss Thurloe, Emma was informed when Nonny got the chance to breathe again, had made her unseen way upstairs, on hands and knees by the looks of her, and taken refuge in her own bathroom. There she had been found by the maids who had postponed share in the search by huddling on their clothes as slowly as possible so as to put in a last-minute appearance. They had insisted too on group action, pursuing a follow-my-leader course that ensured the safety of the individual. Miss Thurloe was now in bed, buttressed with hot-water bottles, with Grace and the hardier maid in attendance.

Nurse Swain had been got away to a spare room, similarly fortified, her reluctant guardians, until Nonny could relieve them, cook and the other maid.

Susan, unexpectedly docile but wearing a reticent look new to her, was persuaded to snatch what sleep might be left from the night that was morning now. Nonny took hot milk to her and fussed in her businesslike way. She so enjoyed a crisis that gave her a free hand in other people's affairs that the girl's lack of response, conspicuous as it was, escaped notice.

Nonny, in fact, was unusually blithe, for after a strenuous search whose failure suggested a kidnapping, Dolly Finch had at last been located, safe if not sound, in Julie Lancret's room, under—of all places—the Frenchwoman's bed. What brought her there, nobody was clear about at present. To Grace's displeasure Mam'selle failed to report the discovery at once. Lancret explained that she had kept Dolly quiet in her room for half an hour because the child was so upset at the thought of leaving it, and because, hearing Dr. Bold arrive, she had thought it better not to interrupt immediately. This seemed sensible enough to everyone but Grace, who contended it was bad for discipline.

"There isn't any," Nonny said, tucking the delinquent up after further dispensations of milk and hot-water bottles. Dolly was in a pitiably nervous condition. She refused to say why she had hidden herself in Mam'selle's room, but declared that when she had gone in the room was empty, that Mam'selle came in later and got into bed without noticing her underneath it, that she couldn't remember what happened next, but thought she must have slept till she was woke later by dreadful screams and a flashlight "making horrible blobs" about the room, and saw Miss Orpen snatch up "a nightdress" from a chair and run off with it. Mam'selle wasn't in the room again when Miss Orpen took the nightdress. She didn't come in till "years after," and then she saw Dolly's feet sticking out from under the bed and hauled her forth. Asked how she had known it was Miss Orpen, she said frankly she knew all the staff by their legs; they all did. "Legs?" Grace said sternly. "Where are your eyes then? You must be like Mammon, who always studied the *floor* of heaven because it was set with precious stones." But Dolly began to cry, and had to be left alone.

It was an interesting narrative from more than one point of view. Emma at least thought so, though Nonny, reporting it with her usual racy comment, dismissed it as plain somnambulism with a dash of pure cussedness thrown in.

Dr. Bold came at 5:20 and stayed an hour and a half. Part of the time he was discussing with Grace plans for Miss Thurloe's removal. She was to go to hospital, where she might be under observation for a few days until a more permanent arrangement had been made. He wanted the Hartlepool sister's address, and her lawyer's too. Grace, with whom Dr. Wick had deposited both as a precautionary measure, gave them to him.

Careful examination of the room made it fairly clear at once that on this, the occasion of Miss Thurloe's worst "upset," the only poison present was the morphine which had found its way into Nurse Swain. Bold was satisfied that the nurse's condition was not serious, and declared she would be as right as rain by the afternoon.

Oddly enough, it was for Susan his concern was marked. Though she had made excellent recovery from Friday's attack, and now at 6:30 Monday morning seemed little the worse for the night's misadventures, he showed a strong inclination to order her to hospital as well. Susan opposed it with vigour, and Grace backed her up impatiently.

"If it was necessary for her to go, she should have gone at once, not now when she's picked up so well."

Bold made a rude noise. "You didn't think I was fool enough to risk moving her then?"

"Well, no," Susan agreed before Grace could answer. "But not now, either, doctor. With Miss Thurloe gone I shall be perfectly all right."

There was a short, pregnant silence. Grace gave her a sharp look. "Why do you say that?" she asked slowly.

Susan spread her hands wide and smiled sweetly. "I—don't know," she said in a tone that matched her head's.

Dr. Bold said nothing.

Taking all things into account, it was, perhaps, not surprising that nobody remembered Miss Wand till eight o'clock.

At that hour, or thereabouts—in the kitchen at Makeways the term had delightfully undefined boundaries—it was usual for the maid who carried up Miss Wand's meals to take her a morning cup of tea. She was in good time this morning because Miss Deakin had reminded her that nobody had paid any attention to the old lady since 10:30 the night before.

She was back in precisely three minutes, the tea slopped over the tray, her face pale and twitching with the shock of new disaster.

"But you *can't* be sure," Nonny interrupted the disjointed tale. "Why, you're hardly there before you're back again! Here—I'll go. Like as not the old lady's got another attack coming on."

She raced upstairs, foreboding lending wings to her feet.

There was no mistake. When the ambulance from Bugle arrived at nine o'clock to take away the weak and unprotesting Miss Thurloe, the school learned that on the opposite side of the house its other old lady lay dead.

All Monday and Tuesday Martinmas lay under a deep hush. Its visit was as unannounced and effacing as a snowfall's that in a world of silence sharpens sound and gives a false significance to movements and words. It could not be entirely attributed to respect for Miss Wand. To most of the school she had been hardly known at all, to none intimately. News of her death came as part of the accepted order of things, like the turn of the seasons, the migration of birds, the sudden crumpling of the petals of a rose after many days. There was no one insincere enough to express a grief not felt, and the dumb, gentle air of the place was less the silence of sorrow than of exhaustion.

Miss Thurloe had gone. That was a fact of far greater importance than that Miss Wand had died. Miss Thurloe had gone—she who had kept the bow always bent with the memory, the fear, the present torment of hysteria. Miss Thurloe had gone—and with her the unacknowledged terror of poison and a poisoner. Miss Thurloe had gone—and Martinmas found itself in that peculiarly enervated condition that is marked by a suspension of thought and feeling, and by satisfaction in one's own stupor.

Even Emma's suspicions acquiesced in the general truce. They had held their ground to the eleventh hour, but with the departure of Miss Thurloe who, coming in like the lion, had gone out like the lamb, their *raison d'être* was finally removed. Perplexity might remain; but it was clear that she was no longer justified in meddling with an affair that had gone out like a snuffed candle. To admit that it was disappointing was not to suggest that she did not feel relief.

Monday afternoon and evening passed, blessedly quiet. There were no lessons; two hastily improvised picnics were arranged, one for the seniors in Lilian Orpen's charge and one for the juniors with Nonny. The older girls asked if they might go into Bugle instead, but Grace refused. Mam'selle, after a solitary walk, pleaded a headache and stayed in her room. Susan and Dolly Finch in their respective beds thought their respective thoughts. Nurse Swain slept till close on tea, woke none the worse for the night before, and after making up her mind to resign the job, found, to her bewilderment, that the job had resigned her.

During the children's absence there were quiet comings and goings, the sound of official treads discreetly ascending and descending Miss Wand's stairs. The funeral was arranged for 2:30 Wednesday afternoon.

On Tuesday an incident after lunch enlivened the inertia for an hour. Dolly Finch's parents arrived by car from Reading and declared their intention of taking her back with them. Grace was at a loss to know how they had been made aware of her recent eccentricities. Whereupon Mr. Finch produced a wire received the afternoon before and handed it over. It ran: "*Please come fetch Dolly. Cannot assure the safety.*" It was unsigned, dated 30th September, and had been handed in at Underbarrow sub-post office, nearly two miles south of Martinmas, at 3:10 Monday afternoon.

Grace, after the Finches had left in an atmosphere of frost, reported the anonymity of the message to Emma.

"'Assure—the—safety?'" Emma echoed. "Really, it doesn't sound English. I suppose you do *know* Mr. Finch? It wouldn't be a mistake to get hold—?"

"Indeed it wouldn't," Grace said crossly. "If you'd ever taken a good look at Dolly you wouldn't ask. And she's not heiress to millions, worth a king's ransom, not she!" With her sneer at money, she managed to convey contempt for those who hadn't got it.

Nor was it possible for the child to have left her bed and the house unnoticed and sent the wire herself.

"I can and will find out, though," Grace said. "Even though Dolly's no loss, that sort of thing can't be allowed. Not that there will be much of a Makeways left when this show is over. Orpen and Mam'selle have both given notice already."

Apparent unconcern with the school's approaching demise contrasted sharply with Grace's earlier attitude. Emma put it down to mere reaction at Miss Thurloe's going, and was afraid for the form reaction might take later.

"But it is over, isn't it?" she ventured, hopeful.

"Perhaps," said Grace darkly.

Her eyes glittered with the old speculative light. She was withdrawn, giving nothing away. But there was about her a buoyancy Emma had not seen before. It would not have surprised her to learn that Grace was already engaged with plans to turn death and departure to good account for herself and her business. She sighed.

It might be all for the best if she were. Self-interest was a wonderful rallying point for nerves frayed beyond endurance.

She made the funeral arrangements. She and Nonny would attend—"You too, Bet, if you like. There's going to be a service in church first." Two prefects would represent the school. That would be all. Miss Wand's lawyer had been wired for, but would be unable to get down in time. Nurse Swain, now completely recovered, was leaving tonight. The dozen or so children would remain for the afternoon in Susan's and Mam'selle's charge. Susan was about again today. Cook, the maids and the boy had got the afternoon off on Wednesday, a placatory gesture Grace hardly hoped would retrieve the domestic situation. The seniors left behind with Susan would get tea, and they would all have a light supper.

All day Tuesday Emma sought and was unable to get a word with Julie Lancret. Since Sunday sympathy had inspired a new interest in her. But the Frenchwoman repulsed all advances. It was not, Emma believed, conscious hostility that drove her to stony silence at meals and the longsighted gaze that saw nothing about her. Resistance to overtures was part of her nature. Expecting no friendship, she could only regard its offer with suspicion.

At six o'clock a large box arrived, the first flowers for Miss Wand. To everyone's surprise they came from Miss Thurloe.

"She wasn't supposed to know," Grace observed. "But there's nothing like death in the house for spreading like wildfire."

Floral tribute was the precise term for the great waxy lilies, uninterestingly chaste and overpoweringly heady.

"The house is going to whiff like a conservatory all night," Nonny said. "She might have waited till morning—but no, of course she'd get hers in first." She read the card: "Not her writing—'With heartfelt sympathy from her sorrowing friend, Maria Thurloe.' H'm—false old cat—though if *them's* her sentiments maybe it's because she feels a twinge of remorse at being the one that killed her."

Emma looked at her in horror.

Nonny laughed, bottling her mirth in conventional haste. "Well, what else? Kicking up bob's-a-dying all round the place and sounding the alert like she did's enough to've given angina to the healthiest heart! I don't like lilies anyway—they make me feel wicked. Give me something more cheerful for a funeral, *I* say, especially when you're burying a gay-go-up like Wandy. These are too be-ew-tiful. The children are sending chrysanthemums, bronzy ones—kind of stuff to brighten a cold day."

Emma agreed about lilies; chrysanthemums too, with their clean, faintly metallic smell, had always seemed to her a grave, intense flower that deprecated the pluck of light fingers.

Nonny went up with the wreath, and after that not a sound broke the silence of the house.

At seven Emma put aside a glove she was mending and left her room for Mam'selle's. Now that the whole affair was looking like a deflated balloon, there was no further need for her to conceal her visit to Ambrosio. It might be that Lancret, with her cry, "And I—*Mon Dieu, mon Dieu*," would be induced to ease her heart to one who, foolishly audacious, shared with her the secret of that evil room.

She made her way to the west wing where she had come only once before. She knew Grace's room. Lancret's was somewhere close by.

How still the house was over here… unbreathing, gentle, though a wind rocked the trees outside and made the pale gleams of autumn sunlight wink in and out on wall and passageway. The hush was like expectancy. She thought of that other afternoon in Churchway, so long ago it seemed, when the sun had greeted her on Mrs. Flagg's attic landing, and she had gone in to read the letters that had changed her life. Now, she must stand on the threshold of another change. Makeways was crumbling. She was not needed. She never had been needed, really. But Grace had been good, and the last day or two, since the strain had lifted, particularly kind and attentive to her…

The intoxicating scent of lilies cloyed her nostrils. Death was up here. She should have remembered. She trod quietly, at the top of a short flight of stairs passing Grace's room, other rooms behind closed doors. She hesitated, unsure. A vague memory of "Mam'selle's over there," before Grace had steered her down again, brought her to a square, low-ceilinged landing as large as a small room. There was a rug in the centre, some chests against the wall. It was flanked by rooms, and at the closed end a window let in the light from the north. Waves of perfume reached her, sickly because immoderate.

She looked left and right. Her usually unerring eye for the allocation of bedrooms up and down the social scale picked out the shabby door, two steps down, as undoubtedly that assigned to Mam'selle. It stood partly open. She was sure to be there.

She went down the steps, raised a hand to rap, prepared to call, "Mam'selle, may I come in?"

The words died on her lips. The door, perhaps from the draught of her presence on the steps, swung in further. It was like the beckoning of an invisible hand. The room was dark, with the subterraneous quality of places curtained by day. But its twilit mustiness made no difference to what she saw. Inside, a huge mahogany cheval-glass stood at an acute angle to the door, almost within touching distance. It was tilted forward. Something dark and smooth and shiny, with a glint of brass, gleamed across it, rigid against the indefinite shadows of the room. Something smooth and shiny and dark, with a white interior... and at the end of the whiteness the light glimmer of a face, clear as day, as day unmistakable.

Like a flower on its stalk, thought Emma, afraid only of the cold calm possessing her. Like a flower on its stalk. She smiled down at the closed eyes of Mary Shagreen.

Not a footfall, nor any sound, broke the silence of death. Emma stepped into the room. Without knowing that she did it, she pushed the door to behind her. She did not notice that it swung open again at once. She was trembling from head to foot, and cold. She was not aware of that either.

She stood perfectly still between the mirror and the coffined bed. Death had taken between his hands the face of Shagreen and smoothed out its tale of age and fatigue. In place of the bloom he could not restore he had left a tenderness, a young and shining content that the faces of the living do not know. The years had dropped away like petals, only personality lingered. It lingered in the little lopsided smile she could still recall, in the nose, the tilt of the chin, the tiny curved hands stubbornly refusing to fold meekly on the shrunken breast. Here, indeed, might be only the shell of her who had once set continents on fire. But it was a shell perfect in line and convolution. It was not even Mary Shagreen come to be an old woman whose last lover, Death, had lain with her. It was Mary Shagreen herself. It was the ghost of the girl who had given her picture with love.

She should have known. She should always have known. Perhaps in her silly, muddled, timorous, ineffectual way she had known something. Perhaps that was why she had agreed that the lilies drenching the room in their cold scent now were the wrong flowers. They should have been roses and honeysuckle, violets and dancing aquilegia, all the blossoms of the Montreux fêtes—"a carnation hit her on the nose and confetti trickled down her neck—she still laughed…"

All the monstrous cruelty of something she began at last dimly to apprehend came over her like a wave of sickness. She moved round the bed and steadied herself with a hand on the dressing table. Her fingers touched something small and hard. Its coldness made her look down quickly. It was the French watch—Shagreen's watch. She must have had it more than fifty years. She remembered the quivering pleasure with which she had handled it as a child, its tiny face, all its delicate conceits, the elegant shepherdess and her spindly lambs with their insufferable air of gentility, the flower chains and lovers' knots. Here they all were, visible even in this brown light. She remembered it had had some sort of an ornamented case—she felt about the table. Yes, here it was—fish skin, gold chased, very old—"a real aristocrat of watches," Aunt Shagreen had said, squeezing her, "not a common little upstart like me, darling!"

Her finger traced carefully the "M.S. from A." that 1884 had had chased upon the 1640 surface. She had never known anything about "A.," but she still recalled father colouring up at the sight of the watch, mother staring down her nose, herself wondering why anything so incredibly fascinating should make grown-ups go "all funny." But Shagreen had charmed it all away.

She could not stand here, always, the watch in her hand, her eyes on the mocking mouth of her dead. There was something she had to do, something she had to stop. She was desperate to see Grace, to speak to her, to— She came back round to the foot of the bed, brushing the cold hands as she passed. She looked up. And there was Grace.

The mirror had caught her even as it held Shagreen. To Emma she was a white face at an open door. The next minute she could not be sure that she had been even that. There was nobody there, only the long whisper of a door closing somewhere.

"Grace, *Grace*," she cried, but only a murmur escaped her lips. She went up the steps again, shutting the door on the dead. The great looking glass mimicked her action and latched it against the living. She broke into a half-run on the landing. That would be Mam'selle's door—perhaps. She could not be sure. She could not be sure of anything any more. She had no time to think of Lancret now, though behind her was a sound she paid no heed to. The shifting patches of sun in the passages were like tantalizing fires of memory, jewels of the past, now here, now slipping through one's fingers. Mary... Mary Shagreen.

She came to Grace's door, tapped on it, opened it the same instant. It was empty. She came out and hurried to the stairs.

She heard only the breath of her assailant. There was a blinding crash inside her head, a light before her eyes, sun and walls and the twinkling pattern of the trees thrown on them spun in a single wheel, she felt her foot float out into space, and herself falling... falling.

Chapter XIV

THE CORTÈGE WILL LEAVE...

The white square dwindled to a pinpoint, and vanished. When it did that, everything was dark again. One's grasp of reality slipped. You thought you had got the world in your hand, and then it slid smoothly away, like a fish. Like a fish with silver scales, bright, dazzling scales. Like a fish with one silver scale, solitary, shining like a star—shrinking to the point of a pin, vanishing. And then darkness.

But not the warm, firm, awaited darkness of sleep. There was nothing stable about this darkness. It moved. It had solved the problem of perpetual motion. It moved like water, in long, slow, successive waves that merged in one another and were lost, and were followed by the same endless pattern—flow, blend, vanish, flow... Water, shot through with flashing bodies, the bodies of the fish that lived in it, silver streaks whose movements were in vivid contrast to the sluggish coil of the water. Here, there, everywhere they swam, cleaving the water, darting out of the dark into the dark, till all of them became a single fish—and you had the world in your hand again.

It swelled to something solid and stable, burning like a lamp in the night, to something God had hung out in the firmament to guide you. It was something right and good. It had lines and corners, the blessed limitations of shape...

The white square dwindled to a pinpoint, and vanished. When it did that, everything was dark again. One's grasp of reality slipped...

Could it be the crystal, growing enormous between her hands, running through them again like a drop of quicksilver? No, for crystals were round, like the world itself. And this had corners, sturdy right angles where the eye that tried in vain to arrest the course of the waves could light for a moment, grateful, on a motionless plane...

Emma found herself staring at a window.

She closed her eyes against the full torrent of the day. But she did not sink again into that unlighted world of curling water and silver fish. Her head ached abominably. Eyes still shut, she put up a tentative hand, groped first about the pillow, then felt the bandage, and under the bandage a swelling above and behind her left ear. She flinched at the pressure of the blundering fingers.

When she opened her eyes next, it was not merely a window, it was her own window. Her thoughts took form and order. She had woke up, it was clear, in the day, not the night. It could not be morning, though, because her room faced east, and now there was no sun in it. She tried to remember what had happened. The effort made her headache worse, but she persisted. Something there had been—in a patch of sunlight, in the west wing. Sun—west wing. Sun in the west. So it had been evening. But, yesterday, today, last week—when? It eluded her like the fish, like the crystal, like the quicksilver, like the blessed, common light of day. Then she remembered the scent of lilies, and it all came back...

Perhaps Emma Betony's greatest virtue was not after all kindness, nor tolerance, nor a practical sense of the brotherhood of man, but the grimmer one of being resolute to complete a job that has become imperative. Added to that now was her conviction that every moment she stayed in the house diminished her chances of ever leaving it. She believed, dispassionately, that her death was intended. No doubt they had summoned the doctor, dressed her head carefully, made her as comfortable as possible. There are more ways of killing a dog...

By dint of setting her teeth and refusing to acknowledge the return of the billows and their gleaming shoals, she managed to turn her head from side to side and survey her room. It looked tidy enough, undisturbed. There was a glass of water within reach of her hand, and when that was gone a full bottle a couple of inches further off. She shuddered. Bedroom bottles had won notoriety in the past days. The water that looked so innocuous—who could say what it was? Better this nauseating, furry palate than that risk…

She no longer hesitated when she knew that she must get up and dress herself. Her ears could detect no sound in the house, though from outside there came an intermittent noise that was perhaps voices. By the condition of the light it could only, she thought, be afternoon. That meant this was Wednesday—Wednesday afternoon, the day and time of the funeral.

A wave of despair enveloped her. She had raised herself up in bed, and now she bent over her knees, clasping her bruised head in her hands. She had planned to stop it, and it was done. At once, her head bowed, her eyes hidden from the light, a phrase Ambrosio had used came unbidden to her mind. "The earth covers all—but you—you—you…"

The earth covered all. All that was left of Mary Shagreen was being committed to its long embrace. But she, Emma Betony, was here. She was alive. She had a tongue in her head still. In Ambrosio's "but" she saw, without arrogance, the inescapable arm of justice.

In the days to come she could not remember how she had got through the process of dressing. At the time she gave no thought to it, but, habit asserting itself, found she had achieved it carefully. While she was fumbling, tying, steadying herself against bedpost and table, she was obsessed with longing for a drink of water. She fought it down. She would not drink again in Martinmas, except water drawn directly from a tap.

The question of luggage was not to be thought of. Her things must stay here, including the suitcase. If she lived she would get them back. But, her purpose clear, her mind was alert enough to grasp the indispensability of certain articles. Though stooping made her sick and she was so long regaining her feet that despair shook her, she struggled with her case till she had extracted from it *Wings of Friendship*. A small lunch-case used for carrying her papers to tutorials was all she could take with her. In with the matrimonial journals she pushed now the photographs of her father and mother and of Shagreen, both the framed one of her own and the mutilated picture she had taken from under the bureau. By daylight recognition had been startling. The writing too was discernible: "To Ronald from Mary, with love."

She found room for toothbrush and sponge bag. Nightclothes she must buy wherever she happened to find herself tonight. She looked in her handbag. She had more than five pounds of the money she had brought away with her. In an inner pocket of the bag was an uncashed cheque for ten pounds that Grace had thoughtfully made out to her as an advance on the first term's salary. She drew it out and, with gentle deliberation, tore it across and across, dropping the pieces into the wastepaper basket.

She bathed face and hands in cold water, tidying the hair she was prevented from brushing by the bandage, took a clean handkerchief from the sachet she added to her case, and dressed herself for going away. All these duties and the thought entailed by each, though the mind appeared to function automatically, braced her against the nausea that returned at intervals.

Getting away from the house might not prove so easy as it looked. She tried to recall who was attending the funeral, who staying behind. But the individual names sidetracked her thoughts and set her trembling.

She opened her door, and listened. There was only the drip of the tap she had heard on her first evening a week ago. Its musical plash sounded like the BBC's interval signal.

It was now or never. Carrying the small case, her handbag, an umbrella, she gave one last look at the room she was leaving that had once held Shagreen, then closed the door on it for ever. Going down the narrow passage to the main one she had to steady herself, laden as she was, touching either wall for balance, as one did in a swaying corridor train. There flashed into her mind's eye the picture of Mary Shagreen doing the same thing—a week ago. A little old woman with a yellow shawl round her head, beauty still in her step, forgetting change and disturbance, returning to the room she had known for years… (How blind, how blind I have been…)

Through the landing window she saw Susan Pollard and the younger children in the garden behind the house. They were standing about, reading from papers. One of them, in imitation of a frog, was crouched and hopping. Rehearsing the play, she thought. She ducked her head on her way past the window to the bottom flight. Susan's back might be to the house, but she was taking no chances.

The passage was clear, but she got a shock as she drew near the office. The telephone started to ring. At the second peal, mustering her wits, she opened the drawing-room door and slipped inside. It was cold, cavernous. Nobody had yet raised the blinds. She leaned against the lintel, her hand on the inner knob, the door not quite shut. Her head was throbbing; against the lids her eyeballs pressed, burning.

Somebody was crossing the hall from schoolroom to office. The telephone pealed again. A voice said, "'Ul*lo*—'ul*lo*." It was Mam'selle then. Emma, in no condition for quick decisions, had to make her mind up at once. If she stayed in hiding she increased the risk of somebody noting her absence from her room. Surely one of them had had word to keep an eye on her. If, on the other hand, she were to creep past the office and out, Lancret, her call done, might emerge at any moment. Nonetheless, she was moved to the second course by so great a repugnance to the thought of lingering in Martinmas that it was like part of the pain that overwhelmed her every few minutes. She heard Mam'selle's voice now only as a distant wash of sound. That meant the office door was closed. She took her chance and came out.

Before she could turn into the hall there was a fresh alarm. The chink of a tray rang out loudly, giving a false impression of nearness. The servants had not gone out then, or not all of them, as had been arranged. No doubt her "accident" had meant a change of plans. The scullery-maid's pipe arose: "*Yew* take it—I've got the 'ot-water bottle to lug up by three."

That would be for herself. With Dolly gone, Susan out and about, and the improbability of anyone else having fallen sick since last night, there could be none but herself in need of a hot-water bottle. In a few minutes they would be entering her vacant bedroom.

Emma sped through the hall to the front door, her thin spinster's figure still deferentially inclined, neat, inconspicuous, never flurried one would have said, umbrella scrupulously rolled, bag and lunch case her respectable equipment, only an inch or two of bandage showing under her hat, and nothing at all apparent of the wild beating of her heart.

In the drive she drew a deep breath that was almost a groan. She schooled herself to walk to the gates slowly, with firm steps. But behind was the grating sound of an upflung window. She would not look round. A voice called, "Mees Betony—Mees Beton-*ee*— come back! *Mais non*—do not run—*je vous donnerai*—" The wind caught up the rest of it and blew it away. Emma, careless of dignity and resolution alike, broke into a stumbling run in spite of the hard core of fire in her head, her uncertain vision, and a weakness in her legs that she was convinced nothing but Spartan treatment to a walk would dispel.

She did not stop running until she had passed between the twin piers and under the vault of trees. This was the end, if she wavered now. Her original intention had been to wait at Underbarrow Halt for the next train to Bugle. Thence she could catch the London train that went via Salisbury. Now she saw that was unsafe. If they looked for her anywhere it would be at the Halt. How easily too description would identify her in such an untravelled spot. Better far to hire a taxi from the garage on the main road and go straight to Bugle. She would reach the garage by following this road parallel to the railway line and passing under the arch about fifty yards further on. On the other side it joined the Bugle road. If by chance there were no more trains to London today she must accept temporary defeat and put up in Bugle for the night.

Walking, with its passionate concentration on every step that was a step nearer freedom, brought her strength for the time being. Those engaged in the exacting business of escape have little opportunity for dwelling on physical disability, however painful. The stabs that drove through Emma's head with horrible regularity and disturbed her vision, punctured but did not divert her thoughts.

When she came to the garage a new idea struck her. This was the route the funeral had taken. She was moved by a mastering desire to visit Shagreen's grave. She was alive to the risk she ran. St. Martin-by-the-Brook was in the opposite direction to Bugle. The funeral would be over by now, but if she let the taxi take her first to the churchyard there was the chance she would meet the cortège returning. Against that she set the fact that none would suspect her of travelling that way. If she sat well back, told him to drive fast… besides which, there was the likelihood they would go back to school by the field-path. On second thoughts she was sure that was what they would do.

Both the garage proprietor and the man who drove her were blessed with indifference to their fares. Emma's age and inoffensive requests, including one for a cup of water, removed her at once from the category of interesting parties. In five minutes she was speeding along the road, giddy with the enormous relief of being conveyed somewhere instead of persuading her feet there against their will.

The main road ran past the lych gate of the church. Emma found she had to get the driver to help her alight. Nursing the flame of his cigarette, he watched her over cupped hands do an odd thing. Instead of entering the churchyard directly, she moved down the length of the yew hedge to a five-barred field gate below it. It was loosely chained and she was soon inside, skirting the churchyard boundary on her way to the small north gate that opened on the Martinmas meadows. She had to make sure that none of them still lingered in the burial ground.

The yard was empty, save for its dead. Not quite, perhaps—for the gravedigger, pausing in his labours, turned his back on them to chat to an acquaintance at the far wall, to chat, to spit on his hands, to share a timely joke. The dead came often, the living rarely enough.

In that quiet place where time had greened the crumbling stone that drew warmth to itself from the sun and gave it back as a kind of bloom on its many-lettered faces, where chestnut and lime and rustling beech bent to the wind, and only the grave yew stood firm, it was not hard to find Shagreen. The new mould glared against the grass, the flowers they had given her looked exotic, out of place. The smell of them hung in a warm cloud about the little space that held her. Here were the lilies looking like marble, wanting only a dome of glass to cover them, killing with their breath the tang of the chrysanthemums the school had sent; pink and white roses in a snug little, smug little wreath from Grace Aram and Nonny—none of it Shagreen. Emma stayed only a minute, long enough to read the lie, as yet unstained by clay, on the brass beneath: "Mary Wand, 1940." Before coming away she plucked from the west boundary wall a piece of hawkweed, slender, eager, soaring like fire against the cold autumn sky. It too had the virtue of long flowering. It too was like a small flame. She dropped it on Shagreen's coffin.

*

At ten minutes to four the platform at Bugle showed more bustle than it had a week ago. A troop train had just unloaded, and all up and down there was khaki waiting for its connections. Emma was grateful for the chance to lose herself in its midst; it was unlikely she would claim attention here.

Inquiry showed that she might either leave Bugle for Salisbury at 4:22 and wait an hour and a half in the city before going on to London, or spend the interval here and take the London train from Bugle. Emma's choice was made at once. Indeed, for her there had been no alternative to consider. Her one aim was to leave the neighbourhood as quickly as possible. Waiting in Salisbury held no known terrors.

There was time to get some tea, to give attention to her person. She was afraid she presented a strange spectacle, and viewed with alarm the discoloration spreading below her temple and round to the cheekbone. There was nothing to do about it, now. Her purpose would sustain her until the time came when she could get treatment and a good long sleep.

The restaurant was crowded, but two soldiers on the point of finishing a snack offered her their table. She felt ashamed of her too ready acceptance, though she was near fainting. She managed to give her order, then kept her head down, her eyes on the bag in her lap, while the hubbub and wisecracks and rattle of cups about her receded like the tide, surging past her ears at an immense distance.

She drank two cups of tea and forced herself to eat a biscuit, sitting there as long as she could, quite still, not looking about her, so as to rally her nerves for the journey ahead. When at length she lifted her eyes it was to see a man and woman at the next table watching her with anxious faces. They looked away as her glance met theirs. But when she had paid her bill and was tucking the Salisbury ticket away more safely in her bag, there was a sound beside her and, looking up, she saw the woman standing there.

"Forgive me," the newcomer said, her tone both abrupt and gentle, "but is anything wrong? Can I help you?"

She did not miss the fright that raced like a cloud across Emma's features.

"No, no—indeed, thank you. I have to catch the next train. A—a slight accident—that's all. I know—it *looks* ghastly—"

"Is no one with you?"

"I shall be all right, really—few changes."

"My husband is a doctor."

This was worse. Emma got shakily to her feet. She gripped the back of the chair with a firm hold. "I won't trouble him"—she saw that she had used the wrong phrase—"indeed, I don't need to." She looked again at the compassionate face, seeing it for the first time. "You are very kind—I have to go now. It's—it's a matter of life—and death…" She smiled, edged away, pleading silently to be allowed to escape.

The woman, with an expression of grave misgiving, slowly rejoined her husband who had risen too. They exchanged a swift, quiet look that did not elude Emma. She got out on to the platform as fast as she could.

There was a big crush here, though as her train steamed in it was evident that the majority were passengers for a later one. The incident in the tearoom had shaken her more than she knew. Spontaneous kindness from strangers is always a little unnerving. When it follows a murderous attack upon oneself, the suspicion of something worse against the person one has loved a lifetime, the shock of meeting with her shrouded body, it may be assumed that it is something more. Emma, pushed and swayed and almost driven into the train, felt the tears running down her face and was too weak to wipe them away.

She thought she heard her name called. But her ears were doing funny things just now. She must not fancy the worst because fear was at her elbow. Somehow she was in the carriage, sinking to a corner seat near the platform because she had not the strength to move further up. She prayed to appear inconspicuous, and closed her eyes against the stately, ridiculous measure the station buildings and all the press of people were executing about her. Her name was called again.

"Mees Beton-*ee*—oh, Mees Beton-*ee!*" It was Mam'selle. She opened her eyes to see Julie Lancret ruthlessly elbowing her way through the ranks of khaki. She saw her dark, tired, inscrutable face, the eyes fixed on her. She prayed for the train to move. Her prayer was answered, for the guard shook his green flag and the whistle tore through the shouting throng. The train lurched, first forward, then back, shook itself in a long tremor, and began to glide slowly—oh, how slowly—out. But Lancret was there, at the window, calling something it was impossible to hear, clutching at the frame, the muscles of her mouth working with that peculiarity an unheard talker's must convey. It made her look extraordinarily sinister.

"Your friend wants you," a woman sitting opposite Emma remarked snappishly, and lowered the window with a thud.

Lancret ran alongside and thrust her hand in. It held a small package hastily wrapped in brown paper, but untied.

"Yours," she gasped—"in the hand when you fall... I don' t'ink it is damaged... I give it to no one else... Oh, *ma chère—bon voyage!*"

Their fingers touched for an instant as Emma took the packet from her. Then she was receding, gone, like the world slipping from her grasp, as the train, gathering speed, left the station behind.

The woman opposite directed a look of reproof at Emma, and swung the window up with another thud.

Emma did not see the look. She was unwinding the paper from her mysterious parcel. Inside was a box that at one time had contained a cake of toilet soap. She raised the flap at the end and inserted her fingers. She drew out what was there and laid it on her lap. It was Shagreen's French watch in its skin case...

After everything had been put away tidily, and she sat with her gloved hands folded in her lap, her thoughts, exhausted, strayed to a kind of dreamland. The small part of her that was still alert and purposeful knew that she was light-headed, but was unable to do anything about it.

She caught herself whispering. It was inconsequent nonsense, but she could not stop. She made a determined effort to regain control, to speak aloud to the passenger in the opposite corner so as to quench this frightening monologue.

"You would call the Thames 'running water,' would you not?" she asked foolishly.

The woman's face that had seemed far away loomed suddenly near.

"I beg your pardon?" she said, frowning.

"And New Scotland Yard 'a tall grey building,'" Emma babbled, unheeding.

"I'm afraid I don't—"

"That will be it. A grey building by running water—Scotland Yard beside the Embankment—" Her voice faded.

The train took it up and beat it out when she could no longer speak. "Run-ning wat-er, run-ning wat-er..." The woman opposite looked highly nervous. She thanked her stars she got out at the next station. She had thought there was something funny from the first—that bandage, and the *foreigner* outside, their faces always so *un-English* and intense. But when it came to talking about Scotland Yard...

Chapter XV

RUNNING WATER

"And that," said Chief Inspector Dan Pardoe, "is *that*. Miss Betony is out of the picture for the next two weeks—*at least*. Got it? Yes, I know—she'd have been invaluable for this sleepwalking kid, as well as the best to tackle Lady Hart in the first place, but we must just lump 'em with the other interviews, Tommy, and hope for the best. The nursing home's definite on that point. Concussion—shock—internal bruising—and her playing about with it all like the very devil to get her story through to us. Women are tough—the old ones, anyway."

He turned the perpetual calendar to its right stop, October 3, and gave it a moody look. A fortnight—October 17. Detective-Sergeant Salt grunted.

"Well, she got her tale in first. Gosh, an' did I think she'd do it?"

"You thought she was crazy. Until you'd heard the evidence. We'll rope 'em in for the attempted murder of Emma Betony, never fear. We've got the witnesses—the Dorset police are seeing to that end of it for us. The story put up to Bold was that she tripped and fell headlong down the stairs. But when Miss Aram and the Frenchwoman got to her she was lying *on her face*, with nothing near that could have struck her, and bleeding from the *back of the head*."

"Huh. What's to do about the old woman?"

"Exhumation."

Salt cocked a homely eyebrow.

"It won't be hard, Tommy. Emma Betony is her sole surviving kin, and Pockett, the solicitor who's been the last to manage her affairs and dispense the quarterly allowance, hummed and hawed a bit, but he won't get in the way. I'm looking after him."

"'Usbands?" Salt said lugubriously. "Shagreen collected 'em, didn't she?"

"About as much to do with it as Noah's Ark. There were legal separations from the last three anyway—maybe those were all there were. They've no claims on her. Only one of 'em's known to be alive still—the old Earl of Wyvoe, and him ninety and over, and about forgotten he ever married. I don't believe anybody forgot quite, though. Take my word for it, it won't be necessary to find the rest. She was a friendless body, no kith and kin she knew where to find—and the temptation was too great for somebody."

"What for? Money?"

Pardoe shrugged. "The what-for is our job."

So the tale started to run, like water. It gathered volume and speed as it ran, it carried with it the flotsam and jetsam of other people's lives and characters, hopes and fears, affections, jealousies, hates, ambitions, all the impertinences of the living that Death no longer resents. So the tale ran its course—like water—like running water. Like the water of Thames that runs by New Scotland Yard.

Mr. Finch looked doubtful. Mrs. Finch fluttered helplessly and waited for Mr. Finch to speak. Mr. Finch spoke.

"It's one of those things one can't see the end of, officer. My daughter is extremely highly strung, now more than ever. If you would confine yourself to questions of—"

"Times and movements," Detective-Officer Crane said firmly. "Yes. Where she went, and when, and whom she saw. That's all."

"And *not*," wailed Mrs. Finch, "about ghosts and goblins and vampires and demons, and wizards and—*things*!"

"No, indeed, ma'am," said the surprised police officer. "We don't exercise any supervision over *them*." But in that he was mistaken.

Dolly was an unhealthy-looking child, a disagreeable white, with round, careful, pebbly eyes that never changed. Physically she looked less than her twelve years, in everything else far more.

"I'm always walking in my sleep," she said proudly. "They can't stop me. They couldn't stop me at Makeways. I used to get very cold feet."

He brought her cautiously round to Sunday night.

"Why did you hide in Mademoiselle Lancret's room?"

She blinked rapidly as if with some nervous affection of the lids, but did not remove her gaze. The effect was disconcerting. Mrs. Finch made noises of mother-love and moved forward. Mr. Finch restrained her.

"It was the nearest," Dolly said.

"Nearest to what?"

"It was the nearest place I could get to."

"Darling!" said Mrs. Finch.

"Don't waste time, Dorothy," said Mr. Finch.

"The nearest place you could get to from what?" said Detective-Officer Crane.

"From the witch," said Dolly.

Mrs. Finch gave a shriek that would not have strained a canary. Crane put out a hand.

"*Please*, ma'am—leave it to me. Yes, my dear—a witch. I see. And what one would that have been?" He affably suggested that warlocks and their covens formed the major portion of his acquaintance.

"We-ell," said Dolly, defying him to laugh, "it was Miss Aram, really. But the wind blew awful all the weekend, an' Miss Orpen says they're always about then—witches, I mean. They take different shapes—*I* might be one, this very minute. *You* might be one." She turned on her mother with sadistic glee. Mrs. Finch uttered another squeak. Mr. Finch rocked to and fro on his heels and looked at Mrs. Finch as though he expected an immediate change in her.

The patient Crane continued. "Where did you see Miss Aram, looking like a witch?"

"You mean a witch looking like Miss Aram," Dolly corrected. "She was coming out of the old lady's room—the old lady who died. We sent her *enormous* bronze chrysanthemums, an' the other old lady sent a wreath too, but *ours* was the biggest, an' Aileen—she's our prefect—Aileen said—"

He got her back to Miss Aram coming from Miss Wand's room.

"She looked *dreadful*," Dolly said. She looked at her mother again. Mrs. Finch squeaked. Dolly smiled. Mr. Finch scratched the back of his head.

"How could you see what she looked like?" Crane asked.

"There's a window on the landing—all ghosty," said Dolly, licking her lips. "Here"—she went on in a burst of generosity, "I'll tell you *everything*."

Pardoe sorted it out later. It was a curious tale, with a flavour nasty enough to satisfy even Dolly. It had started with one of her somnambulistic exercises, time unspecified—but not for long. She must have made her way, past the turn to Miss Orpen's room, up the stairs to that part of the west wing where Miss Aram, Mam'selle, and Miss Wand slept, because when she woke—as she sometimes did on these excursions—she was on the landing by Mam'selle's door, with the wan square of the window shining on her face. Its glimmer of starlight was probably what waked her, unless, thought Pardoe, she knew what she was doing all the time—he wouldn't put it past her. There were sounds, she said, in Miss Wand's room. They frightened her—*terribly*—and her *feet* were so cold—and she sank down, half dead with fright, by one of the big chests where nobody could see her. There were still sounds from Miss Wand's room. What sounds? Voices? No, not voices. Soft, slurry sounds like clothes moving, not like a person at all. And while she crouched there the clock—the big one in the hall—chimed, and then struck three. On the last stroke Miss Wand's door opened—*oh*, how frightened she was then, and her feet *were* so cold—and the witch came out. Dressed in Miss Aram's clothes, of course. What? Oh, dressing gown and pyjamas. That's *nothing* to a witch. She looked straight across at Mam'selle's door, and her face was *awful*. (Squeak, mummy.) She didn't see Dolly, and Dolly held her breath, and her feet were *so* cold. And then she did a funny thing—she meant the witch did a funny thing. What was that? She turned, and very softly locked Miss Wand's door. And then she stalked by and went into the passage beyond, but not back to her own room. How did Dolly know that? Because she would have heard the door close. And she heard her go downstairs into the other part of the house. And that was why she hid in Mam'selle's room. Why? *Why*, because Miss Aram—the witch seemed temporarily to have gone out of her—was somewhere about the house, and so she didn't dare go back to the dorm. So she got under Mam'selle's bed, and there she stayed, and Mam'selle came in and never knew, and she went to sleep till the screams woke her. She didn't know what time that was ("4:15 they began, by every account," Pardoe supplied), but there was a flashlight making awful corpse candles all over the room—

"Making *what*?"

"Corpse candles," Dolly repeated loudly. "Don't you even know what *they* are?"

—and Miss Orpen pinching Mam'selle's clothes (awful frumpy they are too) and skipping off with them, and later on, oh, *much* later on, Mam'selle came in. And Dolly came out from under the bed, and cried, and told her everything, and stayed there a bit. And her feet were so *cold*. And Mam'selle said not to talk about it yet, but to "hold the tongue," only she hadn't said not to tell the police. And after that they put her to bed and made her stay there, and there she was till mummy and daddy came Tuesday to fetch her.

"And are your feet cold?" Pardoe inquired.

"Not half," Crane grinned. "So's Mrs. Finch's."

It fitted with Julie Lancret's account.

She had not been able to sleep Sunday night. Special reason for insomnia? Yes. But not rare. It was always so, now that war had come again. Soon after midnight she heard talking from Miss Wand's room. No, not conversation—a single voice, rambling, occasionally high-pitched. It went on for more than half an hour. She did nothing about it. She did not think it was any business of hers. She had never spoken to Miss Wand. She gathered that the old lady was—what you call it?—queer, just a little, but she had never thought about her. She had not thought about any of them—till it was too late. She was sorry. Soon after half-past twelve everything was silent. Again, however, she did not sleep. At half-past two she thought she heard a sound on the landing. She opened her door and went out there and heard Miss Wand's door being closed. Nobody appeared, so it must have been done from the inside. It was as a rule a door that stood partly open. She thought nothing more about it until she heard Dolly Finch's story.

While she stood on the landing, however, she fancied she could smell fire. It was only faint, but there was the unmistakable pungency of something burning. She put on her dressing gown and followed her nose. The smell grew stronger as she passed Miss Aram's door. She thought it her duty to tell her, especially as she was so near. She tapped on her door and, receiving no reply, went in. She saw that the windows were blacked out and, after calling Miss Aram three times, she turned on the light. There was no one in the room; the bed had been turned down, but not slept in. She came out again, putting the room into darkness and shutting the door, and roamed the house trying to locate the smell of fire. She could not do so. It was true that at that hour it was only faint. It was after 4:30 it became so apparent in the west wing and on the dormitory floor. She heard no one about, everything seemed peaceful.

But she was uneasy. Why? Because of so many people sleeping in the house, and a few of them, she understood, addicted to strange behaviour. Fire was not an impossible result of their carelessness. She visited the bathroom, and was there when the clock struck three, and for a few minutes afterwards ("Explains how she missed meeting Miss Aram, also roaming," Pardoe threw in), and when she returned to her room she had no idea that Dolly Finch was under the bed. She dozed then till a little after four by her watch, when a sound woke her—she could not be sure what, but thought it might be the blind at the landing window. The gale the night before had dislodged it, and the roller bumped. She went out to see, and smelt burning again. She went across the landing and, with memories of the chatter some hours ago, tried Miss Wand's door to see if she was all right. To her astonishment it would not open; the usual trouble was it would not shut. She turned the handle backwards and forwards, but the door was locked. She concluded that Miss Wand, exasperated, had turned the key to keep it closed. She hurried to Miss Aram's room, and did what she had done before—with the same results. No one was there, and the bed had still not been disturbed. Instead of going down the stairs, which would have taken her by Miss Orpen's passage, she turned into the servants' quarters, in case the smell came from the kitchen, and made her way down the service stairs. She was down there when the screaming started. She had seen no one on her travels, nor located the fire—*not then*, she remarked grimly.

The rest of her account corroborated those of Miss Betony, Miss Deakin, Miss Orpen and Dolly. As to the child, she had told her to keep silent partly because she wanted to discourage Dolly's excitement, partly because she thought there was something odd going on in the house and that it was unwise for the children to blab unofficially about the movements of the staff. But, aware that Dolly was not to be relied upon to keep silent, it was she who, on Monday afternoon when the others were picnicking, had taken her walk to Underbarrow and sent the wire to Mr. Finch.

"But why did you suggest the child was unsafe?"

Mam'selle flushed darkly. "Zat make it sairtain zat zay take 'er off wit' dem." When she saw that they did not believe her, she added without being pressed: "Well—Mees Wand has died. Monday I know that. Her door was locked at four in ze morning—Dolly say at three. But when zay find her at eight it is *not* locked. I am alarmed."

"As a matter of fact," said Nurse Edgeworth crisply, "it was I who made the first move. I didn't wait to be told to go. I recognized the inevitable, said I was going, and then was hurled out before I had time to change my mind. There was no other course open to me, even though I had been with her three years."

"Why not?" Pardoe asked, interested. He liked the look of her cool, steady young face, and the unruffled air with which she had studied his card.

"Because it's not a bit of good flying in the face of an aversion of that sort—which gets to be an *idée fixe* in these cases of mild paranoia. By staying on I would have done a great deal more harm than good, though there seems to have been enough and to spare without me. What I really find astonishing is that Miss Thurloe should have died after all."

Pardoe checked an exclamation. "What makes you think Miss Thurloe is dead?"

She stared. "I beg your pardon? Isn't that why you're here? You tell me you're investigating the death of an old lady who was a patient at Martinmas Nursing Home—and then you question me about Miss Thurloe."

"Of course. A reasonable inference. But Miss Thurloe is very much alive."

"Then?"

"It is Miss Wand who died."

"Ah." Nurse Edgeworth said it softly. "Now I see. I am so sorry. But I'm not much surprised."

"No? Why not, please?"

"Miss Wand suffered from cardiac disease of the heart—not badly developed when I was with her, though she had attacks from time to time. And the strain of that sickness, of course, had a bad effect on her."

"Which sickness?"

"There was only one all the time I was at Martinmas. The week Dr. Fielding went away. He was worried."

"What? About Miss Wand?"

Nurse Edgeworth nodded. "He was even afraid she had taken poison. Perhaps food poisoning of some sort, though no one else had the symptoms. She was horribly sick, you see. If it was poison, then the violence of the sickness undoubtedly saved her. Dr. Fielding took away specimens, and samples of the food and drink she had taken that day."

"With what result?"

"Nothing came of it. Two days later the doctor underwent a serious operation. It was thought that he would not live. Happily, though, I hear he has recovered."

"Happily, indeed," Pardoe said. "Tell me, Miss Edgeworth, when Dr. Bold took over the practice, to what extent did he consult you about this alleged poisoning of Miss Wand?"

"He didn't. Don't misunderstand me. I was engaged at the nursing home to look after Miss Thurloe, not Miss Wand. Miss Wand didn't require constant attention, or, perhaps I should say, didn't demand it. But I liked her, and I kept an eye on her. And when the school took over Martinmas, and Miss Thurloe wanted me to stay on with her, I was a bit more attentive to Miss Wand than I'd been before, because

I guessed the old lady would be feeling lonely. But she was never my patient in the professional sense. So when Dr. Bold came I said nothing to him first. I waited for him to refer to her sickness—I suppose Dr. Fielding gave him particulars—and when he didn't, but simply continued to call on her, I didn't consider it my business to bring up the subject. He was clearly not puzzled—and Miss Wand wasn't once sick again during the whole fortnight up to my going."

Pardoe was silent a moment. "So when you left you'd had no professional discussion with anyone about Miss Wand's illness?"

"Only with Dr. Fielding—who'd had to go away almost as soon as it happened. You see, in any case it was Miss Thurloe who filled the picture the last week I was there. But when I went out so abruptly I do remember feeling relief at the thought that Miss Wand would still have with her the maid who was devoted to her."

"Bertha Glass?" Pardoe inquired. "She was at Martinmas for exactly two days after you'd gone."

Nurse Edgeworth opened her eyes wide. "Why, what happened to her?"

"Miss Thurloe turned her out with as little ceremony as she'd used for you."

"What a shame! She was as much Miss Wand's maid as hers, and far more devoted to Miss Wand. Anybody would be, of course. Inspector—it's inquisitive of me, I know—why are the police interested in Miss Wand's death?"

"There is some reason for thinking it was not from natural causes."

"Not angina?"

"Exactly. I can't be more explicit at this stage. You will hear from us again, though. You may be able to give very material help."

"May I? I would do anything to make things right for Miss Wand, alive or dead. One felt like that about her. I admit I should find it hard to believe that she took her own life."

Pardoe checked himself again. "Why do you say that?"

"She was the gayest, most lighthearted, bravest of women. She had no patience with those who shrink from old age. She often said she was so grateful for having had a full and happy life with never a boring minute in it, that she had no time to think about being old. Heart trouble is apt to bring depression in its train, you know, but Miss Wand was never cast down. She had a gallant spirit."

"Those are warm words, Miss Edgeworth. It will please you to know that Miss Wand did not take her own life."

"Then—what sort of accident—?"

"No sort."

She gave him a long, intent look. She said slowly, "Not suicide—not accident... Then—"

"We suspect murder."

"Oh—no."

"Let us hope not. But now you understand why you may be of help to us."

Nurse Edgeworth was white, but still collected. "I never thought—there was no idea—I'm sure that Dr. Fielding never suspected—"

"Never mind that now. There are ways in which you can be immediately useful."

"I'll do my best," she said simply.

"First then—was anything prescribed for Miss Wand's heart trouble?"

"Yes. Nitroglycerine. She took it in tablets of one-hundredth of a grain."

"Were these administered to her, or did she keep them handy and take one when she felt an attack coming on?"

"Yes—I mean, she took them herself. I believe she had some digestion tabloids round mealtimes too. But the nitroglycerine, I know, she kept on her person, and, at night, beside her bed."

"And *angina pectoris* gives warning of its onset?"

"As a rule. In Miss Wand's case always, I think, up to the time she fell sick, because the heart trouble had not reached a very serious stage—but after the sickness she had a nasty attack—heart attack, I mean."

"But in the ordinary way you'd expect her to be able to have recourse to the tablets in time?"

"If she had them with her, or close to her, yes. There's always the chance of the tube being mislaid."

"Yes. Now for the next thing: during the three years you were at Martinmas, do you know if Miss Wand made a will?"

Nurse Edgeworth looked at him with fresh interest. She was silent for some seconds, considering, her brows drawn together. "Strange you should ask that—I mean, I wouldn't have thought of it again. That was why her lawyer visited her—when would it have been?—oh, July, I think. Nearly a month before she was taken bad. I couldn't say positively that a will was made then, but I can tell you what she said to me the day before his visit."

"What was that?"

"I'd looked in to say good-night to her—I always did that. She was kittenish and amusing at that hour. 'What would you think of a giddy damsel like me making her will, nurse?' she said. I said something to the effect that it wasn't a bad thing to do whether you were young or old. 'Ah, you with your orderly mind,' she mocked me. 'You're every bit as bad as Miss Deakin'—that was the school matron. She went on, 'It's true, mine won't give me much trouble'—she meant her will—'for I've only one relative in the world and I don't know whether she's alive or dead!' She bubbled with laughter, and added, 'And it won't give any trouble to her either!'"

"What did you take her to mean by that?"

"Why—nothing in particular. She simply looked mischievous when she said it."

"Do you know what the reference to Miss Deakin meant?"

Nurse Edgeworth hesitated.

Pardoe said promptly, "The truth won't hurt."

"It's really not important. I ran into Miss Deakin herself as I was coming out of the room. She said, 'Is Miss Wand in bed yet? She must go to sleep early, because she's got an important day in front of her. She's going to be a good girl and get her will made all nice and proper.' She was talking loudly, half to me, half to Miss Wand. It was simply her way. I didn't say anything, because it was obviously Miss Wand's private business. I gathered she'd made up her mind to get the will drawn up on the matron's advice, and that that was what she had meant by remarking that Miss Deakin had an orderly mind."

Pardoe made a noncommittal sound. He turned a leaf of his notebook.

Nurse Edgeworth glanced at her wrist watch. "In five minutes," she said quietly, "I go on duty. Is there anything else I can tell you?"

"I'll be quick. A few minutes ago you made a remark I don't understand. You said that what really astonished you was that Miss Thurloe had died *after all*. Why?"

Nurse Edgeworth looked a little impatient for the first time. "But then you know that I didn't understand you were referring to Miss Wand."

"Sorry—let me put it this way. Supposing it *had* been Miss Thurloe who died, why should it have been astonishing?"

"Oh—why, because there was never anything wrong with her."

There was a short hard silence in which they looked at one another.

"But the bouts of sickness?" Pardoe said. "The traces of poison found?"

"Both true," said Nurse Edgeworth, "and both entirely unrelated. Miss Thurloe *was* sick—there's no harm in my saying so since you know already—traces of poison *were* found. But Dr. Bold established that there was no connection between the two things."

The inspector made no effort to conceal his surprise. "Then why the sickness?"

The nurse shrugged. "That wasn't uncommon for Miss Thurloe. As long as I knew her she was a hearty, indiscriminate feeder— frankly, gross would be more correct. The first, and worst, sick turn that week was simply her stomach revolting against high-handed treatment. Afterwards—well, you probably know as well as I that sickness can be produced at will without the aid of emetics. Doctor and I both thought that's what the old lady was doing. She blamed it on me, of course."

"But why did she do it?"

"To win sympathy, which she thought she was losing. That—and jealousy. There was always a certain amount of rivalry between the two old ladies, on Miss Thurloe's side, that is. And Miss Wand had had this really frightening turn only a week or so before which had naturally perturbed us all, from Miss Aram down—and I suppose Miss Thurloe imagined she was getting herself rather less than her share of attention."

"Yet," Pardoe pointed out, "the poison was found."

"Of course it was. In dregs of food and drink, some of which Miss Thurloe had taken—*and some that she hadn't.* But the doctor was satisfied that on none of these occasions had any poison entered Miss Thurloe's stomach."

Pardoe nodded, his eyes bright. Nurse Edgeworth noticed that he did not ask her to account for the curious independence of events.

"One more point," he said, "and then you must go. I'm grateful for what you've told me. Just this—have you ever heard the name Shagreen?"

Nurse Edgeworth looked taken aback at the apparent irrelevance.

"Mary Shagreen," the inspector prompted.

"No." She shook her head. She said again, but slowly, "No. Yet—it's like something—I don't know what—something dreamed and forgotten."

"You come close to the truth," Pardoe said. "Something dreamed—and forgotten."

Beneath the long verandah of the convalescent home, a sun-trap for the first autumn days, an old man seated in a low chair with a table beside it fumbled to regain the thread of his speech.

The inspector looked again at the frail, tired, colourless face, the skin from which all resilience had gone, strung with a multitude of delicate lines, eyes clouded by that gentle detachment that belongs to the last months of life, indifferent to everything but this unhurried decline in the declining sunshine. It was not compassion only that moved Pardoe. He was afraid that this man would die before a jury could listen to his deadly, faltering words. They had the words, however. Moreover, he reflected, jotting down the analyst's name and address, they had evidence that was very much alive.

"My—my memory serves me ill now," the thin old voice went on. "But Dr. Bold will find the address for you, and confirm it."

"Thank you. Will you tell me, please, if there had been anything wrong with Miss Thurloe in the summer, up to the date of your own illness?"

"Nothing—nothing. Only the usual delusions common to her mode of life. It was Miss Wand who required attention."

"Exactly. And now, Dr. Fielding, did anyone besides Nurse Edgeworth know that you had procured for analysis samples in connection with Miss Wand's sickness?"

"No one. The nurse got them for me. As it was then mere suspicion on my part I did not want to alarm those in charge of the school. To—to make a fuss immediately, you understand, inspector, was unnecessary—with nobody else affected in the same way as Miss—Miss—Miss Wand, even if it were food poisoning, which was all I had thought it then. So I judged it best to say nothing till I had a report of the findings. It might so easily turn out to be a mare's nest."

He stopped to draw quick, shallow breaths. The wrinkled hands with their glistening knuckles and long, ropy veins trembled on the arms of the chair.

"No—no—nobody knew," he repeated faintly, stopping all at once to give Pardoe a bright, doubtful look as if he had been caught saying the wrong thing. Pardoe gave him a minute to recover from the effort.

"Dr. Fielding," he said gently, at length, "can you remember what the analyst's findings were?"

"Yes—yes—yes." He nodded testily on each repetition of the word. "Arsenic... arsenic in the remains of the food and in the vomit. It is all in the report—" He gave a long quivering sigh.

Pardoe saw that it would be unwise to press him further. "One other thing, sir," he said quickly, "can you now recall what day it was you received the analyst's report?"

"Alas, yes." He pressed the balls of his fingers to his temples, moistening his lips. "I am much to blame—I—I—it was the day I was found insensible in my surgery. They took me away—no time to—no time for anything. Dr. Bold—I had arranged a fortnight before for Dr. Bold to take over, but at the last I had to go hurriedly. I did not see my locum—he came in on the evening following my departure... I did not think about Miss Wand again... It has all been most—unfortunate..."

His voice had become a shadow, defending, excusing, lamenting the still more shadowy past for which he no longer cared.

"Don't blame yourself," Pardoe said, rising. "As a matter of fact, Dr. Fielding, the prompt way in which you acted upon suspicion last August may turn out to be the most helpful factor in the solution of the case."

"And that's not short of the truth," he said to Salt, when they left the old man to resume his quiet nodding in the sun, the few rings that an announcement of suspected murder had made in his standing pond of thought already fading to stagnation again. "If, unconsciously, Dr. Fielding was one of the chief—what shall I say?—stimuli to the original attack on Miss Wand, he made amends, again unconsciously, by not working out to plan—the poisoner's plan."

Salt looked argumentative. "Seems to me he was just one of those old johnnies past his job, an' not willin' to say so. Now if Bold 'ad been the doc from the start—"

"Things wouldn't look so good for us now."

"No?"

"No. Think it over, Tommy."

"What time approximately did Mary Sha—Miss Wand die, doctor?"

"Not before midnight—not a minute after 1:30. Believe it or not," Bold flung at him. "And that row they had Sunday morning—Miss Aram tells me she thinks high words brought on the attack. They would too."

Pardoe looked contemplative. "About fourteen hours later? Isn't angina quicker on the mark than that?"

He did not wait for an answer, though. Bold was sore, as only an egotist can smart, at the superbly contrived trick that had been played on him, and rubbing it in, Pardoe reminded himself, like recrimination, was futile.

"Died, say, at 1:30—to be as nice to 'em as we can," he went on. "Door locked at 3 A.M.—"

"On the word of a brat."

"All right. I'll be as nice to *you* as I can. Door locked at 4 A.M. on the word of Mam'selle Lancret, who tried it. That do?"

"Nothing will do," the furious Bold groaned. He could not accept defeat. "You're actually telling *me* I've been led by the nose by a pack of women—"

"Not a pack. One to be exact——"

"——since the day I came?" He swore roundly. "That it was never intended to do any harm to Miss Thurloe, yet she *wasn't* doing it herself? That Miss Wand was the chosen victim from the beginning, even before I took over? Then why the *dev*——"

"All right, all right. Keep your hair on. This is how we see it. Dr. Fielding is—was—an old man, a very sick man." Pardoe hesitated, recognizing delicate ground. "He pluckily kept on, perhaps not altogether wisely, saying little or nothing about his health. It was clear he wasn't at all well, but his abrupt departure came as a complete surprise. Before he gave up one attack *had* been made on Miss Wand, in the belief that it would be overlooked by Dr. Fielding. If he had been able to continue in his practice, Miss Thurloe would never have come into the game at all. When Dr. Fielding went, it meant a scrapping of the old scheme directed straightway against Miss Wand, and the adoption of a new one as soon as Miss Thurloe obliged by being sick."

"But *why?*"

"Man," cried Pardoe in the heat of his exasperation, "must I underline everything—hand out bouquets—explain in terms of ABC? *You* don't have to be sore about things—it was because your reputation travelled ahead of you that it became necessary to 'lay off' Miss Wand. You would pretty soon have detected a serious intent to murder, while age and sickness, it had been hoped, would cloud Dr. Fielding's judgement——"

"I get you," the doctor said grimly.

"Glad of it. So Miss Thurloe was chosen——"

"I don't get you there. Why her? Why wasn't I supposed to do the detecting there?"

"You were supposed to—but, detect you never so wisely, all you'd turn up would be spoof. A phoney murder—a phoney suicide—you pays your money and you takes your choice. Isn't that exactly what you did find?"

Bold agreed. He swore again. "And the real thing being planned under my nose—to be done under my nose. *In*solence!"

Pardoe smothered a grin. "Exactly. Because you weren't interested in Miss Wand. Nobody was—much."

"And I *was* interested in Miss Thurloe—infernally. It—seemed not to compare for interest with any other case in the house."

"It was meant not to. Actually, there was nothing interesting about it. All fake—except the old lady herself."

"The biggest fake of all," Bold said.

"Her terrors, I mean. She was picked upon because, with incipient persecution mania, she was the ideal phoney victim."

"I thought she was doing it herself, you know."

"But you let it leak out it might be somebody else?"

"Oh yes—just in case. Like the bloke who took off his hat to the devil. *If* somebody was trying to bump her off—and making, by the way, an incredibly bungled job of it—I'd have 'em know I was alive to all the tricks. I was bothered, I'll admit. I see now how I played into their hands by *letting* myself be bothered with the case. But I couldn't help being—you see, it *had* to be her doing, and yet it couldn't be, it was all out of character."

"Meaning?"

"That persecution mania of her type," Bold said, "isn't marked by suicidal tendencies. That *was* puzzling—it interested me enormously, kept me engaged on her case. *If* you're right—lor' what a fool I've been! *If* you're right—why, that's why she was picked on, because she was terrified of dying, because she'd demand to be saved, because she'd pull the place down about our ears if she thought somebody was going to so much as stick a pin in her—because, in short, she'd monopolize the doctor's attention!"

"You've got it at last," Pardoe said. "Now you know why she never *took* poison. They never intended her to. It only had to look as if she did."

"But how did they prevent her?"

"By planting it in dregs. By *making* dregs if there weren't any—like pouring water away except for the last spoonful—which nobody would bother to drink—and introducing a heavy dose of arsenic to it. It was done when they'd slipped the nurse a sleeping draught, or planted in remains of her food brought down to the kitchen, or in the confusion following her screaming bouts. Don't you see, those screams—they were *cause*, not effect, of the poison? The opportunity of her screaming was seized upon to suggest to you that poison had caused it. Sometimes, Nurse Swain said, she screamed and there was no poison found. Of course—it wouldn't have been easy to scatter it round every time."

"But Miss Thurloe must have known there was another party at work. *She* didn't have sleeping draughts."

"Of course she didn't. Of course she knew. Right at the start, when she was sick from overeating, there was somebody—somebody kind, warning her against a poisoner—showing her what to do to prevent herself from being poisoned—didn't Nurse Swain hear her in her sleep telling somebody to pour away all the water from the bottle? Somebody who swore her to secrecy in her own interests, so they might the more easily catch this wicked poisoner. So she shouted she'd been poisoned, mistrust, fear and hate were sown in her for Nurse Edgeworth, for Bertha Glass, for unknown, unnamed people whose suspected existence and determination to kill her kept her in perpetual terror. Not a pretty game, eh? A weak-minded old woman... But not mistrust or hate or fear of you, doctor—opposite feelings must be fostered there, so that you'd be constantly in demand. So that it would never occur to you that anyone was even thinking about Miss Wand."

"Suffering snakes!... And who d'ye say she really was?"

"Who?"

"Miss Wand."

"Mary Shagreen. A famous dancer."

"Oh… ah. I've heard—something or other. My granddad had picture postcards of her."

"Probably. About the arsenic—"

"Analysis showed every time it had no commercial colouring matter prescribed—no charcoal, indigo, soot. It was white arsenic. That was another funny thing—meant it couldn't have been bought through ordinary, legitimate channels."

"We're dealing with that. Easy to find, wasn't it?"

"I should say. Highly insoluble—especially in the water bottles, the favourite vessels. There was always a noticeable sediment—no attempt at concealment, which, *if* you're right, again fits in. I was meant not to overlook it."

"And what about Miss Pollard?"

"Arsenic—same stuff. In the bottle. The matron had her suspicions and got hold of it. A nasty dose and, unlike the old woman's, actually taken. I'm wondering why, though."

"She was friendly," Pardoe said, "with a girl named Linda Hart, who was expelled. She's told us she let fall on the Friday she was going to see her before Linda left Blandford. It got to the wrong ears. The intention wasn't to kill, but to incapacitate. She was a favourite of the old lady—Miss Thurloe, that is—and there was no objection to involving her in the general mystery."

"To make out it was suicide she was trying on?" Bold raised his eyebrows. "In a fit of repentance after having a go at the old woman?"

"P'raps. Surer to say they'd got her where they wanted her—in bed, instead of gadding off to Blandford and most likely hearing what she shouldn't."

"I wish you wouldn't keep saying 'they,'" Bold said peevishly. "It's catching, too."

"P'raps I won't," said Pardoe, "after Miss Wand's been exhumed."

*

The maid said, "The door wasn't locked. It wasn't even closed. It was standing open an inch or so. It was nearly always like that, or wider."

"That was the way of it," Nonny agreed. "It was wider still when I got up there a couple of minutes later, because the girl in her fright had shut it too smartly, so it swung in further. No, I didn't see if the key was on the inside or not—it certainly wasn't on the outside. I didn't know anything about the door being locked then, so I wasn't looking for the key."

"It doesn't matter," Pardoe said. "Only it would be more interesting if it wasn't there at all. Where was Miss Wand, and how was she lying?"

"In bed, on her back. The bedclothes on top were all topsy-turvy. The sheet and blankets were between her hands."

"What do you mean—'between her hands'?"

"Just that."

"Show me."

Nonny gave him a sharp look. "How? Don't I make myself plain?"

"You mean she was clutching the clothes? Mightn't you expect that with angina?"

"Yes—to the last question. No—to the first. That's what you'd expect. And that's what it looked like. But she wasn't clutching—she wasn't even holding. Her fingers were curled over the clothes, and when we drew the things away we didn't have to touch her hands. There was no grip to loosen."

Pardoe was thoughtful. "A smart bit of observation. Anything else strike you?"

"Two or three things."

"Tell me."

"Her eyes—they were partially open. The pupils were about as contracted as I've ever seen."

"Well?"

"I've done a good bit of nursing. I've seen more than one case the worse for an overdose of bromide. She looked like that to me."

"Look here," said Pardoe. "You made these deductions the morning of Miss Wand's death. Why didn't you voice your suspicions that everything wasn't all right?"

"I did," said Nonny smugly.

"When?"

"To Dr. Bold—that morning. I told him about the eyes, and about the nitroglycerine—you don't know about that yet—but I never got as far as the bedclothes. He wouldn't let me."

"Oh! What did he say?"

Nonny sighed. "He said, 'Woman, because you've pulled it off once, it's no good thinking you can do it every time.'"

"What had you pulled off once?"

"I'd an idea about Susan—Susan Pollard. I didn't believe her illness was plain gastric. I passed over to the doc her water bottle with the drop left in the bottom. Arsenic was found. Just my luck."

"What was?"

"Oh, I didn't put it there in the first place. I mean, that winning fluke was just my luck. Just too bad. Doctors don't like you to tell 'em about their job—not Bold's sort, anyway. I'd been right about Susan, and he wasn't having any more of it. He thinks I talk too much, and he's no opinion of women anyway. I haven't much myself. And by the time I brought these rummy facts to his notice he'd already passed Miss Wand's death as plain heart after hearing the tale I told you just now—about Wandy going off the deep end because we bossed her over wanting to go to church. Coming after her Friday heart attack, an' all. So wild horses weren't going to make him change and say she'd died of anything else."

"I understand," Pardoe said. He had met over and over again that particular form of medical obstinacy that rejects a layman's suggestion on sight.

"And I will say," Nona Deakin conceded, "he had his hands pretty well full Monday with moving Miss Thurloe. As it happened—and, golly, I can't think why it did—she went off like a regular lambie-pie, but not knowing that beforehand through the lack of all previous experience, you might say, we had to prepare for the worst. To give everybody their due, there really wasn't time to think hard about anything else."

"I don't suppose there was. But did Miss Thurloe *have* to go Monday? Why not later?"

"Miss Aram insisted on getting her out then and there when we knew Wandy had died. She'd've been going in any case, but that hurried it on. Come to think of it, you couldn't risk that yelling and screaming with a corpse in the house awaiting burial, now could you?"

"Agreed," Pardoe said sincerely. But how devilishly simple... how devilishly clever! Opportunism... the building up of a superb piece of spoof... again opportunism... all the way diversion, diversion, diversion. The only people whose attention counted having their interest diverted to what didn't matter.

"What about the nitroglycerine?" he asked.

"Oh—just *funny*, that was. She always had it by her, you see, in case of attack. Friday, the old tube was finished. She had a new one. It was by her. But it never was started. I found it on the table close to her bed, close to her hand. She hadn't had one tablet."

"Isn't it possible the attack was too quick and too severe for her to do anything about it?"

"I don't believe it," Nonny said stoutly. "She *always* managed to get one. There'd have been signs she tried, at least—the tube on the floor, or something."

Then, Nonny reported later, the bloke from Scotland Yard asked her a funny thing.

"Do you know the name of Mary Shagreen?"

She stared, shook her head. "Who's she—a film star?"

"She may have been," he assented grudgingly, "if she'd been born fifty years later. As it was, she was a famous dancer."

"Oh. Afraid my dancing days are over. What's she to do with us?"

"Mary Wand was Mary Shagreen."

"What—*Wandy*...?"

Pardoe nodded.

Nonny burst out laughing. "Little—Wandy... I'm jiggered... Well, well—live and learn."

Lady Hart was cold, but not obstructive. When Pardoe, with all the tact at his command, emphasized the importance of what Linda might have to say, she was neither.

"I'm afraid you will be disappointed, though, inspector. I was horrified, I'm bound to say, when Linda admitted to trafficking with this—this person on that unfortunate old lady's behalf. But knowing that, you know all." She added with admirable restraint, "I can quite understand that the school thought it outrageous. In a way I'm glad they did. But it wasn't right to send her away so summarily. My brother and his wife are both abroad, with no chance of returning home while the war lasts—and I feel very much the responsibilities I bear to Linda."

When he looked at the girl's cool, intelligent, unrepentant face, Pardoe understood what she meant.

"My aunt is naturally upset," she said. "But I've nothing to be sorry about. Crystal-gazing and so on doesn't delude me. It's for the old. And if it gives pleasure to old ladies, why shouldn't they have it?" Her voice held the scathing indulgence that is youth's substitute for tolerance.

"I won't answer that one," Pardoe said. "I'm a policeman. But I thought the trouble was that *you* mixed yourself up in it?"

"I didn't have my fortune told."

"No? The teller didn't impress you, perhaps?"

"Yes," she said honestly, "he did. I think Dr. Ambrosio is a remarkable man. That wasn't why I wouldn't have a reading. We'd been told we weren't to, and I kept my promise. I went only for Miss Thurloe. I tried to make Miss Aram understand the difference, but she wouldn't see any."

"Were you fond of Miss Thurloe?" he asked.

Miss Hart lifted her brows. "No—I wasn't fond of Miss Thurloe." Her adolescent reserve managed to convey that being fond of people was mere weakness. "That didn't enter into it. She wasn't well—she was lonely—she was old—"

Hang it all, thought Pardoe, conscious of his own prematurely white locks, is this the way we're to be patronized?

"And she was devoted to your friend, Miss Pollard?" he said aloud.

"She liked Miss Pollard," Linda said guardedly. But he had seen a flicker of anxiety go over her face. She watched him with a slight frown.

"I don't understand—you didn't come here only to ask me if I was fond of Miss Thurloe?"

Too late he saw that the circumlocution he was used to practising among the upper classes had been unnecessary here. Linda studied him with polite amusement while he tried to retrieve the situation.

"I'll get to the point, Miss Hart—there are a few questions I'd like you to answer, please. First, was there any occasion when the man calling himself the Great Ambrosio gave you something to take back to Miss Thurloe?"

"Only her own things—a handkerchief once, once a locket, the last time a brooch—with a written message wrapped round it after the psychometry had been performed on it."

"Nothing else?"

"Never. I watched all the time. There was no chance of slipping in anything I wouldn't have noticed."

"Right. Now will you tell me if you got a phone call from Martinmas early Monday morning?"

Linda was cold. "You probably know I did."

"I *think* you did," Pardoe said frankly. "Who sent it, please?"

"Miss Pollard. It was nothing at all—I mean, nothing at all important. She'd been ill since Friday. I'd not known. She was ringing the doctor for Miss Thurloe at 4:30 that morning, and she took the chance of putting a call through to me. That was all."

"Good!" said Pardoe. "That clears up a point that was puzzling." He went quickly on to his one and only piece of bluff: "Why exactly were you expelled?"

She had not expected that. She flushed slowly. Her eyes that had been critical and steady grew warm with remembered anger. Her composure was gone.

"It was so—so beastly unjust!" The debutante was gone, the schoolgirl back. "To send me away—like that—not even the chance to speak a word to Susan—for something she was doing herself!"

"Who—Miss Aram?"

"Yes. She went to consult Ambrosio too. She was there the day I got found out."

"You saw her?"

"No—not then."

"How did you know she was there?"

"I saw her gloves on the table when he let me in."

Pardoe looked at her with close interest. "You are sure they were Miss Aram's—there was no mistake?"

"I know them well—grey dogskin with black stitching on the backs. I can't even prove it... there's only my word... I'd thought before that was enough—"

"P'raps," Pardoe said gently, "somebody else had sent them along to be psychometrized?"

"Oh no," said Linda. "That couldn't be."

"Why not?"

"Because I was back at Bugle ten minutes before Miss Aram. I'd cycled. I hadn't time to take my things off. She caught me with Miss Thurloe's brooch and the reading made from it—and she was wearing the gloves I'd seen on his table."

"All right," said Pardoe. "What day was this?"

"Last Tuesday week—in the afternoon."

"And what day did you leave Makeways?"

"The next—Wednesday evening."

"Yes. Now, can you account yourself for the lapse of time between? It's said you were expelled at once, but though you left in a hurry on Wednesday, nearly a day and a half went by first, didn't it?"

"Yes. Miss Aram wasn't going to expel me at all—on Tuesday. On Wednesday, when she brought it up again, the sheer injustice of it got under my skin. I flamed up. I charged her with doing what she preached against continually—I told her about the gloves."

"What did she say?"

"It took her breath away. I hadn't said anything before, you see. She denied it, furiously. She said I was lying. She said—she said I had invented a wicked story to discredit her. She was," said Linda scornfully, "completely childish."

"But, my dear," said Pardoe, "why should you be supposed to want to discredit Miss Aram?"

"I hated her," said Linda simply. "I always hated her."

Pardoe was silent a moment. "That isn't the same thing at all," he said.

She looked at him gratefully. "No—one wouldn't bother, would one? And I hate lies too. What I said was true. But there it was—I had to go. I wasn't allowed to see anybody first."

Pardoe got up. "Lady Hart will think I've trespassed too long. Thank you for what you've told me."

"It wasn't very terrible." Linda smiled. "You believe me?"

"I believe you."

She said abruptly, walking in front of him to the door, "Do they wear clothes all alike in munitions factories?"

It was Pardoe's turn to be taken by surprise. "Well—yes—a sort of—"

"It's either that or the A.T.S. for me," Linda said with determination. "After Makeways I want to get into uniform…"

The water went on running… under the bridges, Vauxhall, Lambeth, Westminster, Hungerford, Waterloo—on to London Bridge and past the Tower, carrying to the estuary its endless tale.

And the story ran with it.

On Thursday, 10th October, eight days after Mary Shagreen had been committed to the earth, Pardoe turned the calendar on his desk and summoned Salt.

"Exhumation report's in—here are the findings."

"What? Arsenic?"

"No arsenic was present."

Salt whistled. "All right—break it gently."

"Morphine hydrochloride—five grains."

"Then—?"

"Miss Deakin was right."

"I don't like the way that woman puts 'er finger on things," Salt said. "It ain't nacheral."

Chapter XVI

PACT-AND-PICTURE

P olice Constable Darby was very well acquainted with old
Prosser who kept the pet shop in Thankful Court. He'd had a
Lancashire Coppy from him once, and by gum, was he a beauty? He
was all the more surprised, therefore, since it never occurs to us that
friends may need us in our professional capacity, when returning on
his beat through the Lanthorn on Saturday evening, to be run into
by the old man, shaking from head to foot, his face like chalk, his
words tumbling over one another.

At the third try Darby grasped that Prosser's lodger had been
bitten by a snake, and was in a very bad way. Now, Prosser's lodger
had been engaging the somewhat lethargic interest of the Bugle police
for the last month or two; and, since formal request had been made to
the C.I.D. to take over the Martinmas case which had been plumped
in its lap anyway, that interest had grown into a lively and assiduous
attention. An eye was being kept on the Great Ambrosio. And now—

"Have you sent for the doctor?" Darby panted, breaking into a
run and trying at the same time to support the old man.

He missed the mumble. But when they had run through the poky,
rustling, breathing shop where there was always a curious unity about
sound and smell, and the parrot had whispered, "Would ya be-lieve
it?" and from the parlour the mongoose had watched with bright
unblinking eyes their stumbling ascent of the black stairs—there
was nobody in the room with the velvet curtains except the Great
Ambrosio. And he was dead.

Darby was sure of that before he examined him. What he was not so sure of was the condition of the twisted olive-green body with its handsomely patterned back that lay in the middle of a funny chalk pattern on the floor by the window. As he recoiled, however, he saw that it had no head, and heard old Prosser say: "I killed it. He made me get it—God help me. A—a viper, with fangs. My snakes are harmless—they wouldn't do. And now... and now... what shall *I* do?"

"Shut up," Darby said, not unkindly, and knelt down by the Great Ambrosio underneath the indifferent gaze of Abaddon.

The crystal-gazer lay on his face on the floor, one arm under him, the other flung out, the fingers clawing at the wainscot. He was dressed in his black and scarlet, without the gown, but the left sleeve of his shirt had been cut right up from cuff to shoulder and hung open all the way. He had been bitten on the thumb and forefinger of the left hand. Darby could see the small punctures. A rough tourniquet had been applied just above the wrist, but in spite of it the arm was horribly swollen, boggy, fish-belly white, with bluish patches here and there under the skin that was laced with thin red lines where the lymphatics ran to the elbow and armpit. His face was dark and puffy, the lips cyanosed and much larger than in life.

"Poor *devil*," said Darby, shaken, not knowing how near he came to the truth.

After several efforts he succeeded in turning him over. The old man did nothing to help, but stayed over by the door, whispering inaudible complaints, squeezing one hand hard in the other. Darby felt intolerably hot, for there was a burnt-out oil stove in the room and the atmosphere was stale and still warm. He raised one of the dropped eyelids and looked at the enormously dilated pupil. He got up, telling Prosser to stay where he was. He went downstairs to the shop where he knew the telephone was and, smacking the monkey out of the way, rang up the doctor and the police station. Then he went upstairs again and got the story out of Prosser.

"And you and 'im messed about with it from the middle of this morning till now," he said, incredulous, "without a doctor?"

"He wouldn't let me—he wouldn't have one. We washed it in carbolic. I sucked it for him. He sucked it himself. He seemed better—he was lying down in the bedroom"—he pointed to the curtains on his right—"where he's been sorting things to pack—"

"To pack? What did he want to pack?"

"His—his luggage, of course," the old fellow said, trembling. "He was going away."

"Oh, was he?" the constable said grimly. "Fancy that." He looked down at the wreckage of what had once been a man, and away again quickly. "Well, he's gone *now*—sure enough."

His eyes came to rest on the burning grove and the face to which it was a background. He drew in his breath roughly, letting it out in a gentle solemn whistle.

"What's—*that*?"

Prosser shot at the picture a wild look that did not rise above the flaring ABADDON. He crossed himself. Darby got another shock. He was learning that one does not know one's friends.

"He made a pact with the devil," the old man whispered. The irrelevance of the reply struck neither of them. "But the devil didn't—care."

"You're mistaken," P.C. Darby said, reaching an imaginative height he did not understand himself. "The devil cared too much… Well, I'm glad my old woman can't see it, that's all."

After that the others came, Inspector Thompson of the Bugle force and a doctor who clucked and tcha'd and got as cross as two sticks because Ambrosio and the adder had flown in the face of all the rules. They—meaning adders—weren't venomous in October, he said, only in hot weather, and refused to believe the evidence of his own eyes until he began to look silly. Old Prosser had a sounder lore and a simpler grasp of reality. Though she was even deadlier, he preferred nature to rules. Ambrosio, he said, had kept the stove well alight last night, experimenting with his funny chalk diagrams and chanting invocations that made the animals downstairs restless; and vipers, anyway, were sullen in captivity, a far greater menace than when they crossed your path in the open. And the snake had bitten Ambrosio, and Ambrosio had died, so what was the use of pretending they hadn't?

Thompson and Darby went into the inner room where Ambrosio had slept in monastic austerity. It held only a bed, a washstand, and a small table on which a typewriter and duplicator stood. Both did their best to forget the room afterwards. Ambrosio had been very ill indeed.

There was an open suitcase, an open trunk with some clothes in the bottom. Papers were everywhere. Thompson made a careful collection of them, for the Yard would want the lot, while Darby went through the shelves of a built-in cupboard.

He turned round with a bundle of unsealed envelopes in his hand, from one of which he had taken the contents. "Say, sir, what was he after—a wife?"

Thompson looked idly at the paper, which had been done on a duplicator. It was the October issue of something called *Wings of Friendship*. It seemed to be published by the Pact-and-Picture Club at a place called Whimby-on-Sea. Thompson knew it. It was down by Brighton. He ran through the envelopes. Each bore a typed name and address, each different; each was that of a Miss Somebody-or-other.

"More likely somebody wanting a husband," he growled. He was a family man himself and had to pretend that this sort of thing didn't exist. He stopped suddenly. Among the manila envelopes he was shuffling distastefully, a thin transparent wrapping caught his eye; conspicuous because it resembled nothing else in the heap. It was addressed to a Miss Emma Betony, 12 Museum Road, Churchway. Inspector Thompson's flagging spirits rose.

"Guard all this stuff as you'd guard the crown jewels, m'lad. This"—he tapped Miss Betony's wrapper—"this is the old maid who travelled a couple of hundred miles to tell her story to the Yard, and told it when, the doctors say, *by all the rules*"—Darby grinned broadly at the other room—"she ought to've been dead!"

The ambulance came in under the hour from then. They left the square black room, musty, still, with the glittering pentagram on the floor. Abaddon watched. But like Baal, his fellow, perchance he slept, for he made no sign.

Going down those fourteenth-century stairs with a six-foot-four body was not easy. It was accomplished slowly. From the piano against the parlour wall the mongoose watched with clear, unexcited eyes. The monkey swung himself from a gas bracket and plucked an ambulance man by the sleeve. As they went through the dark shop there was an undertone of scuffling, slithering, and tiny sibilant gossip. The parrot, suddenly inverting his scarlet and grey, said in a loud voice, "Watch your step." One of the men laughed, and then didn't like the sound of it.

They lurched out, silent and depressed, under the lowering sky that was like a lid upon Thankful Court and, as they bore the Great Ambrosio by, the parrot's voice sank to a saccharine gasp, timorous, conciliatory, "Who's there? Who's there? Who's there, I say?"

Chapter XVII

AMBROSIO IS RIGHT

I t was not until 19th October that Chief Inspector Dan Pardoe called on Miss Betony.

It was early afternoon, and she was sitting up, unbandaged, only a faint discoloration round her eyes, in a chair by the window in the Wimbledon nursing home to which they had taken her more than a fortnight ago.

"I've been able to see people since Thursday," she said, when they had talked for a few minutes. "Julie Lancret came, and Susan. You very nearly didn't find me here at all. I'm going out on Monday."

"Fine," Pardoe said. "And in spite of everything, nothing more than what I expected. I knew you would come through with colours flying."

He looked at her thoughtfully, with an admiration that was part bewilderment. He felt like pinching himself as a reminder that only the will to live of this thin, gentle woman with the sensitive movements had brought toppling down the ingenious scheming of a cold-blooded murderer.

All Emma said was, "I've the bad penny's trick of survival. I always had. But now, I felt I must struggle to get better. I couldn't let her be responsible for my death too. Because it has all—been my fault."

"Nonse—" Pardoe began, but she silenced him all at once with a stern gesture that he was no longer surprised to find in character.

"Don't," she said. "It was my fault—I shall pay by carrying with me always that knowledge." Her voice was low and unstrained. "It was I who, never knowing it, made Grace Aram reach out in forbidden directions for the satisfaction she was denied in her youth. I—"

"No," Pardoe said, as definite as she. "That won't do, Miss Betony. Nobody can do that to another person—we're all free agents ultimately. The most—the worst—that can be said is that your stories of your aunt helped to determine the direction of the trespass." He smiled to lighten the load of their gravity. "Don't let's lose our sense of proportion when so much of it elsewhere's been going overboard. Murder would never be committed if only people kept that sound. Killing isn't so much a question of want of humanity as want of proportion. If only all of us realized how much—and how little—things mattered."

"But it was only I," she said, "who told her of Mary Shagreen. She would have known nothing but for the fact that I glamorized her."

"The key to this," Pardoe replied, "was character—as to so much else. The impact of character on circumstance, circumstance on character. You must look to Grace Aram's proud, lonely, jealous nature, impinged upon by early poverty, neglect, sense of inferiority, a hobnobbing with things she was made to understand were for ever out of her grasp—worse, out of her right to expect—and her consequent exaltation of those things, the wrong things. She saw material wealth as an end, not a means. She saw a life without it as failure. *You* didn't do that to her. You were not responsible. You gave her Shagreen—I may call her that? She was a great woman—you gave her Shagreen as a contributor to the gaiety and beauty of living. She saw Shagreen as a woman who had got *out* of life those things Grace herself most prized and couldn't have, the things which, unluckily, hang out the most specious signs for the rest of us to take note of. Shagreen was a great giver. Grace Aram saw her as a successful taker. She would be one too. She made her plans accordingly. Do you understand?"

"Yes," Emma said.

Pardoe said, "She kept her always in sight, of course—after those chance encounters in Switzerland."

"All those years ago," Emma added. "Yes, she must have done so—till my aunt changed her name. And at that time—why," she broke off as a new thought came to her, "why, even then, she must have hoped to make contact with her for her own ends, and that was why she didn't mention her when she wrote to me."

Pardoe knew nothing of this. She told him—of the letters from Lausanne that had never brought news of Mary Shagreen.

"But Grace thought she had told me. She forgot she kept it a secret at the time, and so when she blundered my first evening at Martinmas and thought it was *I* who had forgotten her letters, she was obliged to tell me about both times she had seen her. I've puzzled over it a great deal, though it seems a little thing, perhaps. Because Grace would *never* have left Mary Shagreen out of a letter—unless with an ulterior motive. And if that were so, one had to ask oneself what the motive could be."

Pardoe looked at her with the admiration he had felt from the beginning. "Sound stuff, Miss Betony. Just now—you said you didn't want Grace Aram to be responsible for your death too. Did you know at the time that it was she who attacked you?"

"It was the last conscious thought I had—'Grace has done this to me.' You see, as soon as I knew who Miss Wand was I knew it could only have been Grace all along."

"Why?"

"Because she was the only person in Martinmas except myself who was interested in Mary Shagreen."

Pardoe nodded. Salt would have said there were no flies on Miss Betony.

"True," he remarked. "Inquiry's shown that no one knew Miss Wand's identity except Doctors Wick and Fairman and her last lawyer, Pockett. When Grace Aram saw her on the lawn as she was leaving Martinmas after viewing it—and, incidentally, intending to turn it down—she didn't recognize her at once. She made an excuse for crossing the grass close to her, and a little later said to Dr. Wick, 'You have Mary Shagreen here then, the famous dancer?' A question in that form is difficult to deny convincingly. I doubt if Dr. Wick at that stage considered denial worth while. She may even have detected a note of excitement in Grace Aram's voice and thought that it might tip the balance in favour of letting the house. Anyway, she said, yes, she had, but urged Miss Wand's desire for secrecy and obscurity—later, of course, Grace Aram observed both in her own interests. The doctor was amazed then at the change that came over her. All at once she was finding every kind of advantage in taking the house she had just now rejected, and pretty soon was mad to get it."

"I know," said Emma. "That was something Miss Deakin couldn't understand—why she'd turned down places so much more suitable than Martinmas from every point of view. You saw, perhaps, if you looked at the foolish paper I left with you, it was one of the questions I jotted down on Sunday—before I knew who Miss Wand was—and scribbled out, though it was still legible, because it made me miserable to harbour suspicions of Grace."

"Your paper was invaluable. I used it all the time."

"Oh." Emma grew pink. "I put down just what came into my head."

"You had your finger on all the salient points except one—though you did all the work for it, and left us the lazy reward of spotting the answer."

"What was that?"

"You never saw—how could you have seen?—that the answer to all the oddities of the attacks on Miss Thurloe was that they were a blind for something else, a fake to camouflage a real crime from the too sharp eyes of Dr. Bold. But you got very 'warm,' as the children say, in point 9 of your review of the case—indeed, you kept touching on it all the way through."

"And if Dr. Fielding had stayed on—but no, you've said the end would have been the same."

"Shagreen would have died—yes. Sooner, not so painlessly. When Bold's coming upset the scheme, and a new one had to be prepared, clever selection was made of a poison that didn't simulate the symptoms of arsenic, which was being used in the fake poisoning."

Emma was silent in the face of ingenuity on a scale wickeder than any she had conceived.

At length, burking the name a little, she said, "It was Ambrosio who supplied the arsenic?"

"Packets bearing the name of a foreign chemist were found among his belongings. Traces of the powder have been found among Miss Aram's things, including some actually inside one of the gloves Linda Hart saw that day—I suggest she brought small packets away with her by slipping them inside her gloves while she was wearing them. Ambrosio had been a member of a travelling show—I think you knew that?—Ehrenstein and Watt, a very big 'do' run by German and American partners. They had an audacious reputation. They toured the continent thoroughly. This stuff was easy to smuggle in—"

"Oh yes, of course," Emma said. "In Steiermark and on the borders of Hungary and Croatia they eat it, you know—apparently without ill effects! I was governess once in a family abroad whose under-gardener came from a hamlet near Graz. He used to be teased about his nice complexion, and he put it all down to munching white arsenic, of all things!"

Pardoe laughed. "They get immune in time—by taking certain precautions."

She gave him a timid look. "The—the motive against my aunt—it was for the sake of the money which was coming to me? It was from *me* they hoped to get it?"

"Yes," said Pardoe. He looked uncomfortable. He examined his nails, lifted his brows till the creases ran up to his white hair. "I—Miss Betony, the whole thing was directed against *you*. Shagreen—the death of Shagreen—that had to be, of course. But their scheme *began* with that."

"I know," Emma said.

He gave her a quick look of such youthful relief that she smiled.

"Don't 'fash' yourself, inspector, as my dear mother used to tell us. I've worked it out while I've been lying here—there was nothing else to do. Ambrosio meant to marry me, didn't he?"

"Yes," said Pardoe.

"Oh dear," she said, sighing, "no wonder he gave me such a nasty look on the stairs that day. It was beginning to come to me then, what was meant by it all. I knew, of course, that somebody was anxious for me to consult him—and then, when I got there, seeing that note on his pad set me thinking. 'E. B. about 2:30.' That was all it was, and the old man's talk about his being engaged. It meant somebody had let Ambrosio know I was coming. I'd only announced my visit to him after breakfast that morning, so it must have been passed on to Thankful Court by telephone or wire. But I had told only Grace, who had arranged the time for it herself, and had asked me to keep it secret. When I saw what that implied I felt more afraid then than I had at any time."

Pardoe picked up the paper on which she had enumerated the points of the case.

"You had your eye on Ambrosio right enough," he said. "I think you soon knew who the person was who was coming into your life."

"I suspected—it was clumsy of him to introduce him so soon."

"He had to. It filled his thoughts. They were pressed for time.

The Miss Thurloe business was almost exhausted, you see, like a vein of ore. And *you* had been most—unaccommodating, hadn't you, by resisting those invitations to Dorset?"

"Oh yes," Emma said. "And afterwards," she gripped her hands tightly, "I supposed—Grace needed me."

She did, was Pardoe's grim thought. "That was why you got *Wings of Friendship*," he said abruptly.

"To—persuade—to get me out of Churchway?"

He nodded, his eyes on the window and the red and gold ampelopsis crisping at the edges.

"In insolent—flimsy covers," he said in a slow, savage voice. Emma looked at him in surprise. Pardoe was silent. He had not told her they had found the October number ready for post to her, in the hope that by being forwarded to Martinmas by Mrs. Flagg it would give verisimilitude to its earlier appearances and point away from the real culprits. He recovered himself by sudden irrelevance.

"I looked up Ambrosio, the name, I mean—"

"Oh," Emma interrupted, talking fast to cover her embarrassment, "he asked me once if I knew what it was—his name. He didn't say, though."

"I thought I remembered something, something that fitted this Ambrosio. The original is the chief character in a highly flavoured eighteenth-century novel—a Capuchin monk. He made a pact with the devil."

"Abaddon," Emma said with a shiver. "The angel of the bottomless pit. He thought I didn't know."

"He was a diabolist," Pardoe said shortly. "More to the point where we're concerned, he carried on his trade in Brighton, till things got too hot there. And Whimby-on-Sea is only three miles away. In that discreet spot he was the secretary of the Pact-and-Picture Club—he couldn't get away from pacts, could he? It's a quiet, smug little locality—chosen by him to inspire confidence. He posted your copies in Churchway, of course, to make you believe your unwelcome correspondent was close at hand. It was diabolically astute."

"Yes." Emma blushed. She was thinking, with the desolation of friendship betrayed, that Grace had been the only one to know of that foolish adventure of hers long ago, in the other war. She said bravely, "And since he was intending to offer marriage, it's quite clear to me why he grew so distant when I used the words 'happy ever afterwards' about the crystal-reading. They're used in the stories as a conclusion to marriage only. He was hating it all, and, bless me, yes—he must have thought when I said that that I was anticipating it too!"

She laughed, a little hysterically. Pardoe smiled.

"You have a vivid imagination, Miss Betony," he said.

"No, not really." But she was calm now. "I see what's there. It isn't comfortable, always—but it's safer. And all that to me about not taking the independent line, and about looking on the crystal as a warning—it was really veiled threats."

"It's over," Pardoe said quickly. "You see, he *had* to have money. If he could get money then he could develop his cult on the lines he dreamed of, acquire for himself the power he wanted and felt he was capable of wielding."

"Yes. And his odd remark, 'For *you*?' when I said the crystal gave me a gloomy picture—"

"Was meant to imply it was gloomy for himself. He was, I'd say, sufficiently psychic to know that your character, your way of life, were going to be obstacles to the achievement of what he'd planned."

"Grace must have consulted him before," Emma said, reluctant to speak her name.

"She'd visited him in Brighton. Her restless, hungry, acquisitive spirit liked that sort of thing. Some indiscreet word, some disclosure during a reading, may have opened his eyes to her ambition, may even have placed her a little in his power. That type of man gets golden opportunities for blackmail. But, however it was, Ambrosio wasn't the moving spirit. That was Grace Aram. He wanted money—she could supply it, one day, through Mary Shagreen. She wanted money too, but first she wanted poison—he could supply it, at once, without any tiresome regulations. He promised excitement too—substitutes for what Grace had lacked at the right time to have them. To try too late to enjoy pleasure is to invite disaster. But that is what men like Ambrosio trade on—the longing to have again not a misspent youth, but a youth that never was coined at all. They promise something more exciting than renewal. He probably exercised to the full the peculiar fascination of his calling. But—he was instrumental. She was the instigator. It was she who made that swift, masterly change of plans on Dr. Fielding's departure—she who set in motion the Thurloe business—she who moved at once against Shagreen when the hour was ripe. Those words they had in the morning about your aunt not going to church, her own decision to leave Martinmas—those things precipitated action."

"That disagreement in the morning," Emma said, "—I see now why it was. Grace was determined I shouldn't have the opportunity of recognizing Miss Wand, and if we both went to church I was bound to see her, of course. As it was certain I should be going, the only thing to do was to keep Miss Wand at home. When I said I was rather late for the first service, and suggested coming to the next, Grace wouldn't hear of it."

"She couldn't," Pardoe said. "She dared not. She was afraid to leave you in the house with Shagreen when nearly everyone else would be out of it. A bad conscience summons a host of bogies. You *might* not have gone anywhere near Miss Wand, but, guilty, Grace Aram could not chance it."

"She kept very close to me that day." Emma's voice shook a little. "Why—why should she lock the bedroom door?"

"She couldn't—" Pardoe began. He broke off, looking anxiously at her pale face. "Isn't this too much of a strain for you? We can leave it—"

She shook her head. "I want to know."

"It is your right to know. Grace Aram locked the door to postpone the finding of the body. The less time for everyone to think about Miss Wand's death the better. Miss Thurloe was going away in the morning. They must find Shagreen then. She'd gone into the room not earlier than about 2.30, for she wouldn't have risked a longer stay than half an hour—it was probably only a few minutes—and Dolly Finch heard her coming away at three. Her task was to make it all look unsuspicious, like angina. Morphine being an uncertain poison, she hadn't been able to tell how long it would take for the dose to prove fatal, so she gave it a wide margin—your aunt did not die later than 1:30, probably some time earlier."

"Then she had to unlock again?"

"That was easy. She'd slip along there when they were all trying to snatch forty winks after an exhausting night. What she forgot, of course, when she was staging things in the room, was the tube of nitroglycerine, which ought to have been meddled with. Not of the first importance, perhaps—but it engaged Miss Deakin's attention, and in conjunction with other things was suggestive to a sharp mind."

Emma sighed. "Such a lot of things to think of... How can people take so much trouble to be wicked? And Nurse Edgeworth and the maid, she hadn't dared risk their noticing things."

"No. Miss Thurloe had to be served by strangers as soon as it was necessary to turn her into a decoy for Dr. Bold. So fear and dislike of her attentive nurse and maid were sown. In both cases devotion to Miss Wand was an even greater stumbling block, but because Miss Thurloe was a prey to suggestion it was she who was made the instrument of their dismissal."

"Speaking of nurses"—Emma put a hand to her head—"Grace said something about the other nurse on Sunday night. I thought it strange. She said, 'Nurse Swain has drugged herself—'"

"An interesting remark," Pardoe said, "especially to a psycho-analyst. She knew it was she who had put the morphine in Nurse Swain's nightcap—she'd administered smaller doses frequently before, as we know—and at the crisis of her affairs, when the crime she had planned was done, she told that lie, not caring much whether it confused the issue or not, but simply as a measure of self-defence, a sort of reflex action."

"I'm afraid," Emma said, "she lost her head after my arrival. I suppose it was just that—the crisis was approaching. Nothing else can explain that search of my room—I don't know now what for."

"I do," said Pardoe. "You found an old faded photograph of your aunt under the bureau, didn't you? Miss Deakin says that after Miss Wand was moved from that room—by the way, she'd never once complained about Miss Thurloe's carryings-on and had no wish to make a change—Grace Aram made an inexplicable fuss about a photograph of Miss Wand that had apparently been lost in the move from one room to another. It's noteworthy that Miss Wand herself made no inquiry. In fact, when she was asked why it had disappeared from her room she'd even forgotten she had ever had such a photo. The matron was at a loss to understand why such a trifle should interest *Miss Aram*—and showed her surprise, I suppose, for nothing more was said about it. But your room was searched—at an admirable opportunity when attention was concentrated on Miss Pollard and you were waiting for the doctor to come. Your recognition of that picture was a grave risk, especially as you already possessed a photograph of Shagreen in her youth and would be able to compare them. For all she knew you might have come across it even by then, and hidden it in some book or box. All things are possible—to a guilty conscience."

"I wonder," Emma said slowly, "why Grace was so anxious for us to believe that Miss Thurloe was the victim of a poisoner and not doing it herself?"

"Gave everybody more to do," Pardoe said, "wondering who the poisoner could be." He smiled grimly. "Public interest wanes in a prolonged suicide—it's like those 'positively last appearances' that go on for ever. Besides, it was an audacious bluff. It unconsciously built up a bias *for* Grace Aram. *She* couldn't be the poisoner because she'd suggested there *was* a poisoner."

He gave her a quick, warm look. "Miss Betony—I'm sorry. I'm making you tired. I run on."

"No, no," she said. "I was only thinking. Do you know, I had one small clue in my hand all the time, but I'd forgotten—I've only remembered it in the last day or two. Wand was my grandmother's maiden name. She married twice, and was the mother of my mother and Mary Shagreen."

"If Grace Aram had known that," Pardoe said, "she'd have had further cause for worry." But he sounded absent. He was looking uncomfortable again. "I'm not doing my duty. Now that you're able to see people again, Mr. Pockett the solicitor is paying you a visit. Meantime—" He flushed suddenly under her quiet gaze. "Mr. Pockett will have full particulars, of course—Miss Betony, you—you haven't counted on—you won't be disappointed if things don't turn out quite as was expected?"

"Inspector, what are you trying to tell me?"

"Mary Shagreen was a poor woman."

In the silence that followed, Emma's face relaxed, her eyes softened. She took a deep breath. She smiled.

"Oh—just for a minute I was afraid. I was afraid you had another blow for me."

"I said poor." Pardoe repeated it slowly. "Grace Aram made a mistake. She did what she did—for nothing. All that wealth—there had been a great deal—but it was gone, chiefly in speculation by Pockett's unscrupulous predecessor."

"Oh." Her eyes shone. She was intent, he saw, with a new thought. "Then—Ambrosio *was* right—in spite of himself. He said I should never be rich. Only the funny thing is, he believed I was going to be... He said that, of course, to make me think when the time came that his interest in me was *dis*interested, if one can put it that way!"

Pardoe was watching her steadily. He caught himself saying against his will, "Don't you mind?"

"I'm glad. I'm—*glad*. I'm too old to be rich now. I wouldn't know what to do."

Pardoe found nothing to say while he prepared to take his leave. Then he suddenly blurted, "I've no business to ask you—I'm going to ask you just the same. What *are* you going to do, Miss Betony?"

"I like being asked. Any plan I make is more real to me if I speak of it... There will be a little, I think? Yes. Well, added to my own, it will let me do great things. I shall venture on a cottage, I think. I've always wanted that. If the war weren't on, perhaps though, I'd rent a little house and shop—I fancy that too. But this doesn't seem the time to start in business, does it? And women are wanted for other things. Maybe I can fit in to one of them."

Pardoe looked at her thin, eager face. He thought of Mary Shagreen going out like a candle, a flame to the end. He thought, involuntarily, of Linda Hart, young, aloof, her words, "She was lonely—she was *old*—" The child had dared to pity age.

Emma went on, "There's something else. I may—I would like to—if she is willing. I saw her—yesterday. Julie Lancret. We talked a long time. She told me of them all, Yves and the others—oh, nothing to do with this story. There's not much we really know about one another, is there? I—I don't suppose your work would be so hard if we did. Well, I think we might set up together, find something to do together. It will be a sort of *entente cordiale* till the larger one is mended again." Her eyes grew bright and reminiscent. "She told me that her father was a butcher's assistant who liked fruit and hens better, and turned smallholder. It's good to know. You have to be careful about these things still, don't you? And her grandfather was an *épicier* in a small way in Flers. I don't think she would fall out with a greengrocery, do you?"

Pardoe, who had no idea what she was talking about, said he didn't think so. He would have agreed with anything Miss Betony said.

THE END

*Also available from Moonstone Press
by Dorothy Bowers*

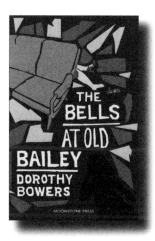

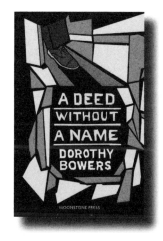

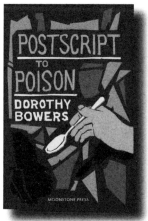